HIGH ROAD
(DAVID WOLF SERIES BOOK 15)

JEFF CARSON

CROSS ATLANTIC PUBLISHING

Copyright © 2021 by Jeff Carson

All rights reserved.

No part of this book may be reproduced in any form or by any electronic or mechanical means, including information storage and retrieval systems, without written permission from the author, except for the use of brief quotations in a book review.

THE DAVID WOLF SERIES IN ORDER

Gut Decision (A David Wolf Short Story)– Sign up for the new release newsletter at http://www.jeffcarson.co/p/newsletter.html and receive a complimentary copy.

Foreign Deceit (David Wolf Book 1)
The Silversmith (David Wolf Book 2)
Alive and Killing (David Wolf Book 3)
Deadly Conditions (David Wolf Book 4)
Cold Lake (David Wolf Book 5)
Smoked Out (David Wolf Book 6)
To the Bone (David Wolf Book 7)
Dire (David Wolf Book 8)
Signature (David Wolf Book 9)
Dark Mountain (David Wolf Book 10)
Rain (David Wolf Book 11)
Drifted (David Wolf Book 12)
Divided Sky (David Wolf Book 13)
In the Ground (David Wolf Book 14)
High Road (David Wolf Book 15)
NEW Dead Canyon (David Wolf Book 16)

1

The boy twisted the handlebars of his bike hard as he looked over his shoulder, and when he swiveled his head back, his balance went off-kilter.

Wolf could see he was going down, but there was nothing he could do but watch the carnage unfold.

"Careful!" Wolf said reflexively, but his words were already smothered by the crash of bicycle on pavement, the slap of the boy's skin on concrete.

He rushed forward, ignoring coffee spilling out of the lid's sip-hole, searing the back of his hand.

"Are you okay?"

He knelt, setting down his coffee and the bag containing his breakfast sandwich on the cold concrete, assessing the boy at ground level.

The boy struggled, whimpering, his leg caught in the wreckage of his BMX bike, his body weight making it worse with every movement.

Wolf grabbed him by the armpits and picked him up, relieving the pressure. The bike lifted, freed itself, and clattered back to the ground.

"Are you all right?" he asked, setting the boy down.

The boy was seven or eight years old, with a mop of straw-colored long hair erupting from a sticker-covered helmet. His jeans and short-sleeved shirt were too skimpy for an October morning at nine thousand feet.

Wolf looked down the sidewalk lining Main Street, vaguely remembering another boy who had passed before noticing this kid crash and burn. He spotted the boy three blocks away, pedaling hard and receding quickly into the distance, looking like an older version of the young boy next to Wolf, with a mop of hair flapping in the wind and also wearing short sleeves.

He checked his watch, which read 7:25 a.m. "It's early for you to be riding around without a jacket."

The kid ignored him, bending over to pick up his bike.

"You going to school?" he asked. "Where's your backpack?"

No answer.

"Is that your brother up there?"

The kid got onto his bike, bumping his handlebars hard into Wolf's leg.

He stepped back and watched the kid push away, standing on his pedals and cranking as fast as he could. He bunny-hopped off the curb, then wheelied up on the other side as he swerved around some pedestrians.

"You're welcome!"

The boy continued his blitz up the sidewalk, gaining more speed, jumping and swerving around obstacles with expert precision. It was amazing the kid had fallen over in the first place. He was a BMX savant.

He bent over to pick up his coffee and sandwich and noticed part of the bag was under his foot.

"Damn," he said, lifting his hiking boot, noting he'd squashed a good third of the sandwich inside.

He stared up the sidewalk, the kid a forgotten memory, now

wondering if he should walk and get another sandwich or if this one was salvageable. He was famished and he had time before the meeting scheduled at 8:30, but he had also left his jacket in the office and was chilled to the bone. Although the western mountains were bathed in bright morning light, setting the whole valley aglow, the sun had yet to rise fully above the eastern wall of mountains, leaving the town in the deep Chautauqua River chill that had built up overnight. The mashed sandwich would do.

Another breeze kicked up, sending gold coin aspen leaves brushing against his legs and out onto Main.

He walked another block, sipping his coffee and thinking about food and kids on bikes, until he reached the Sluice-Byron County building. At four stories high, and half of a town block long, the window-covered structure looked like the Empire State Building in comparison to the squat gold rush era buildings lining the rest of Rocky Points, Colorado's Main Street.

The automatic doors slid open, and he stepped inside, bag in one hand, coffee in the other.

"Is that mine?" Tammy, the long-time lead dispatcher and receptionist going all the way back to the days of the old building, put her hand out over the reception counter, her hand grasping in a "gimme" gesture.

He smiled, not breaking stride. "Yours is down the street."

"Yeah, yeah." She raised up an issue of *Guns and Ammo*, flipping a page. "Hey, that DA from Crow County just went up."

He stopped and turned around. "It's 7:30."

"So?"

"He's an hour early."

"Oh, so you don't have time to eat that." She smiled, her hand extending out again. "Wait. Why is there a footprint on the bag?"

He eyed the front of the reception desk, which had a cotton

spiderweb hanging off it, a googly eyed paper spider taped to the center. "I thought you hated Halloween decorations."

She flipped another page. "You know how it is. We're grandparents now. You get in the mood for all that childhood crap again. How's little Ryan doing? Walking yet?"

He smiled despite the mood the super-punctual Crow Valley DA had brought on. "He's good. And yeah, he's running everywhere I hear. And Zelly?"

"She's a terror." The phone rang and she waved as she picked it up. "Sluice-Byron County Sheriff's Department ..."

He walked to the elevator bank and rode up to the third floor. Once out and into the hallway leading to the main squad room of the sheriff's office, he kept his eyes down, his mission to reach his office door without being noticed by the sheriff.

It was a losing proposition. Sheriff Heather Patterson was as observant as she was smart, which was why Wolf had hired her all those years ago as a detective, and was why she had stepped into his previous role of chief detective when he had moved up to sheriff, and why she ended up swapping with him, taking the throne in the sheriff's office once Wolf stepped back down to chief detective. To say she had her finger on the pulse of everything that happened in the building was an understatement. She was a pacemaker attached to the heart, a microchip inserted into the body of the department, reading its vitals every second of every day.

And she had adopted former sheriff MacLean's policy of leaving the blinds open so everyone in the squad room could see her inside working, and she of course could see out, and her office was at the end of the hallway, and she was probably looking at him right now.

Then again, maybe she had closed the blinds for the meeting. Sometimes she did that, giving her and her visitors a sense of privacy when discussions turned to delicate matters. He snuck a glance and regretted it instantly, as Patterson thrust up her hand, waving it overhead at him through the glass.

He nodded vaguely, sliding his eyes back to his door. He twisted the knob and slid inside.

"Detective Wolf!" he heard just as the door slammed shut behind him.

He paused for an instant, deciding the timing was just believable enough that the noise of the door would have drowned out the sound of Charlotte's voice, and sat down behind his desk.

He quickly unwrapped his sandwich, pulling hard to separate the paper from the smashed portion. The wrapper had held up, keeping the meal inside edible, albeit a bit misshapen.

He took a bite, and then another. He sat back and chewed, savoring the sensation. His refrigerator at home was bare, so once again he hadn't had anything for breakfast. On any normal day he would have eaten at least an hour ago. On top of that, he'd scrounged for dinner last night because of the same bare refrigerator, so by morning he'd been murderously hungry.

There were three knocks on the door. "Sir?"

"What?" He took another bite.

Silence.

"Come in," he said in a pleasant tone.

Charlotte opened the door and poked her head inside. "The sheriff wants to see you."

"Thanks. Tell her I'll be down in a few minutes."

Ignoring him, she walked inside, leaving the door swinging open behind her as she sat on the arm of the loveseat. "She told me to bring you down."

Wolf stared at her as he took another two bites. Charlotte Munford-Rachette, a deputy and office manager, was married to Wolf's detective, Tom Rachette, which meant she had a master's degree in BS detection, how to deal with it, and more patience than a kindergarten teacher. There was no other explanation the marriage lasting long as it had otherwise.

She sat poised on the couch arm, back straight, eyes confident and looking out the window. "Supposed to snow later," she said. "Did you hear?"

Wolf grunted in acknowledgement, studying Charlotte. Back when MacLean was in charge, she would have poked her head in, said her piece, and left. Now she took her job much more seriously, carrying an air of authority with her new role of office manager. Not that he minded any of that, he was just hungry, and he wasn't moving until he'd ingested every crumb of the sandwich.

He took his time chewing and swallowing this time, took a sip of the coffee, and then another.

She eyed her watch, then stood up and went to the window. "It's a nice view from in here."

He ignored her, finishing his sandwich in another two bites. He wadded up the paper and dropped it in the trash.

"Ready?" she asked.

"Yeah, yeah." He stood up and grabbed his coffee, took another sip. "After you."

She walked out of the office and down the hall at a fast clip, him trailing behind a couple paces. A dozen steps later they reached the squad room and she broke away.

"Thank you, Charlotte," he said.

She waved over her shoulder, sitting back at her desk, at least that's what he thought she had done. The sun had broken over the thirteen-thousand-foot eastern peaks of the Chautauqua Valley and was now streaming in through the floor-to-ceiling windows, setting the cathedral-like space ablaze with blinding light.

Wolf turned away and looked at the sheriff's office, blinking as his retinas adjusted.

Patterson watched his approach while continuing to chat with the silver-haired man sitting across from her.

He walked to her opened door and knocked twice at the entrance.

Patterson nodded, her hands bridged in front of her, a smile hiding impatience. "Come in, detective."

Across from her sat the Crow County elected District Attorney, according to the text message Wolf had received from Patterson last night, inviting him to this meeting.

Wolf entered, his hand out to shake. "Hello."

"Detective Wolf, you remember District Attorney Gabriel Bluthe, of Crow County?" Patterson said.

Wolf did not, but he nodded anyway. "Good to see you."

"We met in Aspen a few years ago at one of those conferences," Bluthe said, standing and shaking with a calloused hand that wrapped around Wolf's like a tightened lasso.

Bluthe looked to be in his mid-sixties, thin, a shade shorter than Wolf's six-three height. He wore a button up and a bolo tie, jeans and cowboy boots, and had a silver belt buckle that looked like it belonged on a heavyweight champion.

"Please," Patterson said, "take a seat."

Wolf sat down.

In the years that Wolf had spent behind the sheriff's desk he felt like he'd aged a hundred years, and he distinctly remembered looking in the mirror back then and being shocked at the sight of the wrinkles at the corners of his eyes growing deeper every day. The job seemed to have the opposite effect on Patterson. She seemed to gain strength and vitality from her position behind that desk, her blue eyes bright and wide, her posture straight, her jaw raised with poise as she tented her fingers.

"Thanks for coming down, David," she said.

"No problem," he said.

"I'm sorry I'm early," Bluthe said. "I guess I was in a bit of a hurry to get things going this morning. I didn't sleep much last night, so I was in the car and driving north way before the crack of dawn." He chuckled.

"So, what's happening?" Wolf asked.

Bluthe's face went serious. "Kind of a doozy of a situation we have going on down there. We have a dead body of a young man, aged twenty-two." Bluthe paused. "And it's the sheriff's son."

Wolf sat back heavily, his eyebrows raised. Memories swirled in his mind and a name came out of his mouth unbidden. "Mustaine."

Patterson stood up and silently began shutting the blinds around them, blocking out the view of the squad room. Delicate matters and all.

"That's right," Bluthe said. "Sheriff Mustaine's son, Bennett. He was twenty-two years old."

Wolf's own son Jack was around that age. He shook his head before that thought progressed any further. "Mustaine must be devastated."

"He is."

"What happened?"

Bluthe rubbed his forehead with the knuckles of one hand. "Friday night he went out for drinks. Never came home. His body was discovered Sunday morning some distance away, lying in the back seat of his truck. One shot to the head. Pants were down, as if he'd been in the midst of a sexual act. Lying on his front. There is evidence the body, or the truck, rather, was moved after he was shot. And there is evidence the truck was wiped clean, at least, the steering wheel, handles, upholstery, etcetera. So, it could be everything was staged, including positioning the body to appear the way it did. Anyway ... we got an anonymous call traced to a nearby gas station cell phone."

Wolf's mind flashed back thirty years to the high school

football field. He felt the slam of Clark Mustaine's body, heard the punch of his helmet hitting his chest and face mask, the murderous grunt. He thought of slamming to the ground, the wind knocked out of him, writhing for air for agonizing seconds, teammates hovering over him with concerned faces.

"You okay?" Patterson asked.

"Any suspects? he asked, snapping back to the moment.

"Right. Well, it's fuzzy. He was at a bar, left right around the same time as some girls his age."

"And what do they say?"

"The two women contend they left after Bennett, completely separate, that there was no connection."

"And does their story check out?"

Bluthe switched legs, crossing the other one. "So, here's the part where I explain why I'm up here talking to you." He smiled without teeth. "I hear you know Mustaine from your high school football days."

Another flash memory of Wolf standing next to Sarah after a game, Mustaine and his pals walking by with gloating grins.

Bluthe popped his eyebrows. "You did know him, didn't you?"

"Yeah."

"You played against him. That's what my friend in Ridgway told me. He said you were a quarterback."

"That's right," Wolf said.

Bluthe shook his head. "My God, son. I'm sorry to hear that."

"Why?" Patterson asked.

"I take it you've never met Clark Mustaine in your short time in office, Sheriff?" Bluthe asked.

"No. So, what? Is he big or something?"

"Yes. He played Division One football. For Ohio State. Was even drafted into the NFL but got injured in camp before he was ever able to play. I'm sure Detective Wolf can tell you more." Together they looked at Wolf.

"Yeah. We played together. He was ... large."

"He's six-foot-six," Bluthe said. "Pure muscle."

"Wow," Patterson said. "You played against him?"

Wolf nodded.

"So how about Bennett Mustaine?" Patterson asked. "He must have been a big kid, too."

Bluthe nodded. "Like father like son there, yes ma'am. About the same height. But he was leaner. Bennett also played for Ohio."

"Just like Daddy," Patterson said.

"Almost exactly like Daddy, only he blew out his knee sooner. Bennett was injured in his sophomore year. It ended his college career. He dropped out and came home to Crow Valley."

Wolf reeled his thoughts back. After high school he himself had gone on to become quarterback at Colorado State, but after his dad died, he'd quit football and gone into the military. On one occasion he'd watched Clark Mustaine play college ball on national television in an MWR tent overseas. Naturally, as one who'd been smothered repeatedly into the ground by Mustaine, Wolf had kept tabs on the big man's career, watching him shine at Ohio State, leading to him getting drafted in early rounds by the Kansas City Chiefs, ultimately getting injured in training camp before he'd gotten his chance on the big stage.

However, Wolf hadn't followed his son Bennett's similar rise in the high school and college football ranks. Wolf knew Mustaine had become sheriff down in Crow County, but any more details about his life were beyond him.

"And now you're up here," Wolf said, bringing the conversation back to the case.

"Right. And I'm up here." Bluthe pulled his mouth into a line. "Sheriff Mustaine is upset, obviously. Hell, I have two daughters, grown and moved out. I couldn't imagine if something happened to them." He shook his head. "I mentioned there were two women who were at the bar Friday night with Bennett, or allegedly with Bennett, who also left about the same time. Their names are Valentina Johnson and Carrie Whitlock, also twenty-two years old, same age as our victim.

"Anyway, while Mustaine was questioning Valentina, he put his hand around her throat, then pushed her up against a wall. Allegedly."

Patterson whistled softly.

Bluthe nodded.

Wolf thought about Mustaine's large hands gripping his own facemask, the full weight of his body pressing down, all while emitting psychotic spit-laced screams. It didn't take too much imagination to know the fear Valentina must have felt.

"And after he talked to Valentina, he went up to the ranch. Uh, that's where Carrie Whitlock lives. Nola Whitlock—that's Carrie's mother—wouldn't let him in through the gate. As far as I can gather, he raised some serious hell. I'm not exactly sure what happened there to be honest, the details I've heard are blurred. Everyone's on edge. And meanwhile, we have a potential killer on the loose."

Bluthe turned in his chair, facing Wolf. "The bottom line is, we have a situation where the sheriff is way too close to this investigation, and we need outside help. That's all there is to it."

Wolf nodded. "And you want me? Why? How about CBI? FBI? State police?"

"This is a delicate situation, Detective. People are looking to me to bring in help, and it's gotta be the right kind of help. The FBI? I can't bring in a bunch of suits who know nothing of the situation. Or CBI?" He made a disgusted face and flipped his hand. "Anyone who isn't intimately connected here I'm not bringing in. It would only pour gas on the flames. You know Mustaine. You have a history with him."

Not the kind of history you're thinking, Wolf thought. "What makes you think Mustaine and I are intimately connected?"

Bluthe upturned his hands. "I have to admit I know nothing of you and your relationship, other than you played football together. But that's more of a connection than anyone else."

He stared at Wolf.

"That, and I was DA up in Ouray County until a year and a half ago when I moved down to Crow County. I was there when you helped my good friend Sheriff Roll during that whole God-awful incident up in Ridgway. You and I never met, but I kept tabs on what you guys were doing from afar, and I liked what I saw. So, I guess you could say *I'm* intimately connected with you as far as I'm concerned." He sat forward, his plea apparently over.

"You're new in Crow County," Wolf said.

"A year and a half." He looked at Wolf. "So, yeah. I'm still the new guy. You can see how bringing in the wrong kind of person to help might … multiply that whole gas on the fire scenario. But I'm not going to sit back and let what's happening get any worse."

"And you've told Mustaine that you're bringing in outside help?" Wolf asked.

"I have."

"I'm sure he took that well."

Bluthe chuckled, but said nothing.

"He's not going to like having me down there," Wolf said. "We played against each other, but we didn't like each other. And you want me to come in, an outsider, and investigate his son's death, telling him to stand down? To relax, I have it covered?"

He shook his head, thinking about what he would do in a similar situation. He stood up, walked to the window, and looked outside. If his own son had been killed and he wasn't getting the entire picture, he figured there would be no stopping the rampage he would go on in search of the truth. He'd been in that situation with his brother years ago.

"I'm not asking you to come in like it's a hostile takeover. I will smooth over the back end. I will talk to him and let him know the importance of bringing in the outside agency to help. It's for his son, really. If he steps over the line on the investigation, justice might not be served. We're just looking for cooler heads, as it were. It's a benefit for everyone."

Wolf stared outside, keeping silent.

Bluthe got up from his chair. "Listen. It's a tough sell, but it would be a big help to our office, and to me. Right now, we have a dead young man and a father looking for answers, and possibly some citizens in danger because of it. I'm not asking for an answer right now, but sooner than later would be appreciated. The situation is only getting worse."

"And if I don't help?"

"I guess I'll try Gunnison County, but I don't like them as much as you. And if they can't help, I guess I'll go to the feds."

They sat in silence for a beat.

"We'll discuss this and get back to you, okay?" Patterson stood up and moved to the door.

"Thank you, Sheriff," Bluthe said, holding out a hand.

Patterson shook it. "I'll walk you to the elevator. David, if you could stay and wait for my return?"

Wolf stood at the window as Patterson walked with Bluthe out into the squad room and down the hall.

A minute later Patterson came in and Wolf sat back in the chair opposite her desk.

"Well?" she said. "What do you think?"

"I think I already said it. It's a difficult situation. Maybe impossible."

"Nothing's impossible. Difficult? Sure."

"And what I didn't say with him here is this guy's a real asshole. Class A."

"Bluthe?"

"No. Mustaine."

"What happened? He smack you around on the field or something?"

"Something like that."

She sighed, letting the breath out in a musical note of disappointment. "Okay. You don't want to do it. I'll tell him you have other more important stuff to do. After all, we do have ... what's your team working on right now? Two stolen bikes?"

She waited with raised eyebrows until Wolf nodded.

"I'll tell him you're busy with other cases. I'll tell him you're just not up for—"

"What's in it for you?" he asked.

She sat forward, putting her elbows on the desk. "What are you talking about?"

"I know how it is behind that desk," he said. "You're playing for points here. Using me as your chess piece."

Her eyes flared. "You know the writing is on the wall out there. People are already bitching about how I'm dropping the ball on this, how I'm too soft on that, how I have no experience and I shouldn't be sitting behind this desk. Oh yeah, and let's not forget this is the desk you put me in when you decided you didn't want this job anymore." She stared at him, then took a deep breath, the red in her face fading to pink.

She stood, turning her back on him as she looked out the window.

After a while she said, "You know about the guy in town?"

"Waze?"

"Yeah, Waze."

Wolf knew. Gregory Waze was a wealthy, single man in his fifties, attractive to the ladies, charismatic, semi-retired, with a history in law enforcement and politics. He was renting a house down the valley along the Chautauqua River. It wasn't long before Margaret Hitchens, who was the mayor and Patterson's aunt, had discovered his true intentions: to gain full residency so he could run for sheriff in the next election.

Last year Patterson had won sheriff uncontested, which was basically the same as being appointed by those around her, and already a rival was gunning for her position. Now Gregory Waze was in town, ready to fight. The man had backing, lots of money from lots of donors, and they'd set their sights on Sluice-Byron County to further their political agenda.

"So what?" Wolf said. "You got him. As Rachette ... or Yates ... would say, he's a douche."

She turned around and sat down, rolling her eyes. Then she put her face in her hands. "I'm not sure I can do it, if I'm honest."

"Do what?"

"All this bullshit. This sucking up to DAs in neighboring counties, loaning out my best detective to get on his good side, so that maybe this fruitcake can help me in this upcoming election."

"I don't think you were supposed to say that part out loud."

"And all this pressure ... did you know Margaret is talking to all sorts of people? Shit, she's already appointed herself as my campaign manager and is out there raising money on my behalf. There're like, millions of dollars getting handed back and forth. For an election in a small town in the middle of the Colorado Rockies? For me?"

Wolf let a smile tug the edge of his mouth and sat in silence.

Patterson stared at her desk, and then blinked out of

thought and looked up at him. Her eyes had lost that cock-sure glint from earlier.

"My mother," Wolf said.

"What about her?"

"If I go down there, I need somebody to keep an eye on her." Last year his mother had moved from Denver to Rocky Points so he could keep an eye on her. Her cognitive abilities were beginning to wane in her old age and his concern was too much to allow her to stay on the Front Range anymore.

Stubborn as his mother was, she had refused to move into his house, insisting on renting her own apartment in town along the river. The arrangement made things easier and harder at the same time.

"I thought that she had that nursing company, or whatever, looking after her?" Patterson asked.

"They are. But I like to check on her when they're not there. You know, in between."

Patterson nodded. "You're a good son."

He said nothing, thinking he probably checked on her so much because he was making up for leaving her to fend for herself so long down in Denver. There were much better sons out there in the world.

"My aunt can keep an eye on her," Patterson said.

"Between being mayor, your campaign manager, real estate mogul, and ... whatever else that woman does, Margaret has time for looking in on my mother?"

"She owes you guys. She's getting a ton of money from the sale of that house."

He frowned at the non sequitur. "What house?"

Patterson's eyes widened for an instant, but her face remained blank. "Nothing. If my aunt the mayor doesn't have time for keeping an eye on your mom, then my aunt," Patterson quoted her fingers, "the woman who was good friends with your mom before you were even a thought, as she likes to tell you, surely will."

"Yeah. Sure. I guess. I just hope Margaret can handle her. You know, mentally. This case could take a while."

"It will be fast, I'm sure," she said.

"Well, as long as you're sure."

"With your skills? In and out." There it was again—that cocksure glint in her eye.

He looked past her out the window, then rolled his eyes. "Fine."

"Great. Thank you." She pulled out a card and slid it across the desk, tapping her finger. "This is Deputy John Normandy's phone number. He's your liaison down there. They'd like you to get started today. It takes two hours and fourteen minutes to drive down there according to my phone. Give yourself a few minutes to gather your stuff at home and you should be there by two this afternoon. Call him," she pointed at the card.

Wolf stared at it. Then slapped his hand, pulled it back, and scanned Patterson's loopy handwriting written on the back of DA Bluthe's card. He stood and put it in his pocket, eyeing her suspiciously.

"What?"

"Were you just putting me on? Playing the sympathy card to get me to agree to do this?"

"What?" She frowned. "No. What?"

"Tell me the truth."

"I always tell the truth, David. You know that."

He narrowed his eyes. "A bunch of money from the sale of what house?"

She looked at her watch. "I have a meeting in a few minutes. Can you leave the door open? And keep me posted." She turned to her computer monitor and began typing.

He left, but not before stopping in the doorway and turning around.

"Yes?" she asked, keeping her eyes on the monitor.

"You owe me."

"Oh, I think we're pretty much even, don't you?"

The way she said it was convincing. "This had better be *in and out*. And if this guy tackles me again? Then you owe me."

2

Wolf went to his office, shut the door, and sat in his chair. As he sipped his lukewarm coffee, his thoughts drifted back to high school.

It had been the Homecoming game, junior year. Wolf and the Rocky Points Wildcats had lost that game by ten points to the Alamosa Mean Moose, Wolf had gotten his ass beat by Mustaine, and the score would have been much, much worse if it weren't for Wolf making a few lucky passes that had earned them two touchdowns.

Clark Mustaine had been a year older than Wolf, a senior with Division One coaches knocking on his door, a one-in-a-million athlete every top football school wanted a piece of, and every athlete he played against wanted to stay away from.

Mustaine hadn't been as much of a factor the year before, but somehow he'd grown taller and bulked up to the size of a grizzly, with about as much speed and ferocity. His blitzes had been relentless, devastating rampages that bowled through his offensive line. Wolf had normally been good in the pocket, quick and calm under the pressure of the defense, but with Mustaine, Wolf had felt gut-quickening pressure that made him falter or second-guess himself. Over and over he was smothered to the ground that game. He still remembered the fear on his teammates faces in the huddle, the nervous banter, the blame and finger-pointing.

"You were supposed to block him!"

"No, you were!"

And then there had been after the game.

Wolf had that old pickup, and he and Sarah were sitting on the tailgate, Sarah with her arm around him and consoling him, Wolf trying to act like he was fine even though his neck had seized up and his head felt like it had been kicked by a bull.

"Nice game out there," Mustaine had said, walking past with three of his teammates.

"Thanks. You too," Wolf had said. And then, for some reason, he'd said, "You got me pretty good out there."

Which made Mustaine stop and smile. "Yeah. I did, didn't I?" And then Mustaine had looked at Sarah and licked his lips. "What are you doing with this loser, sweet cakes?"

Wolf had jumped off the tailgate and got into his face, or the lower half of his face, and said, "If you talk to my girlfriend like that again I'll push your face through your skull."

And then Wolf's father had appeared out of nowhere, asking if everything was all right. Mustaine had grinned, knowing he'd won again, Wolf forced to hide behind his father with his sheriff's badge and gun on his hip.

Of course, the truth was Wolf had been lucky his father appeared, and he knew everyone else knew it—Mustaine, his father, and Sarah. It was a wound to Wolf's pride that was still tender to the touch.

That had been the extent of his conversations with Clark Mustaine, even up to now. But Wolf knew the gist of what the big man had been up to. Since that game Mustaine had been drafted to Ohio State, had a shining collegiate career, and then been drafted to the Kansas City Chiefs, only to be injured in training camp before he'd gotten a chance to play. After that Mustaine had moved back to Colorado, gotten into law enforcement, and become sheriff in Crow Valley.

Wolf had seen the big man in passing at law enforcement conferences numerous times, never acknowledging him, not once, nor did Mustaine acknowledge him. They both pointedly avoided eye contact. They both knew exactly who the other was. They both thought of that night in the parking lot every time they saw one another, and Wolf's muscles tensed every time, waiting for a confrontation that had started decades ago to conclude.

"Hey you."

He turned to the door and saw Piper Cain standing in the doorway.

"Hey, what are you doing here?" He rose, looking her up and down.

Piper Cain was a satellite deputy stationed in the adjacent valley, on the outskirts of Sluice-Byron County in the town of Dredge. She was also Wolf's girlfriend of the last ten months. To see one another usually took some planning, and a lot of driving for at least one of them. To simply pop in was startling for sure, but it was the outfit that threw him the most. She normally wore jeans, a tan button up uniform shirt, and hiking boots, her fanciest accessory an old watch her father had given her. Now she was dressed up like she was due in court or something, with dark slacks and a jacket hugging her slim figure, a silver necklace framing her slender, tanned neck, her dark hair cascading down in a shimmering sheet on her shoulders.

Her large obsidian eyes glinted as she smiled, and Wolf sensed a nervous tension in her expression.

"I have a meeting with Patterson in a few minutes," she said. "I can just say hi and that's it."

"Oh." He met her halfway and wrapped his arms around her. "What's the meeting about?"

"Work," she said.

"Ah. So why the getup? I mean, don't get me wrong, you look great. I mean, you look amazing. Why not your normal uniform?"

"It's more of an interview."

He frowned. "Oh." They had been together two days ago, eating dinner in town, then spending the night at Wolf's house. They had spoken yesterday on the phone. This was the first he was hearing of an interview with Patterson.

They both knew she was looking to move to Rocky Points. Some day. But that day was an amorphous, sometime-time-in-the-future date. Right now she lived with her father in Dredge, in the house he had built with his own two hands. His dream home. And because he was not well, suffering from Alzheimer's disease, she'd been hesitant to sell the house her father built and move him somewhere he had no roots, even if she was miserable so far away from where she yearned to be.

A delicate matter. One that Wolf thought a therapist might help her sort through better than he could, so he'd offered himself up as a sounding board when she wanted to vent about it, but otherwise stayed generally silent on the subject.

"For a job here?" he asked.

She looked at him, an unreadable expression on her face. "Yeah."

"Wow. I had no idea. That's great."

"Yeah, well, I don't have any offers yet. I didn't want to talk about it, you know?"

"Right. I get it."

She kept close, pressing into him. Her eyes skipped side to side, studying his. "I'm sorry I didn't tell you. But I didn't want to..."

"You didn't want to jinx it."

She opened her mouth, then closed it. "I'll see you tonight, right?" She let go and backed away, looking at her watch.

"Yes. Wait. No, I have to leave. I have to go to Crow County to help with an investigation."

Her face dropped. "Oh. Okay. Then...call me."

"I will."

She turned to the doorway.

"Wait," he said.

"What?"

He stepped up and kissed her again on the cheek. "Go get her."

Again, she gave him that unreadable expression, and Wolf had the sense he was being studied.

"Bye." She left down the hall, as Rachette and Yates came up from the other direction.

"Hey, what's she doing here?" Rachette asked, pushing past him into his office.

Wolf watched her walk down the hall. She greeted somebody as she walked through the squad room, looking beautiful in the sunlight as she laughed and waved. Then she curled into Patterson's office, disappearing behind closed blinds. He went back into his office, and Yates and Rachette who had already made themselves comfortable in the chairs at his desk.

"We're hiring again," Yates said. "Looks like she was dressed for an interview or something."

Wolf sat down behind his desk, thinking of the look Piper had given.

He reset his mind, looking at the two men in front of him. Both of his detectives filled out their seats, Rachette with a gut that had blossomed last year and seemed to be gaining momentum, and Yates with muscles that stretched the sleeves of his uniform shirt to the point of tearing.

"I tell you what," Rachette said. "It's kind of nice to have your significant other working in the building. It's great rolling over at night, seeing them sleeping next to you, then seeing them in the kitchen at breakfast, then in the squad room, then in the hall every time you're going to take a piss."

Yates slapped him on the shoulder. "Dude."

"Sorry. I mean, yeah, that's awesome, though. She'll what, then? Be a detective? Working with us? Now that would be weird."

Wolf said nothing.

Rachette continued. "And she's going to commute from Dredge? That seems like a long-ass drive to come into work every day."

Yeah. It did. Unless she sold her house and moved to Rocky Points.

Patterson's earlier words echoed in his head. *She owes you guys. She's getting a ton of money from the sale of that house.*

Is that what Patterson had just been talking about? Had Margaret sold Piper's house? Should Piper ever hire a real estate agent, she would undoubtedly hire Margaret, as everyone in Wolf's circle of influence would have done the same.

She owes you guys. She's getting a ton of money from the sale of that house.

As in, Wolf had been responsible for Piper hiring Margaret to be her real estate agent, so Margaret owes him, as well as Piper?

It was unlikely. He wasn't even aware she was selling. Then again, he hadn't known about the job interview either. What the hell was going on?

"Sir?" Yates was snapping in the air, waving his hands.

"What?"

"We were gonna talk about the bikes," Rachette said.

"Okay. Yeah. The bikes. How are you guys coming on that?"

A couple days earlier two young men had come in, reporting stolen mountain bikes. It wasn't exactly murder, but it was the only crime they had going in Rocky Points at the moment.

"We don't have jack shit," Yates said.

"Wait a minute now," Rachette put up a hand. "We know the locks were cut."

"So you've read the report," Wolf said. "That's what you've done so far."

"Correct."

"We're going up to resort now," Yates said. "We're not complete invalids."

"You want to ride along?" Rachette said.

"I'm headed down to Crow Valley."

"Why?" Rachette asked.

Wolf told them about Sheriff Mustaine's son being found dead.

"Whoa," Yates said. "So why you?"

"They want outside help."

Yates gave his partner a quick glance. "You need one of us to tag along?"

"No, thanks. You two keep me posted, and I'll do the same." Wolf stood up and grabbed his jacket off his coat tree and slipped it on. "Do me proud while I'm gone, gentlemen."

3

Wolf parked in the parking lot of his mother's apartment complex and got out of his SUV, stepping into cold air smelling of the Chautauqua River that burbled in the grove of aspens behind the buildings.

The lot was nearly empty, either everyone who owned the places were down in Denver until the ski season, or out at work at this mid-morning hour. He jogged to the cavernous first floor hallway that led to his mother's unit in the back of the building.

He knocked and waited for an answer. When none came, he knocked again, and put his ear to the door. Inside he heard the television blaring, but still no movement.

With a sigh he pulled out his key and let himself inside.

A cacophony of sound poured out, a hooting audience blaring out of the television speakers in the other room, the dinging of a bell, music.

He walked through the entryway to the living room and knocked on the jamb.

His mother sat with her back to him in her lounge chair, transfixed by the screen.

"He-llo!"

"Oh my!" His mother jumped in her seat, twisting to see him, a blanket dropping to the floor from her lap to the floor. "What are you doing, David? You scared the crap out of me!"

He held up his hands, eyeing her phone on the table, inaudible to anybody watching *The Price Is Right* at that volume, the light-up screen invisible since it sat behind her line of sight.

He picked up the remote control and muted the TV. "Mom."

"What?"

"I've been calling you."

"So?

He sat down on the edge of the couch, elbows on his knees. "So...I need to speak to you. Your phone is sitting right here, but you can't hear it because your television is about to blow a speaker. I'm surprised no one's called to complain."

She shook her head, mirroring his expression. "So, come over and talk to me. Looks like you just did. Good job."

She got up from her chair and grabbed the remote control from where he'd set it down.

"You have a doctor's appointment tomorrow."

"I do?"

"Yes."

She pressed the mute button, unleashing the sound of a bell and siren wailing over a crowd going wild.

"He won!" she yelled, arm up in triumph.

He watched an elderly man on the TV hug a woman in a swimsuit while his wife tried to get in on the action. He studied his mother, joy exposing her teeth in a wide grin, leaning forward on her recliner, hands clapping softly together.

"What did he win?" he asked, seeing the boat, car, and trip to Hawaii telegraphing the answer already.

"His bid was fifty dollars under! He got both of them!"

Wolf eyed the screen, realizing there was a bit more

commotion than he was used to seeing at the end of an episode. "Huh. Lucky him."

"What?"

"Lucky him!" He got the remote off the chair arm and lowered the volume. "Listen. Mom. I'm leaving town."

"Okay. Where to?"

"Down south a couple hours. Crow Valley."

"Place is beautiful. Your father and I used to go through there on the way to Durango to visit my mother."

Wolf eyed her closely, as he always did when she pulled perfectly lucid memories from her brain with no effort like that.

"Listen." He stood up. "Are you good? Are you doing okay?"

"Yeah. Why?"

"Margaret is going to come over and check in on you when I'm gone."

"What about Trevor?" she asked, referring to the man from the nursing service that checked in on her six days a week.

"Trevor will still stop by. But so will Margaret."

"Fine. Whatever."

He went into the kitchen and started rummaging, making sure she had enough food. There were three bunches of bananas on the counter, and when he saw one inside the refrigerator, he stood staring at it.

"What did you have for breakfast?" he asked.

"Oatmeal," she said.

"And for lunch?"

"I haven't had it yet. It's only ten."

"I'm wondering what you are going to—"

"I'm going to have toast and peanut butter." She was standing now at the threshold of the kitchen, her tone stern. "Right after I watch my shows."

He nodded. "Why do you have three bunches of bananas on the counter and one in the refrigerator?"

"Because I forgot that I already got bananas."

That didn't really explain the four bunches of bananas, but he figured he'd let it go.

"How's Piper doing?" she asked.

He shut the refrigerator. One time she'd accidentally called Piper Sarah, her mind latching onto his high school sweetheart-turned-wife and the mother of his only son, now at rest in the cemetery overlooking Rocky Points. He had corrected her that time and she'd remembered every day since.

Piper's father was suffering from dementia, though in Wolf's estimation he was much worse off. Piper was constantly astonished at how far her father had slipped away from his former self, while Wolf was constantly astonished at how well his mother seemed to be holding it together. He had decided a while ago that the return to Rocky Points had been just what she needed.

But, then again, there was a bunch of bananas in the refrigerator. Three outside. Why didn't Trevor catch the repeat purchases?

"David!"

"What?"

"I asked you a question."

"What?" He opened the refrigerator again and took out a sparkling drink, realizing he had probably played out this scenario a thousand times in his life, his mother yelling at him to listen as he ducked into the refrigerator to turn his back on her.

"I asked if she's found a job yet?"

He looked at her, cracked the can open, and sipped the tasteless sparkling water. "She has a job, Mom. She's with the Department out in Dredge."

Her forehead crinkled as she thought. "I thought you said she was getting a job in town."

"I said one day she might. Right now she's staying in Dredge because her father built that place up there."

She waved a hand. "I know, I know."

She pushed him out of the way and ducked into the refrigerator. "I'm hungry now."

He watched with growing satisfaction as she expertly prepared herself toast and peanut butter, complete with a banana perched on the side of her plate.

"When are you going to marry her?" she asked.

He swallowed some sparkling water, just managing not to choke.

"Geez. That bad of a question?"

"No. I just ... we're not getting married, Mom. We've been dating for less than a year."

"She's the one," she said, taking a bite of her toast. "You two are that annoying couple."

"Ah. Glad you like her, Mom."

"You guys sit there and cuddle, and laugh, and kiss, and think nobody's looking."

Wolf said nothing.

"I love her," she said, straightening in her chair. "Don't you love her?"

"I think so. Yeah. Sure. Mom, chill."

"So why don't you put a ring on her?"

Because I'll never put a ring on anyone again.

"Listen," he said. "I have to leave town for a few days. Trevor will be here, and Margaret will come check on you, too."

"You said that earlier."

He nodded. "I'm glad you remembered."

"The doctor says my memory is doing better," she said.

"And you go see him tomorrow, remember," Wolf said. "Trevor will come pick you up."

"I do? Again already? I saw him a couple days ago."

He looked at her, his smile fading as he saw she was dead serious. It had been over two weeks since she'd last been to the doctor. "It's been a few more days than that. It's just another checkup."

"It's beautiful today," she said, staring out the window.

He followed her eyes to the river flowing outside, shimmering reflections of the sun glinting off its eddies and swirls, aspen leaves falling, dislodged by a passing breeze.

"Yeah." He thought about Sheriff Clark Mustaine, and what he must have been thinking about this day. "I have to go, Mom."

"Be good."

"I'll try," he said.

4

The clock said 11:32 when Wolf summitted Williams Pass, the southern rim of the Chautauqua Valley with all its trials weighing on Wolf's mind falling out of sight in the rearview mirror.

He coasted, the switchbacks cutting down through dense pines until the road flattened at the bottom, stretching out into a straight edge cutting along the floor of the immense valley where the trees gave way to sage brush.

Almost an hour later he reached the outskirts of Ashland, and then he was through, and on highway 50 heading towards Gunnison.

Traveling west, Monarch Pass had a few inches of snow blanketing the ground between the dense pines, remnants of the fall storm they'd had a few days ago that had missed Rocky Points.

After summiting, he dropped down into the Gunnison Valley, out of the pine trees and into more sage country covering gradual hills that hugged the meandering Tomichi Creek, and then before the town of Gunnison he headed south on highway 820.

It was about this time he began looking at his laptop screen, which showed a line leading to some coordinates where he was to meet Deputy John Normandy of the Crow County Sheriff's Department, who himself was scheduled to meet Wolf at the spot where Bennett Mustaine had been found.

The highway snaked along a tributary of the Gunnison River between basalt cliffs. Driving was easy, pushed from behind by a north wind that buffeted the trees. As Charlotte had alluded to earlier, weather would be moving in later according to the forecasts, and clouds were building in the rearview.

An hour later the line on the screen told him to hang another right at a gas station that squatted off the right side of the highway, so he did, heading west up a dirt road that climbed into hills covered in Rocky Mountain Junipers and Piñon Pines. A few minutes later, and at least a thousand feet of elevation gain, the trees turned over to pine forest, which thinned as he came into a sparsely covered valley surrounded by hills.

The end of the computer screen line came up fast after that, and right at the spot, out his windshield, was parked a brown and white painted Crow County SD truck.

As he slowed a young man who looked to be in his twenties climbed out of the vehicle, giving a friendly wave. Wolf parked behind him and got out.

His back creaked, and his legs felt stiff. As he put his arms over head and stretched, cold air burrowed under the bottom of his jacket, knifing through his shirt beneath. The air was light, carrying on it the scent of pine and maybe a bit of moisture.

Wolf eyed the sky to the north and saw it was darkening between and beyond the mountains, and a dark gray smear on the horizon was sliding in on the wind from Wyoming.

"Cold, eh?" The man said. "It's coming."

Wolf nodded and shut his door. "I'm Wolf."

"I'm Normandy."

They met at Wolf's front bumper and shook hands.

Normandy had a lump of chew in his lip that bent his smile sideways. His eyes were blue and bright, and he squinted hard in the overhead sun. His blond hair was cut short under a Crow County SD ball cap, his face clean-shaven, which Wolf found to be an exception to the norm in his department.

"Perfect timing," Normandy said. "I just got here a few seconds ago."

"Excellent."

Wolf turned his attention to their surroundings. Here they were in a valley surrounded by low mountains. A dry wash cut along the right of the road, then crossed under the road about fifty yards up where a steel bridge spanned the gap, before continuing along the left side into the distance.

"That's Dry Wash," Normandy said. "We're flush with original names around here." He pointed to the wash on the right, and to a spot that it weaved into an outcrop of rocks and disappeared. "He was found up inside there. Through those rocks."

Wolf nodded. "Are we walking?"

"It's a bit too far for that. Hop in. I'll drive."

Normandy's truck was clean and warm, smelling of chewing tobacco, fast food, and aftershave. Wolf had been in worse.

After they crossed the bridge Normandy hit the brakes and eased to the side of the road.

"Hang on." He steered the truck off the shoulder, down a two-track that looked recently well-traveled, to the flat, sandy bottom of Dry Wash.

"Lots of tracks." Wolf looked out the window, seeing not only the spaced tracks of four-wheel vehicles, but the tell-tale signs of dirt bikes as well.

"Yeah." Normandy spat in a can. "This is part of the network of motorized vehicle trails that lead from way down in Silverton all the way up north, past Steamboat. Shoot, I don't know how far it technically goes, but I bet you could get to Wyoming on this track. A lot of dirt bikers and Jeeps take it every year. Then of course, we've been up here the last few days. Shit, there they go now."

Normandy slowed to a stop as two dirt bikers came revving around the corner from behind the rocks he'd just pointed out.

The bikers fishtailed and slowed to a crawl, waving as they passed, their bikes loaded with dirty gear, then revved up and disappeared in a cloud of dust underneath the bridge behind them.

"Dirt bikers called it in," Normandy said.

"So I hear. Anonymously?"

"Yep. There's a gas station you had to pass on the way up. That's where they made the call. Can you imagine coming around the corner on one of those things and seeing a truck, then looking inside and seeing a dead body?"

Normandy edged forward again, bumping over rocks and through depressions.

"Who took the call?" Wolf asked.

"Deputy Garcia. She's usually manning the switchboard for us."

Wolf said nothing.

"I've been thinking about that call," Normandy said. "I don't think it was anybody involved. I mean, it seems like somebody drove the body up here to hide it. So, why call it in once you get it hidden up here? You hid it, then tell the cops where to find it? Doesn't make sense. And besides...there was the way Bennett was found inside the truck."

"And how was that?"

"Pants down." Normandy spat again. "Had to be somebody

he knew down in town. Just doesn't fit, I feel like, that if somebody shoots and kills him, why call it in?"

Normandy sped up for a few seconds, then slowed as they reached a narrow point of the wash, the way forward with a four-wheel vehicle turning rocky.

"Hang on now." Normandy's truck edged up and over some jutting granite, then the tires slammed down on the other side. "That's always the doozy there." He repeated the process with the back wheels, then sped up and around the bend.

"There it is." Normandy slowed to a stop.

Basalt formations on either side of the wash framed a scene of wide-open land just beyond, covered in brown, yellow, and rust vegetation. A ring of crime scene tape fluttered and bounced, hooked to rocks and shrubs, bowing back towards them on the thrashing wind.

Normandy shut off the engine. "That's where his truck was." The rock formation where he pointed was at its steepest and narrowest. The ring of crime scene tape covered more than three quarters of the distance between the rocks, meaning the dirt bikers they'd just seen would have just barely squeezed past.

Normandy reached behind him, grabbed a manila folder, and handed it to Wolf.

Wolf opened the folder, revealing a stack of photographs.

The first picture looked like it was taken from the same vantage they were at now, looking identical, save different weather in the photo and Bennett Mustaine's full size model truck covering most of the gap ahead.

The next photograph was of an open rear door, exposing the misshapen, blood and brain-covered skull of Bennett Mustaine. There was a close-up of the tan leather seat beneath the body.

"Can you see that seat beneath the body?" Normandy asked.

"He was moved," Wolf said.

"Very astute." Normandy spat softly into his can.

"DA Bluthe told me about it this morning, but I see now. He was shot, bled out, and then the body slid around in the back seat as somebody drove his truck up here."

Wolf flipped through more pictures, which showed different angles of the body and some photos of the interior. There were a dozen or so focused on Bennett's right hand, which dangled off the bench seat and lay on the floorboard. Next to his hand sat a Glock Model 30.

Another photograph showed a single spent casing wedged between the front passenger seat and the center console, tucked way down where people drop their valuables when they need them the most.

He flipped to another series of photos.

"His pants were down," he said under his breath, again seeing for himself what the DA had already mentioned.

The young man's jeans were unbuttoned and pulled down to his knees, and a T-shirt bearing the logo reading *P&B Pizza* rode up his torso, exposing the pale flesh of his buttocks and back.

"Clearly in the middle of a sexual act with somebody," Normandy said.

"Or staged to look that way," Wolf said. "Bluthe also said the scene was wiped down. If he was moved, if it was wiped down, we can't trust anything we're looking at."

"True."

There were some photographs of the ground surrounding the truck. There were footprints, lots of them, and tire marks from multiple dirt bikes.

"I think the forensic team was taking those photos to show how difficult it was to read the ground," Normandy said. "I don't think they came up with anything by looking at it. And then I'm not sure we did a very good job with walking around the truck, to be honest. I'm not even sure what that crime scene tape is doing out there."

Right now it indicated the wind had gotten stronger.

"We don't get much death down here," Normandy said. "Shit, I've only seen one dead body in the four years I've been here, and that was an old man who died on his couch."

Wolf finished looking at the photos, handed the folder back to Normandy, and popped open the door.

Normandy followed his lead, climbing out of the truck.

They stood in silence, the wind pushing through the natural wind tunnel, flapping Wolf's jacket collar against his face.

"It was pointed that direction," Normandy said, "away from us. So they must have driven up the same way we came in."

Wolf had already seen that in the photos, but he let the young man talk. "They," he said.

"Had to have been more than one person," Normandy said. "Whoever drove the truck up here, and then whoever drove that person out of here. Right?"

Wolf nodded, looking down. Normandy was right, they hadn't done a very good job, leaving dozens of footprints of every shoe style and size.

"Me and Mustaine looked up and down the wash for footprints, you know, away from all these other footprints. We didn't find anything."

"Mind if I look for myself?"

"No, sir. Of course."

Wolf walked to the ring of crime tape and looked in, seeing tire tracks suggesting a tow truck had come in and pulled it out —a big truck coming in, stopping, lots of commotion, and driving away the opposite direction with a heavy load.

"They pulled it out with a tow truck yesterday," Normandy said, watching him.

The sheer number of footprints made it impossible for Wolf to decipher anything. He walked past the ring of tape and through the gap in the rocks. A gust of wind hit, sending grains of sand hissing along the ground, the cold knifing through his clothing, the crime scene tape humming.

He kept his eyes on the ground and heard Normandy follow behind. The wind thrashed them, spilling over the sides of the wash, which were ten or so feet at their tallest points. Above the banks the trees thinned, giving way to low shrubs and grasses carpeting gentle slopes that had turned them warm, earthen tones of autumn.

The occasional elk and deer had printed the floor of the wash, all of it crisscrossed with the tread of dirt bikers and the occasional boot and shoe track.

Further down the human foot traffic dissipated, save two lines of prints. Wolf picked them up and followed the new trail.

"That's me and Mustaine," Normandy said. "We walked here looking for prints, too."

Wolf nodded and continued, his chin tucked in his jacket against the chill, following the tracks on the ground. Mustaine's were heavy, one of the legs twisting and dragging a bit at the toe with each long step, while Normandy's were lighter, his toes pointed inward slightly.

They walked in silence for another fifteen minutes, following Mustaine and Normandy's tracks to their terminus, then beyond. When it was clear there were no other human tracks to be found, Wolf climbed out of the wash and up a long slope that blocked the horizon ahead. He walked ahead, curious to see what was on the other side of the rise, where the ground flattened and the wind blew even harder.

Layers of mountains and valleys rose into view, the most distant ones blotted out by the encroaching moisture. Curtains dropped out of the clouds in the distance, sweeping over the landscape, heading straight for them.

"They say it might be a couple inches that falls today and tonight," Normandy said.

"Let's head back," Wolf said, his curiosity satisfied.

Back at the car, Normandy opened the door, cursing as the wind tried to push it closed on him.

"I'll take the way we came in on foot," Wolf said.

"Okay. I'll follow."

Normandy got in and fired the engine while Wolf walked down the wash toward the bridge, and his SUV, in the distance.

At first there were dozens of footprints, too many to make sense of, before they thinned out after fifty or so yards. Wolf kept walking, his boots sinking in the sand, scraping on the bedrock that poked through in places, kicking round river rocks. The footprints whittled down to two sets, Normandy's and Sheriff Mustaine's.

Normandy crawled behind him in the truck, the exhaust whipping past Wolf in spurts.

It was much the same in this direction, with footprints thinning out as the distance grew from the scene, but here there were more vehicle tracks than the other direction, wiping everything out, even Mustaine's and Normandy's.

Normandy kept a patient crawl behind him.

A short while later Wolf decided that was good enough and stepped to the side of the road.

"Well?" Normandy asked through the window, pulling up beside him.

"Nothing I can see." Maybe a better tracker could have unraveled the mess, but not Wolf.

He popped open the door and got inside. It was jarringly still, save a breath of warm air flowing out of the vents.

"Not really much to learn, I guess," Normandy said. "But that's the spot."

They drove back up onto the dirt road and over the bridge, then to Wolf's SUV.

"Three o'clock," Normandy said, pointing to the dash clock. "Undersheriff Elan set up an appointment for this afternoon at four-thirty to see Bennett's truck. They have it sitting in the town impound still. He figured you'd want to see that."

"He figured good. How about the body?" Wolf asked. "I'd like to see that, too."

"That's what he also figured," Normandy said. "But the coroner's not back in the office until tomorrow morning at eight. We have an appointment set up for then."

"Okay, we have until four-thirty. An hour and a half. How far is it to drive down to Crow Valley?"

"Took me about forty minutes," Normandy said. "But that was the fast way. I'm supposed to take you the long way back."

"What's the long way? And why?"

"I think it's best you follow me. We'll take that turnoff about a quarter mile down the road. It's County Road 309-B, but everyone calls it High Road around here. A bit more romantic, you know? You would have passed it on your left on the way up."

Wolf nodded, not recalling the turnoff. That's what following a red line on a computer screen will get you—real life out the window passing by unnoticed.

"It's a two-track jeep trail. A bit rough in spots, but not too bad."

"After you," Wolf said, popping the door and hopping out.

5

The snow came straight at Rachette's windshield, making the world outside look like they were in the Millennium Falcon heading into light speed.

"How much longer do we have?" Rachette asked, leaning forward.

They were on their way to talk to the two men who had their bikes stolen. The theft victims worked at the base of the resort, both in the same lift ticket office, an office that was only a few miles from the town of Rocky Points, a drive that usually only took fifteen minutes, but they'd been driving for at least twenty into the white maw of the storm that had descended into the Chautauqua Valley.

"We're here," Yates said, pointing at the first buildings of the resort village as they emerged from the whiteout.

Rachette slowed and parked at the wood-constructed structure with the loud paint job, intimate with the lift ticket and season pass office in question, and their astronomical price increases over the last few years.

While Rachette shut off the engine he watched Yates, wearing only a flannel pushed up to his elbows, get out without hesitation and shut the door. The last couple months his partner had been going on about exposure to more cold weather and its importance to immune system health.

No thanks, Rachette thought as he zipped up his jacket all the way, donned the winter cap over his closely shorn head, and exited the vehicle.

The snow fell hard and sideways, stinging his face. He squinted to see and leaned forward, walking across the street fast toward the building.

"Damn it," he said to himself. It was times like this when fond memories of Nebraska fall weather came back to him, where the snows of winter were still a couple months away.

Before long he was underneath a covered walkway and out of the elements, joining Yates at the entrance to the office.

Yates opened the glass door and walked in, and Rachette stepped in behind him.

The air inside was warm and dry, smelling vaguely of food. A young man sat at a reception desk. He had long blond hair that looked like it was housing wildlife, a nose ring, and tattoos on his arms edging out of his long-sleeved Rocky Points Resort t-shirt.

The kid saw the badges and guns, straightening in his chair.

"We're here to see Jake Morhaus," Rachette checked the piece of paper in his pocket, "and Theo Anders."

"I'm Theo," he said.

Rachette nodded, looking closer at Theo Anders. Rachette had seen this young man around town over the last few years, but he'd never spoken to him.

"Is Jake around?" Yates asked.

"Yeah. Just a second." Theo got up, revealing he was tall and thin, and walked into a row of cubicles in back. He peered over a workspace wall and spoke softly, then came back with another young man, presumably Jake, in tow.

Jake had the same look as Theo, tattoos on his arms, fit-looking, but with hair cut shorter than his friend and standing a few inches lower.

"Hi, I'm Jake," he said.

"I'm Detective Rachette. This is Detective Yates. We're with the sheriff's department."

A woman in her mid-forties leaned out from another cubicle, eyeing Rachette and Yates. "What's happening?" she asked.

"Hello, ma'am." Rachette nodded.

She stood and walked up behind Theo, extending her hand. "I'm Trisha. I'm the manager of the ticket office. Is this about the bikes?"

"Yes ma'am." Rachette took her hand and shook. It was wiry, her grip like iron. She wore no makeup, her long brown hair pulled back in a ponytail, wearing the same basic outfit as Theo and Jake. She was pretty, not in a drop-dead gorgeous way, but she had big blue eyes that were electric.

She turned to Yates. Neither of them extended their hands to one another.

"Howdy partner," she said with a smile. "Fancy seeing you here."

Yates's skin turned red, and it wasn't the cold weather exposure.

After a brief silence Trisha cleared her throat. "It's crazy. I keep telling them, they shouldn't have parked them on the other side. They could have locked them up right there and kept an eye on them all day."

She pointed to a floor-to ceiling window behind them. Beyond the glass was a hibernating ski lift barely visible through the fog and flakes, and, much closer, a bike rack.

Rachette nodded, sliding a glance to Yates again. Yates stared out the window.

"So, what's up?" Jake asked. "Did you find the bikes?"

"No, not yet," Rachette said. "We're just looking into it, and my partner and I wanted to ask you two a few questions."

"Yeah sure," Jake said. "Shoot."

"Actually, can we see exactly where these bikes were stolen from?"

"Uh, yeah." Jake looked at Trisha.

Trisha shrugged. "When the big law men call, you gotta answer." She looked at Yates.

"Let me get my coat." Jake walked back to his cubicle.

Theo pulled his coat from the back of his chair and slipped it on.

"You still have a phone, detective?" Trisha asked Yates.

Yates kicked his foot on the carpet. "Yeah. I mean, yeah."

Rachette gave his partner some space to flounder and went to the window. The bike rack outside was a good thirty feet long, with two more racks behind it. He knew this was the ski lift that took the downhill mountain bikers up in the summer months, so there would have to be plenty of bike parking space here.

"Ready?" Yates asked.

Rachette turned around and saw Yates and the two men waiting, the woman known as Trisha no longer in view.

They walked outside and back into the elements, following Jake and Theo down the covered walkway until they came to a tunnel between a darkened clothing shop and a condominium building.

"This way," Jake said, waving them into the tunnel, and into a hard headwind that funneled straight at them.

Rachette ducked his head, hands shoved into his pockets, following until they came out the other side and into a wide base area. Here two chairlifts sat idle in front of the main ski lodge. In a couple of months, when ski season was in full swing, this zone would be choked with skiers and snowboarders, music blaring, the smell of burgers cooking in the air, but now it sat quiet and deserted.

Jake stopped, gesturing to another bike rack lined up against the wall of a restroom building. "Here it is. Here's where we had our bikes parked."

Rachette turned his back to the snow, looking at the rack, then left and right at the closed clothing shop and condominium buildings. "Why did you guys park here?"

Jake leaned sideways and pointed. "We were eating breakfast down there before work. We ride in from town from that way. And sometimes we stop for food and coffee first before we go to the office."

"Where?" Rachette asked, leaning sideways with Jake and seeing nothing but a closed ski lodge building.

"On the other side of that lodge there's a coffee shop. In front of that other lift down there."

Rachette held up his hand to cover the snow and saw a silhouette of the ski lift on the far side of the base area.

"So you parked here and walked all the way over there?"

Jake nodded.

Theo said nothing.

"And you said you rode in from that direction? Why didn't you stop at the coffee shop as you were riding past?"

"Well, we come in on the road. On the other side of that tunnel."

Rachette frowned.

Jake shrugged. "It was kind of a last second decision. We decided to park our bikes between the two places, you know, between work and the coffee shop, and walk there."

Theo said nothing.

Rachette blinked, trying to follow the strain of logic, but shook his head, giving up. "Okay, so you locked the bikes up here, and went down there to eat. Then you went to work, walking past the bikes on the way back to the office, leaving them here all day?"

"Yeah, we know." Jake shook his head. "In hindsight it was dumb. I mean, damn, we didn't think anybody would come up and cut the locks here. It's out in the open."

Rachette looked around, doing a full circle in place. If he were to step close to the restroom building, the structure was tucked in and angled so it was out of sight of the buildings next to it.

"Actually, you can't see a single window into any of these buildings from here," he said. "It's out in the open, but it's pretty secluded, too."

Jake turned around. "Yeah, I guess you're right."

Rachette raised his eyebrows. "Yeah."

Theo seemed preoccupied by his feet. Rachette looked down and saw the tall, silent young man was rubbing the sole of one shoe against a dark smudge on the other shoe's toe. When he saw Rachette was watching him he stopped and looked around.

Rachette wondered if he was stoned, if they were both stoned. That would explain the lack of logic these two operated with.

"The report said you found the locks cut at the end of the workday," Yates said.

"That's right," Jake said.

"Were there any other bikes parked here, when you locked them up?" Yates asked. "Any other bikes here when you got back and saw they were gone?"

"No, sir," Jake said. "It's pretty dead after the summer season's over. The lifts are closed. Not many bikers."

"Did you ask around if anyone saw anything?" Rachette asked. "Anybody working in the lodge? Or in the condos?"

"No, sir," Jake said. "Everything's locked up for another few weeks until ski season starts."

Rachette looked at Theo, realizing he hadn't said a word since introducing himself earlier in the office. "Is that right, Theo?"

"What's that, sir?"

"Nothing. Just seeing if you're awake. Listen, we have the descriptions of the bikes on file in the report. But do you guys by chance have a photograph of the bikes?"

Jake shook his head, sucking in a breath skeptically. "I can't think of a ... wait a minute." He pulled out his phone and began tapping buttons. "I do have pictures of a ride we did down in Durango this summer. Maybe there's a photo of us there...just a second."

Jake tapped and swiped, while Theo continued his ice statue impression.

"You don't have any photos?" Rachette asked Theo.

Theo shook his head.

Stoned, Rachette thought again, surer now than ever.

"Here. Here's a photo of mine, and one of Theo's too."

Jake pointed the screen toward them, displaying a photo of Jake sitting on his bike, his arms in the air, stopped at the top of a mountain. The bike beneath him was clearly visible. "And here's a picture of Theo. It's not as good, but it's all I have."

He swiped, showing the next photo, with Theo sitting on his bike atop the same mountain with a group of friends. Theo's bike was a diagonal view, some of the details lost in glare, but it was better than nothing.

Yates relayed his phone number and Jake texted him the photos.

"I hope you catch the guy," Jake said, pocketing his phone.

"No guarantees," Rachette said. "Only an idiot would steal a bike and then ride it around town or sell it online. But, of course, only an idiot would steal a bike. We'll cover all the bases."

Rachette and Yates said their goodbyes and walked back to the SUV, but not before stopping at the doors of the condo buildings and ski lodge, finding them both locked tight.

Once back at the vehicle Rachette sat behind the wheel, cranked the heater, and rubbed his hands in front of the vent.

"What do you think?" Yates asked.

"I think those two have gotta lay off the pot brownies. Maybe they can keep track of their valuables a bit better."

"No shit."

He shifted into drive. *"Partner."*

Yates shot him a warning glare, but he pretended not to notice.

"So, what now?" Rachette asked.

"I don't know. I guess we start checking the internet."

"I'd feel better about that if we had some food in us."

Yates eyed Rachette's gut. "Of course you would."

Rachette shot him a warning glare of his own, but Yates pretended not to notice.

6

After thirty minutes of brisk driving over rutted, rocky jeep trail, snaking through dense forest, Wolf and Normandy emerged in a clear spot on the side of a gradual-sloped mountain, where the majesty of the terrain stood in full view as far as the eye could see.

Normandy slowed to a stop, got out, and walked towards Wolf's vehicle.

Wolf rolled down his window, letting in a blast of cold wind.

"We'll get out here for a second. I want to show you something about this view." He pointed to the west, down the slope toward the lowering sun, and to a meadow on the valley floor below.

Wolf shut off his engine, got out, and followed Normandy to the shoulder of the road.

"That's the Whitlock Ranch," Normandy said, pointing down.

In a clearing in a meadow far below stood a rectangular one-story house, and a larger rectangular tan out-building. The grass surrounding the place still had some green color blotches to it, and around which cattle dotted the land like tiny black ants.

"This is why Mustaine's so suspicious of Carrie Whitlock. She was at the bar that night, and she lives right down there." Normandy pointed back the way they had come and shrugged. "Pretty close to his body."

"Carrie Whitlock was one of the two women at the bar who left around the same time as Bennett," Wolf said, refreshing his own memory.

"Correct, sir. And Valentina Johnson was the other woman."

"But Valentina lives down in town, correct?"

"Yes, sir."

There was activity down at the ranch, two figures walking through the yard from the out-building toward the house.

They both stared downward, until a flake of snow swept by on the wind, and then another.

"I'd like to talk to them," Wolf said.

"Now?"

Wolf looked at him.

"I mean, yeah, sure. We can go down and talk to them." Normandy looked at his watch.

"We're up here now and the weather's rolling in," Wolf said. "We may as well take advantage of us being here. If we're late to see the truck I'll take the blame."

"Yes, sir. Sounds good to me."

"Do you think that Carrie Whitlock will be there now?" Wolf asked.

"I think she's there. She works at the ranch full time, and with the risk of having a run-in with Mustaine if she goes down into town?" He chuckled. "Yeah, I bet she's there."

"Let's go."

The trail sloped down gradually, switching back and forth a few times as it descended. At the bottom the two-track met up with a much wider and well-maintained gravel county road.

After a short drive through lodgepole pines they came upon the Whitlock Ranch.

The house was surrounded by tall game fencing, and three barking golden retrievers ran alongside them on the other side of the wire mesh as they pulled up. Normandy took a turn off the road onto their driveway, which led across an expanse of open field, then stopped at a wooden and wire gate closed shut with a chain, completing the full enclosure of the house.

He stopped and got out. The air had gone completely still. It smelled of cattle dung, grass, and moisture. Snow fell straight down in pellets, making a whooshing sound as they landed.

The dogs barked until quieted by a woman using a sharp German command.

The woman stood on the covered porch, watching them with narrowed eyes. A rifle leaned against the house just a foot from where she stood, clearly placed for effect. She looked to be in her early fifties, healthy and strong looking, with sandy-blonde hair and tanned skin. The front door was open, and behind her stood a young woman of about twenty, along with a teenaged boy about eighteen. They all had similar features, similar builds, clearly all related.

"Hello Nola!" Normandy said.

"Is *he* coming here?" She asked.

"Mustaine?"

"Yeah, Mustaine."

"No, ma'am."

Though the static of the snow dropping, Wolf could see she took a deep breath, looking relieved. She turned around and said something, and the young man disappeared into the house.

"This is Detective David Wolf," Normandy said.

The three dogs came to the fence and sat, curious onlookers to the conversation.

"He's down here from Rocky Points. He's going to help us with the Bennett case."

She said nothing.

Wolf cleared his throat and waved. "Hello."

She nodded.

"I was hoping I could have a word with you. Maybe we could come in out of the cold for a few minutes and chat?"

"No thanks," she said. "We've already had our chat with the cops. I'm not interested in having another."

Wolf eyed their front yard, which was strewn with rusted farm equipment, parked in neat rows, rather than the haphazard mess Wolf had seen in many other rural abodes.

The outbuilding had a large roll door that was open, revealing the interior. Inside stood an antique tractor, cleaned to its original green color, all the rust removed.

Wolf took a stab. "You restoring this stuff or something?"

Nola Whitlock folded her arms. "The boys restore old farm equipment and we re-sell it. Helps pay the bills."

The young man returned in the doorway, another young man behind him, slightly taller and older looking.

"That's Carrie, Kent, and Cruz," Normandy said, just loud enough for Wolf to hear.

"That must be Kent, Carrie, and Cruz," Wolf said to Nola.

Nola nodded, or at least Wolf thought she did. It was tough to tell. The snow was getting worse. What he did know was that she was basically saying nothing.

"Anyway, nice to meet you," he said, now feeling like he was talking to a wall. He chuckled. "You sure we couldn't come up to the porch and have a word with you? It would be nice to get out of the snow."

"We've already told you guys what you need to know. I'll

repeat it for you, since you're new. But Carrie came home at eleven Saturday night. Valentina drove her. Valentina went back home. That's that."

"Okay," Wolf said. "Is that right, Carrie?"

Nola turned around and snapped at her under her breath, resulting in silence from Carrie.

"We don't need to talk to you," Nola said. "We know our rights. We already tried talking to Mustaine, and he stood right where you were, threatening us. Telling us we had to let him in, then he threatened to break in, and that he'd start making us talk. We heard what he did to Valentina. You think I'm stupid? You think I'm going to put my children in danger?"

"I understand. I heard about what happened."

"Then you'll understand." Nola turned around and shooed her kids back in the house. She gripped the handle, then ducked out. "You two have a good day now." And she shut the door.

The dogs stood up and started barking, three gentle animals turned rabid on a dime. Wolf and Normandy backed away from the fence.

"O-kay," Normandy said. "And that's the Whitlocks."

"Where's the husband? Their father?" Wolf asked as they headed for their vehicles.

"He left ten or so years ago."

"Gotcha," Wolf said, eyeing the house through the fence. The front door was still closed. The dogs were still barking, pacing back and forth.

"You were here with Mustaine when he came up and threatened them?" Wolf asked.

"I was, but only for about half the conversation."

Wolf shook his head. He wanted more. He wanted to know exactly what had been said when Mustaine had come up. But here and now was not the place or time.

"She's a tough one," Normandy said. "They all are, those Whitlocks."

"Mustaine really spooked them, eh?"

Normandy said nothing, but he nodded, then looked at his watch. "Well, on the bright side, with our conversation being so short, we have plenty of time to get to the garage."

Wolf eyed the house. A curtain was drawn back, revealing a pretty young woman's face looking back at him. Carrie. Her eyes were wide and unblinking.

"We'd better head down the canyon," Normandy said. "Before this gets too much worse."

Wolf nodded. "Okay. I'll follow you."

He walked to his SUV, eying the window again, seeing nothing but the drape swinging to a stop.

7

Wolf followed the tire tracks that were cut into the snow, feeling a bit of relief that Normandy had seemed to come to his senses with his speed. The way down to Crow Valley became steep, and although visibility had been reduced, he could still see some big drop-offs on the side of the road.

There was no one else on the road. It was desolate country. Or maybe people were just smart around here and weren't driving in this mess.

A few minutes later they were out of the canyon and into a huge sage- and shrub-covered valley that reminded Wolf of the valley south of Williams Pass. Here the snow thinned to a wisp, the bulk of the storm still not reaching here for whatever meteorological reason. The visibility opened up to miles again, revealing a wall of mountains to the east on the far side of the valley, the tops obscured by clouds.

The road went ruler-straight as Wolf coasted down a slope behind Normandy, toward traffic running perpendicular on a highway in the distance.

Crow Valley was a mass of low buildings choked by trees.

Wolf wondered where all the beauty was his mother had been talking about. Probably behind all these clouds, or his mother was mistaken. It wouldn't be the first time, especially lately.

His mind wandered to home, and his heart quickened thinking about Piper. What had happened at the meeting today? Was she going to be working at the department now? He pulled out his phone and dialed her number. Her phone rang through his speakers three, then four times, then went to voicemail. He left her a message and told her to call him back, then focused on the town ahead.

In and out. Patterson's promise of a quick case echoed in his mind.

He was still a mile or so from being *in*, and as far as a way *out*, that was like the landscape hidden behind the surrounding clouds, completely unknown.

Soon the dirt turned to pavement, shiny and wet, and then they were inside the town limits.

There were some cars on the road, not exactly the rush hour traffic that choked Rocky Points during ski season, but more than he would have guessed. What did everyone do in this town, he wondered?

He followed Normandy to the highway where they hung a left, heading towards the northern outskirts of town, and then slowed and took a right at a large building and parked in the lot.

The garage was the size of a small airplane hangar, black corrugated metal with two white roll doors, one open, emitting a bright glow into the fading daylight.

There was one Crow County SD SUV parked outside of the building, which Normandy and Wolf flanked as they parked.

Was it Mustaine's vehicle? He was about to find out.

He had given this some thought, and the only way he could see this working at all was if he came in offering assistance.

There would be no sense coming in with the intention of taking over, even if that's what he was officially doing. In reality, this was Mustaine's son, and this was Mustaine's case.

If it were Jack, Wolf would not welcome somebody from the outside coming in for the express reason to push him aside and take over. No, Wolf would not welcome that at all.

Wolf got out into calm air, just as cool as it had been thirty minutes ago up at the Whitlock Ranch. It smelled of diesel fumes and moisture.

Two men walked into the open doorway. Neither of them was Mustaine.

"That's Undersheriff Elan," Normandy said, walking with Wolf across the parking lot.

"How are you?" Elan said, walking forward. Elan was short and wide, a few pounds overweight but light on his feet. He was in his fifties, with blonde hair and glasses. Behind the lenses shone confident, intelligent eyes. He held out his hand.

Wolf shook it. "David Wolf. Nice to meet you."

"You, too. This is Dr. Donald Traver," Elan said. "He's our head forensic technician in Crow County."

Traver was thin, in his sixties, and taller than Elan. He also wore glasses, and his handshake and expression said he wasn't too excited to be there. Or was it for Wolf to be there?

"Back here," Elan said turning and waving them inside.

The building was tall and bright, and smelled strongly of diesel, with an undertone of rubber. A school bus sat parked, its hood removed, along with two snowplows, one of which was being worked on by a pair of mechanics.

They headed for the rear of the building, where pole-mounted floodlights surrounded a full-sized red pickup Wolf recognized from the pictures as Bennett Mustaine's. Crime scene tape threaded a circle around it all.

"Here's Bennett's truck," Elan said unnecessarily.

"Here you go." Traver handed over a box of latex gloves and ducked under the tape, Wolf following.

"What did you think about the scene?" Traver asked.

"I didn't see much."

"Too many footprints," Traver said. "Between the dirt bikers and all the personnel that showed up on scene it looked like a stampede had gone through there." He led Wolf to a folding table stacked with photographs. "I may have found some swept tracks here," indicating a photo of sand, with a depression that might or might not have been a footprint.

"That one's not the best. But see here?" Traver gave Wolf another one. "See that? Looks like a push broom mark to me. It was windy last weekend. So, it's inconclusive. But my gut's telling me somebody had the foresight to wipe their tracks. Looking at the truck, I wouldn't doubt it."

Wolf took his word for it and looked at the truck.

Traver put the stack of photographs down and walked toward it. "You can see here in the back seat where we found him." The doctor gestured to the rear door.

Wolf walked up and looked in. All the doors were opened, and the lights were positioned to illuminate every inch of the interior.

"See the blood there?" Traver pointed at the seat. "And up there. Above your head."

Wolf looked at the ceiling and saw spatter, a lot of it.

"He was here," Traver said, fire in his voice. Wolf dismissed his earlier perception of a slight to be just the man's quirks. Traver pointed at the seat in front of Wolf. "On his knees. Pants down. He was shot in the right temple. The gun used was Bennett's personal handgun. A Glock thirty loaded with Federal HST two-thirty grain. The exit wound was large and messy. He bled out on the back seat, went down face first."

There was a piece of string running from the rear of the

front passenger seat to the ceiling, where it met a hole in the roof of the truck, marking the trajectory and origin of the bullet that traveled through Bennett Mustaine's skull.

Wolf backed away and went around to the other rear door.

"You can see here he bled out onto the seat, and there was a lot of smearing of the blood. That suggests to me that the body was driven to the spot those dirt bikers found him. The blood pooled at the back of the seat, suggesting the vehicle was parked at an upward angle when he died. But look here. You can see the marks, rhythmic rocking back and forth, forward and back of the body hours after he was shot."

Wolf eyed the marks.

"The blood had dried in the shallower spots," Traver said, watching Wolf. "But not so in the deeper puddling. That part was smeared over the dry marks. So, it's clear he was driven to the spot where he was found hours after death."

Wolf nodded. "And no prints?"

"None, other than a few of Bennett's on the rear tailgate, and some other obscure parts in the back. The gun was wiped clean. The door handles, all four of them, most of the exterior doors, all of the interior except for the blood. I did find yellow fibers everywhere inside, wherever it was wiped. Seventy percent to thirty percent ratio of polyester and polyamide. They used a cleaning agent that had ... well, I could list the ingredients, but I narrowed it down to a common multi-surface spray that could have been any of three different brands. It's all in my report."

Wolf nodded again. "What else? Anything definitive? Anything leading to a suspect?"

"Nothing."

Wolf waited for further explanation, but none came. "And GSR? Did you find any on his hand?"

"We found gunshot residue on his right hand. But as you

know GSR tests alone cannot indicate the shooter. It takes analysis, and what we have is a crime scene that has been tampered with."

"Does it look like suicide to you?" Wolf asked.

The word seemed to make the doctor visibly flinch. He gave Elan a quick look.

Wolf followed his eyes and saw Elan was looking at the garage ceiling.

"It could look like that," Traver said. "But it also looks like he could have been putting his hand up to block the shot." Traver pantomimed the motion. "That would explain the presence where it was found."

"How about stippling?" Wolf asked. "Was there any powder tattooing on his hand supporting that theory? That would be a way to rule that out, right?"

Traver stared down at the vehicle seat, as if looking through it.

"Doctor?"

"Yes. No. I didn't see any myself. But only if his hand was in close proximity to the blast of the gun would there be stippling. But I'm not the coroner. You'll have to talk to Dr. Carl. He's the expert on that kind of stuff. Not me."

Wolf eyed him, then Elan and Normandy. Everyone seemed to be avoiding looking at everyone else. Suicide was not a popular theory. Got it.

Then Dr. Traver seemed to see something interesting at the garage door. He turned and walked toward one of the mounted flood lights with a hand up to block the onslaught of illumination. "It's snowing now. I have to leave. I'm sorry. I told you, Undersheriff, I have to go. You have everything I know in my report, and in those photographs."

Dr. Traver snapped off his gloves and put them in a trash can as he walked away, not waiting for a response from Elan.

The Undersheriff's face went red. "I'm sorry. He's a bit strange sometimes. He has to make a drive down to Silverton tonight. It's going to be brutal in this weather. He was freaking out about it before you got here."

Wolf nodded. "It's okay. We have everything in the report, right?'

"Right."

Elan's cell phone chimed. "Just a second, I have to get this. Hello?"

Wolf walked around the vehicle as Elan talked on the phone. It sounded urgent, and Wolf kept one ear toward the conversation as he inspected the interior of the truck some more.

"... okay ... send Alvarez. I'll be back soon ... he's here ... and?"

He stared some more at the trajectory string. Given the position of the body when it was found, if there was a shooter they must have been sitting in the front seat as they shot Bennett in the head, with their arm over the headrest and down low, or they reached around the seat. Which would have been difficult to make that upward trajectory shown by the string and the spatter. But not impossible.

"Okay. Okay..." Elan said, a bit of annoyance in his tone. "When in the afternoon?...no, have you talked to him? Okay, okay, we'll be back." Elan put the phone back in his pocket.

"Everything okay?" Wolf asked.

"Not really. The snow's hitting. You know how it is. We're already starting to get calls." He looked at Normandy. "Alvarez is heading out to a collision on mile marker one-two-eight."

"You want me to join him?" Normandy asked.

"No. You'd better come back with me, in case something else pops." Elan looked at Wolf with raised eyebrows. "I'm sorry, we have to get back. Are you coming? Or I know it's been a long day for you, you can come in first thing tomorrow."

Elan went to a power strip and flipped a switch, shutting off the floodlights.

The garage went momentarily dark, then Wolf's eyes adjusted.

Elan led them outside. "Later, Chad!"

"Later!" a man yelled, waving out from under one of the snowplows.

They walked outside, and into thick wet flakes of falling snow. "Where's Mustaine?" Wolf asked. "I was hoping to have a word with him."

Elan stopped and looked at him, ducking his head away from the snow slanting down. "Well, that's a good question. We haven't seen him for a couple days."

"Really," Wolf said.

"Really."

They continued across the parking lot. Wolf wanted to call it a day and start first thing in the morning, to go sit in a motel bed in his underwear, with some food, the television on, but he also wanted to get this thing over with. In and out.

"I'll follow you back," he said. "I'd like to talk to you guys some more about what's happened so far."

Elan nodded. "Follow us."

8

The Crow County Sheriff's Department building was small, a boxy place made of brick with two front windows that glowed yellow in the evening dimness.

Wolf parked next to Normandy and Elan, noting there was a cruiser and an SUV also parked there.

They walked through the lot, Wolf squinting against the flakes as they blasted his face, wondering if Mustaine would be there.

The suspense was raising his blood pressure, and he wanted the scene over with.

"Mustaine's not here," Elan said. "He drives a truck."

Wolf nodded and followed him inside, thinking Elan was reading his mind, and that he thought he heard a bit of relief in the Undersheriff's voice.

They walked into a large room where five desks were situated at various angles. A uniformed woman was seated at the first desk. She looked up at Wolf, then the others, then turned her attention back on her computer screen. Her skin was brown and her hair black, and her long fingernails were painted bright pink.

"This is Deputy Garcia," Elan said. "This is Detective Wolf, from Rocky Points."

She smiled, but to Wolf it looked more like a wince, or something somebody does when they smell something terrible.

"Nice to meet you." He shook her hand, one of her nails scraping against his wrist.

A man sat at another desk against the back wall, looking up from his computer.

"Alvarez," Elan said. "I thought you went out to one-fifteen."

"State troopers' on scene. They have it covered." The man named Alvarez nodded at Wolf. "Hi."

"Hi. I'm David Wolf." Wolf walked over and offered a hand.

Alvarez stood and shook it. He wore a tight uniform shirt that hugged a broad chest, suggesting he spent a lot of time in the gym. His grip was firm, his eye contact deliberate. Wolf pegged him in his late thirties or early forties.

Normandy went to his desk and Elan to his, while Wolf stood awkwardly in the center of the room.

"You can take one of those chairs," Elan said, pointing to a cracked plastic seat on the other side of his desk. "Still no sign of the big man, eh?" Elan asked nobody in particular.

"No, sir," Garcia said, keeping her eyes on her computer screen. She typed fast despite the nails.

The room descended into silence, and Wolf felt acutely out of place as he looked around. There was a door on the rear wall that was open, revealing a darkened office inside. A nameplate read *Sheriff Mustaine*.

Wolf eyed the squad room walls surrounding them. There hung a half-dozen landscape photos of, presumably, Crow Valley and the surrounding area. The photographer made it look beautiful, he had to admit. There were deep canyons lined with aspens, a high mountain lake, some snow-veined peaks.

"My father took those photographs," Normandy said.

Wolf nodded. "They're nice. What about case photos, though? You guys have a board set up? A room for the investigation?"

"Mustaine didn't want that," Elan said.

Wolf raised an eyebrow.

"Last thing he wants to see are pictures of his son's dead body up on the wall," Garcia said.

"I see," he said slowly. "So, I've heard a bit of information from the DA about what happened, I've seen the spot where you found Bennett. I've seen the truck. I've seen pictures of his body at the scene. And now I've met you guys. But I haven't met Bennett."

They sat silent.

"So, what have you got on him? I hear he played football like his father, and that you found him dead up in Dry Wash. That's about it."

Alvarez cleared his throat. "Age twenty-two. He grew up here in Crow Valley. Played football. He was Mustaine's only child, so we always heard about his sports achievements. He was a good athlete growing up. Let's see ... went to college to play football, you know that, got injured, and came back here."

"Where did he live?" Wolf asked. "With whom?"

"Alone," Elan said. "Across the highway, in a house on the southern side of town."

"Friends?"

They looked at one another, and Alvarez took the answer. "He hangs out with Paco Nez, I know that. All the other high school jocks he used to hang out with pretty much left. Other than that…I guess that's something to look into more."

"Who's Paco Nez?"

"Paco owns a pizza shop with Bennett," Elan said. "I guess I should say owned."

"Interesting," Wolf said.

"Yeah," Alvarez said. "Mustaine didn't approve of it too much, but he helped with some seed money to start it up. Wanted to help get his son on his feet and all."

"Where's Bennett's mother?"

"She's not in the picture." Elan gestured to the others. "They would know better than me. I've only been here a couple years."

"She left a long time ago," Alvarez said. "Moved out east. I don't know the story there. I just know she's not in the picture."

"Did Bennett have a record?" Wolf asked.

There was a palpable pause now, and it seemed like everyone was simultaneously holding their breath.

Elan cleared his throat. "He doesn't have a record."

Wolf nodded. "Okay, let's go back to Friday night, and the investigation so far. What happened, start to finish? What have you got?"

Garcia, Alvarez, and Normandy said nothing, clearly deferring to Elan.

The Undersheriff cleared his throat. "Sure. Of course." He got up and walked to a table set against one of the walls, carrying a coffee mug from his desk. "Coffee?"

"No, thanks."

Elan poured himself a cup from a carafe and came and sat back down. "We got the call Sunday. In the morning. Garcia took it."

Wolf looked at her.

"It was some guy," she said, turning around in her chair. "He wouldn't give me his name, just the location of the truck and dead body. He said he and his friends rode past it on their dirt bikes. I asked him to come in to give us an official report, but he hung up. The number was from the payphone at the Shell station north of town."

"Did the caller mention Bennett Mustaine by name?" Wolf asked.

"No, sir," Garcia said. "He just said they saw a dead body. Male."

"We're going with the theory they had nothing to do with it," Elan said. "They just didn't want to get caught up in hanging out with us."

Wolf nodded. "So that was Sunday morning. What next?"

"So we went up there," Elan said.

"All of you?"

"I stayed here," Garcia said.

"The rest of us went up, with Mustaine." Elan looked at his desk and shook his head.

"So, Sunday was spent on site. Dr. Traver and his assistant came up and processed the scene."

Normandy got up and handed a manila folder to Wolf.

Wolf recognized it as the same one he'd seen earlier that day in Normandy's car.

"That's yours," Normandy said. "I forgot to give it to you earlier."

Wolf leafed through the pictures again while Elan continued.

"As far as the investigation goes," Elan said, "that first day we were all pretty shell-shocked. We just kind of sat around up there, watched the scene be processed and taken away. Mustaine took it very hard. A couple of his friends came in to try and console him, but he turned them away. He sat in his office that whole night. I'm not sure he slept. He was just staring." Elan's eyes widened, and then he shook his head. "On Monday we started our investigation. Me, Normandy, Alvarez, and Mustaine."

"And Garcia?" Wolf asked.

"Garcia is our dispatcher. She stays in house."

"Gotcha."

"Our first goal was to figure out when Bennett was last seen. And we came to the conclusion he was last seen Friday night at the Tavern. It's a place over on Main."

"And how did you come to that conclusion?"

"We talked to Paco Nez," Elan said. "Like we said, Paco runs the pizza place with Bennett. They were partners. Best friends."

"How long have they been friends?" Wolf asked.

Alvarez fielded the question. "They're longtime friends from high school. Maybe earlier. I'm not sure."

Wolf nodded.

Elan continued. "Paco told us Bennett was the first to leave the pizza shop, and Paco stayed to close up with another employee."

"Time he left?"

"Bennett left around nine-thirty. And he reported to Paco he was going to go have some drinks at the Tavern. Paco said he was going to join him once he closed up."

Elan sipped his coffee, gathering his thoughts.

"So, we made our way down to The Tavern, and we spoke to the bartender. He happened to also be working Saturday night, so he confirmed Bennett was there. He produced a receipt that showed Bennett paying at 11:15 pm, and the bartender said he remembers him leaving immediately after paying.

"He played pool with some of the local men. And we learned that Carrie Whitlock and her friend Valentina Johnson were sitting over there by the table, conversing and having drinks of their own. We perked up to that, because... there's a supposed history there between Carrie and Bennett."

When the explanation didn't come, Wolf asked the obvious question. "What history?"

Elan, Normandy, and Alvarez looked at each other.

"We don't really know," Elan said. "It was Mustaine who

was pretty adamant on the whole thing. Mustaine says they 'had something going'. I'm not sure what he means."

"Bennett used to hang out at the Whitlock place, I think," Alvarez said. "I remember him hanging around town with Kent and sometimes Carrie."

Elan gestured to Alvarez. "There you go."

"But that's the extent of my knowledge on the subject," Alvarez said.

Wolf nodded. "What next?"

Elan sipped his coffee again. "So Mustaine was asking about Carrie and Valentina, and we realized that they left right after him. Their credit card receipts said they left at..." He frowned, looking at the other two.

"Eleven twenty-one was Carrie's," Normandy said. "Valentina didn't have a receipt. Carrie paid for the two of them."

"So eleven-fifteen for Bennett," Wolf said, "and eleven-twenty-one for Carrie and Valentina. They left about the same time," Wolf said. "How about when they were at the bar? How were they acting?"

Elan shook his head. "Everyone we spoke to said nothing out of the ordinary. Just a few cordial laughs."

"Cordial laughs," Wolf said.

"Yeah, I don't know. Nothing out of the ordinary."

"Flirting?" Wolf asked. "Cat calling? That type of thing?"

Elan upturned his hands.

Wolf pointed to a pen on Elan's desk. "May I?"

"Yes, sir." Elan gave him the pen and pulled a yellow legal pad out from his desk drawer. "Here you go."

"What's the bartender's name?" Wolf asked.

"Barry," Elan said. "And the waitress on duty was a woman named Shannon."

Wolf wrote that down. He also wrote *Paco Nez*. "What about Paco? He came to the bar, right? He was there too."

"He came after Bennett had already left," Elan said. "We confirmed his story with the bartender and the waitress."

Wolf nodded. He wrote down, *Carrie Whitlock*, and then *Valentina*.

"Johnson." Elan pointed at the note pad. "Valentina Johnson."

"Thanks." Wolf wrote that down. "So how about other people leaving at the same time? Were there any?"

"No," Elan said. No further explanation seemed necessary.

"And you're sure about that?"

"Mustaine grilled the bartender hard about that. Nobody else within thirty minutes left the bar. And that was an older woman nobody knows anything about. She seemed to be an out of towner."

"Okay," Wolf said. "You found out Valentina and Carrie left about the same time. Then what?"

"We went to go talk to Valentina," Elan said. "Have you heard about that?"

"Bluthe said Mustaine got physical with her."

Elan looked at the darkened window, then back to Wolf. "Yeah. You could say that."

"What happened?"

"We left the Tavern and went to the auto parts place down the street. Underhill's Car Parts," he said slowly. "Valentina works there weekdays, and we went in to talk to her. She was..."

"She didn't know what she was getting into," Alvarez said. "She started mouthing off to Mustaine, saying she didn't like pigs, and all that."

"She didn't know what was going on," Elan said.

"So she says," Alvarez said.

"I was there," Elan said. "She was shocked to hear about

Bennett's death, in my opinion. Like I told you, I don't think he slept a wink the night before, and with Bennett's death..."

"What happened?" Wolf asked.

"He started asking about what she had been doing Saturday night. She said she'd been at the Tavern and she went home. Simple as that. Then she kind of corrected her story, saying, 'Oh yeah, I took Carrie home.'"

"Does she live up near Carrie?" Wolf asked.

"No. That was the fishy part. Valentina lives here down in town. Carrie's way up the canyon living at her ranch."

"Okay," Wolf said. "What did she say about that?"

"She insists it was normal for her to go pick up Carrie and drive her home later at night. She says she's done it all her life, since she had a driver's license. That's when...well, that's when Valentina said some things."

"She's a feisty bitch," Garcia said.

"Thank you, Garcia. She is definitely a strong character, and she let Mustaine have it. Like Alvarez said, she was calling us pigs, and she said she didn't want to talk to us anymore, that she thought it sounded like she was being interrogated for something. And that's when Mustaine put his hand on her throat and pushed her up against the wall."

The room went silent save for Garcia's typing. Then Elan cleared his throat. "He pinned her and started yelling how his son was dead, and he wanted to know what she knew, or he was going to pull her head off."

Garcia stopped typing.

"We did what we could to get Mustaine off her, and he relented. But he was..."

"He was pissed," Alvarez said. "He was Mustaine."

Elan eyed him. Alvarez shrugged.

"And then what?" Wolf asked.

Elan sipped his coffee again. "Then there was the Whitlock

Ranch. We went from the car parts shop and drove straight to the Whitlocks' to talk to Carrie." Elan stared into his memory. "Mustaine was quiet. Didn't say a thing the whole way up. We got up there, and he was acting much cooler. We were all a bit on edge, wondering if he was going to do anything rash. But then they had that big front gate closed and locked.

"At first Nola came out and talked, and Mustaine was insisting to talk to Carrie. And she ended up coming out, and Mustaine was gripping the fence, and, well, he got upset again. We didn't get very far with talking to them."

"And he threatened them, too," Alvarez said. "He didn't exactly pull his gun, but he put his hand on the handle. Was making like he was about to. Was demanding they open the gate, or he was going to break in and make them talk."

Elan looked at him, then lowered his eyes and nodded. "It was bad. Nola had her gun, her kids had theirs. Poor Cruz, the youngest one, he was scared shitless. Mustaine yelled, and then he kind of broke down crying. The Whitlocks went back inside and locked themselves up."

"I thought we were going to have an old-fashioned shoot-out on our hands," Alvarez said.

"Thanks, Alvarez." Elan's voice was heated now.

Alvarez turned to his computer and got busy typing something.

"And then what?" Wolf asked.

Elan picked up his coffee to sip it but put it down. "Mustaine cooled off. We all came back here. Mustaine drove alone, I came back with them two. Then we went to the coroner. He wasn't done with his autopsy yet, so Mustaine had nothing to do there, so we came back here. We called and spoke to the wireless company to get some cellular and GPS data from Bennett's phone."

"And what did they say?"

"We don't have it yet," Elan said.

Wolf frowned. "What's taking so long?"

"Summit Wireless is saying there're technical issues that are beyond their control."

Wolf had seen the same company drag their feet on multiple occasions, for the same non-reason.

"Needless to say, Mustaine was unhappy about that. Let's see, what else...later we went and saw what Dr. Traver had come up with over in the garage, and we heard about his theory of the body being moved. The wiping of the front, and it was clear there was serious foul play going on. Mustaine said nothing through the whole presentation, just stared at Dr. Traver. That is, until Traver brought up the GSR found on Bennett's hand and arm."

Elan looked at the window again, nothing but their reflections staring back at them.

"Traver had the theory that Bennett shot himself?"

"He mentioned it might be a possibility," Elan said.

"And Mustaine didn't like the theory," Wolf said.

Elan nodded. "Correct."

The room went silent again.

"But Traver said it could have been the other way, too," Elan said. "That somebody could have shot him and the GSR got on him that way."

"So, what else?"

"We came back here. I tried to convince Mustaine to get some rest. We had a long, long day. I'm not sure if he did or not. He went into his office and shut the door for the next few hours. When I went to get dinner, I asked him through the door if he wanted something. He didn't answer, so I went." Elan shrugged. "When I got back, he was gone. And I haven't seen him since."

"Me either," Normandy said.

Wolf eyed Alvarez, who shook his head.

Garcia looked at Wolf. "Nope."

"When he didn't show up yesterday, I called and talked to Bluthe about it. And now you're here. Welcome to Crow Valley."

Wolf smiled, tiredly. "I'm happy to help."

"What do you think?" Elan asked.

"I think Bennett's cell phone records would help."

"They're supposed to be here no later than tomorrow afternoon," Garcia said. "I've been on the phone with a guy over at Summit all day and he assures me they'll deliver tomorrow."

Wolf flipped through the folder. "Where's the autopsy report?"

"Mustaine has it," Elan said.

Wolf closed the folder. "Then a conversation with the coroner at eight a.m. tomorrow will help. What else? Have you found any more leads today?"

Elan shook his head, looking embarrassed. "No."

Wolf appreciated the honesty. He looked at Normandy and Alvarez, then at Garcia, and back at Elan. They all had dark circles underneath their eyes. Their hair was greasy. Elan's uniform had stains on the front, as did Normandy's.

"I'll go get some rest and I'll be back tomorrow morning before the coroner meeting at eight," Wolf said.

Elan nodded. "We'll be here."

"You'll be resting, too, right?"

"Alvarez and Normandy," Elan said. "Why don't you head home. You're on call in case, but he's right."

They stood and put on their jackets.

"And Normandy, Alvarez," Elan said.

"Yes, sir."

"Take a shower, too."

Wolf looked at Garcia. She continued to tap on her keyboard, her nails clicking softly.

"It's our turn for overnight shift," Elan said. "We'll be okay. We'll rest in shifts. We have a bunk in the records room."

Wolf said his goodbyes and followed Normandy and Alvarez out front. It was still snowing but not as hard as before. The temperature had dropped, though, and ice was forming, crunching underneath his boots.

"Where are you staying?" Alvarez asked.

"The Mountain Inn, or something like that?" That reminded Wolf he had to check the email he'd received from Patterson to confirm.

"The Mountain Light Inn," Alvarez said. "It's on Main. It's a real shit-hole."

"Oh, great."

"But they're all shit-holes in Crow Valley," Normandy said. "So really you're doing the best you could."

Alvarez turned toward Wolf, squinting against the snow. "You think he was shot, or he offed himself?"

Both men looked at him, youthful faces covered in slight beards, eyes bright and curious. Wolf felt old.

"I think that's a good question," he said. "Get some rest and we'll find out tomorrow."

9

The Mountain Light Inn was a one-story L-shaped building located along the highway-turned-Main Street.

He parked in front of the office and got out, feeling tired, but now hunger had fully set in, and he would have to do something about it.

He noticed The Tavern sign beckoning, a yellow rectangle with black letters, two blocks away on the same side of the road.

He walked into a brightly lit lobby that smelled like deodorant spray, and the musty scent it was trying to hide. There was a breakfast area boasting two cereal dispensers and a basket of fruit. He would be eating out for breakfast tomorrow.

"Can I help you?" An elderly woman came out of the back room wiping her hands on her pants.

Wolf checked in without incident and grabbed the key from her outstretched hand.

"It's the farthest room you can get from here," she said. "Number twenty-seven."

"Thanks. Where can I get a good dinner around here?"

"Well, we have the Chicken House right next door there." She pointed. "And then next to it there's the Tavern."

"How's the food at the Tavern?"

"It's delightful."

"Delightful," he said. "Great. Thanks."

"Sleep well."

"I will," he said, exiting outside.

Room twenty-seven had two queen beds, the walls decked out in brown and green wallpaper, not exactly the shit-hole Normandy had promised, but nothing to boast on social media about.

He dropped his bag, turned on the heater under the window, then departed for the Tavern.

His boots crunched, smashing tiny, rounded ice stalagmites rising from the cracked concrete.

As promised, he passed The Chicken House first, and with salivating mouth he looked through the windows. The bar bustled with a Wednesday night crowd, a dozen or so men and women talking and mingling, a few patrons playing pool, televisions flickering on the walls.

Ahead, the Tavern looked darker, with windows deeply tinted, barely showing the atmosphere within. *Seedier* was the word that came to mind. But as he approached, he watched the door open as two people left, releasing a sliver of bright light, the sound of music, and laughter from within. The parking lot was filled more than its neighbor a snowball's throw to the north.

He walked past two men and women smoking cigarettes outside the front door and went inside, into a room that was better looking, smelling, and feeling than he imagined. The air was dry and warm, saturated with the smell of bar food. The music was turned to a volume that allowed people to speak at a normal level.

HIGH ROAD

"Can I help you?" A smiling woman with bleached blonde hair pulled into a top of the head ponytail asked.

"Table for one."

"Booth okay?"

"Perfect. Thanks."

She walked and Wolf followed, eyes of the patrons following the outsider with a gun on his hip to the booth.

"Here you are. My name's Shannon, I'll be helping you tonight. Can I get you a drink?"

Shannon.

He ordered a Sprite and looked over the menu. There was a French dip sandwich that looked pretty good. He was surprised to see they had a kale salad, with a picture that made it look like something right up Piper's alley.

"You had enough time to choose?" Shannon asked, coming back with his drink.

"Is the French dip good?"

"It's really, really good." She smiled, writing in her notebook. "French dip it is?"

"Yes, please."

"Fries or salad?"

He ordered the salad. Piper would have been proud.

She looked up from her pen pad and did a double take at something behind Wolf.

"Salad?" A deep voice asked.

Wolf felt the floorboards bending next to him before he saw Sheriff Clark Mustaine walk into view.

"Oh, that's right, you've always been soft. I forgot." Mustaine sat across from Wolf, his bulk of at least two-hundred-fifty pounds of muscle sending a jolt up Wolf's legs as he landed on the bench opposite him and scooted into position.

Two thumps rattled Wolf's drink, spilling some, as Mustaine put his arms on the table. He wore a uniform top, sheriff's badge gleaming in the overhead lights, short sleeves stretching just below the point of exploding into thread smoke, his biceps looking like two honey-baked hams.

His neck was thicker than Wolf's thigh, and his head was square and large topped with a buzz cut, hair matching the reddish-brown hue of his beard and moustache.

"Sheriff," Wolf said with a nod.

"Sheriff." A somber expression colored Shannon the waitress's face. "How are you holding up?"

"Oh," Mustaine sat back, eyes closed, letting his arms fall to his sides, "I've been better." He smiled tightly.

"Can I get you something?" she asked.

"I'll take my usual."

"The burger or the slab?"

"Your choice." He waved a hand, an emperor dismissing his servant.

She slunk away, stopping at another table on the way, her face brightening like it was on a dimmer cranked back to high.

Mustaine's bright blue, red-rimmed eyes flicked around the room, beyond Wolf, up to the television. He was taking everything in, and Wolf was flooded by another memory of the man on the football field, jumping, growling, chomping at the bit behind the defensive line. He realized Mustaine's eyes were what he remembered most.

That, and the crushing body weight, and rage.

"How are you doing, Sheriff?" Wolf asked.

Those eyes slid to him. "Not good."

"I'm sorry about Bennett."

Mustaine's eyes went a little wider. He stared at Wolf, his jaw moving forward and back, as if wondering if Wolf was somehow taunting him. At least that's how Wolf read it.

"I have no idea what you must be going through right now.

You know I have a son of my own. About the same age." Wolf shook his head.

Mustaine leaned forward, slowly, until his head was over his arms. The bench beneath him creaked like it was about to snap.

"Thank you," Mustaine said.

They sat there for a beat, staring at one another.

"Here you go, Sheriff." Shannon put a mug of yellow beer in front of him. "I'll be back in a bit with—"

"I don't want this." Mustaine sat back, anger twisting his face. "Take it away. I'm not celebrating today with a beer. Today is definitely not a day to celebrate."

Shannon's face went white. "Of course not. Okay. Yes, I'm sorry." She snatched the beer from the table, the liquid sloshing onto her shirt, but she ignored it. "What would you like?"

"Your choice," he said, again with a dismissive wave.

She flicked a glance at Wolf and walked away.

Mustaine kept his gaze on the television behind Wolf for a short while, then looked at Wolf, his eyes narrowing slightly. "I haven't seen you in a while."

Wolf nodded.

Mustaine stared. Wolf held his gaze.

"How's your father?"

"Dead."

Mustaine's eyes shifted back to the television behind Wolf. "Sorry to hear that."

"Thanks."

"I hear you're going to see him tomorrow," Mustaine said. Wolf assumed he meant Bennett.

"That's right. I have an appointment set up for eight to see the coroner."

"And you saw the place we found him, up on Dry Wash."

"Yeah."

"And you saw his truck."

"Yeah."

"I'm sure you heard from Traver about the GSR on his hand, and how somebody moved him hours after they shot him, and then wiped down the vehicle."

"Yeah."

"So you can see there's definitely some foul play going on."

Wolf glanced at the television behind the bar. It was showing highlights of last weekend's Broncos' loss. When he looked back, Mustaine was looking at him.

"You can see that, can't you?" Mustaine asked.

"I have to admit it looks like foul play."

"Damn straight. Somebody killed my son."

The room seemed to go quiet as Wolf stared back into Mustaine's eyes.

"What?" Mustaine asked.

"What do you think about that GSR on his hand?" Wolf asked.

Mustaine's head tilted forward as he looked at Wolf, his eyes half covered by his pronounced brow, a maniacal expression reminding Wolf of Jack Nicholson frozen in the snow, an axe across his lap, right down to the jaw jutting forward, bottom lip slack, revealing his lower teeth.

"The way I see it the GSR is from somebody shooting him," Mustaine said. "The GSR is on his hand because his hand was close to the shot. He could have been putting his hand up to block it. Could have been scratching his chin at the time. There's no way to know."

Shannon came over with a tray. She put a burger with a side of fries in front of Mustaine, then placed Wolf's French dip in front of him, walking away without a word.

Mustaine put up a finger and turned his head a few degrees, keeping his eyes on Wolf. "Shannon."

Shannon was at the table next door talking, writing something on her pad.

Mustaine raised his hand higher and turned his head, and the effect was like an electric prod.

She left the other customer in mid-sentence and came over. "Yes, Sheriff?"

"Please get Barry over here to talk with us."

"You got it."

Shannon went behind the bar and said something into the bartender's ear. Barry the bartender let go of a beer tap, put down a half-filled pint, and walked over to their table, wiping his hands on a towel.

"Barry," Mustaine said, still not taking his eyes off Wolf, "this is Detective David Wolf. He's down here from Rocky Points, helping us out with the investigation into my son's murder. Can you please repeat what you told me you saw Saturday night?"

"Uh, sure. Yeah." Barry pulled the towel off his shoulder and began wrapping it around his hand.

"Who was he with?" Mustaine asked.

"Right. Yeah, he was alone. Came in alone. But he was playing pool with some of the local guys."

"Who did he talk to?"

"You're referring to the girls?"

"Yes."

"He was, you know, talking with Valentina Johnson and Carrie Whitlock. They left, the two girls, and shortly thereafter—"

"They left first?" Mustaine turned to him.

"No, wait. Bennett left first, sorry. I'm just ... Bennett left first, and then Carrie and Valentina a few minutes later."

"Time?"

"Excuse me?"

"What time did he leave?"

"I gave you the receipts. You have those, right?"

Mustaine stared at him.

"They, uh, I think it was about eleven. Eleven ten or something like that? I don't remember, sir."

"And the girls?"

"I think the receipts showed it was a few minutes after him. Like, six or seven minutes later."

"Did anybody else leave with my son?"

"No, sir."

"What about other people. Did anybody else leave at about that time?"

"No, sir. I think we figured out that the only other person was that woman. She left much earlier than he did. And she was sitting at a table."

"Thank you, Barry. You can get back to work now." Mustaine waved another dismissal.

Barry the bartender left and went back behind the bar, and, Wolf noticed, never once looked back toward their table. None of his coworkers came to him asking what they had been speaking about. Nobody looked their direction, not a single patron in the place or any of the employees.

Mustaine leaned back, hands upturned. "Not much to go on, I admit. But when you talk to those girls, Valentina and Carrie, then things get interesting."

"Yeah?" Wolf said.

"Yeah. Valentina says she took Carrie home. But I think it was a different scenario. Carrie and my son have a bit of history."

Mustaine picked up a French fry and put it in his mouth.

Wolf realized he hadn't touched his food. It hadn't even occurred to him. He looked down at the sandwich, which looked better in person than it did on the menu picture. Next to it sat the salad, which looked decidedly worse, brown lettuce propping up wilted tomatoes and some carrot strings, a dollop of Italian dressing splashed on the side of the bowl.

"God damn. That's the funniest thing I've seen in a long time." Mustaine smiled, the maniacal tinge to his eyes disappearing for a moment. He threw another fry in his mouth and picked up the burger. Took a bite.

They ate in silence for a bit, both watching the football highlights, staring off in different directions.

Wolf choked down the salad and then dug into the French dip. The sandwich was perfect, with a fresh roll that was just as crisp as it was chewy, the meat inside tender, the au jus flavorful but not too overbearing.

"I haven't heard about Carrie and Bennett's history," Wolf said, wiping his mouth.

Mustaine dropped his attention back to Wolf, looking like he'd been pulled from a disturbing memory. "Yeah." He cleared his throat. "He was going over there to the Whitlocks' ranch back in high school, and then every once in a while when he came home from Ohio. He was hanging out with her little brother to get close to her." Mustaine smiled. "I told him. 'You gotta be more direct. Just ask her out.' He was softer than his old man. Had too much of his mother's blood in him."

Wolf noticed Mustaine's jaw flexed again as he looked up at the television.

"What happened to his mother?" Wolf asked.

"My wife?"

"Yeah."

"Bitch left." Mustaine exhaled and pushed his plate forward.

Wolf nodded. "Okay. So, what else leads you to believe Carrie was involved with your son's death?"

"I can spot a liar, and she's lying. So's Valentina Johnson.

They're both lying about what happened that night, and I'm going to prove it."

"And what did they say happened that night?"

"They say they went home."

Wolf waited for more explanation, but none came.

"Anyway, it doesn't matter." Mustaine wiped his mouth and tossed his napkin on the table. "I'll get Bennett's phone GPS data tomorrow. I guarantee it's going to show him going to Carrie Whitlock's. Once I get that, I'll have probable to get a warrant for Valentina and Carrie's phone records, and I'm certain everything's going to be mapped out, showing exactly what happened Saturday."

Wolf nodded. "Makes sense."

"Yeah." Mustaine's eyes slid down, his gaze locking on Wolf's. "It does."

They sat in silence for a beat. Wolf eyed the room for Shannon, who was nowhere to be found.

"What doesn't make sense is why you're here," Mustaine said.

"I was asked to come down and assist."

"Yeah, right. You're taking orders from that little girl you guys have for a sheriff up there now."

"Sheriff Patterson."

"Whatever." Mustaine's eyes sparked with amusement again. "What's the matter? You couldn't cut it? Had to hand over the reins to the little girl to take over for you?"

Wolf smiled without teeth. "Something like that."

Mustaine stared at him, then he leaned his head back, the bench creaking as he pulsed with laughter. "You remember that last game we played against each other up in Donkey Points?"

Wolf nodded.

"So do I." Mustaine stared at him, his face going cold. "I got you pretty good that game. Kicked your ass."

"It was a close one. Closer than the scoreboard told."

"No, I mean, I kicked your ass."

Mustaine smiled, the gesture fading rapidly, and they were back to staring at one another.

Wolf was pulled back in time, to the high school stadium parking lot with Sarah, and he could tell Mustaine was there in his mind with him.

"You fuck with this investigation," Mustaine said, "you fuck with me in any way on this, and I'll push *your* face through *your* skull. You got that?"

Wolf blinked. "I'm here to help, Clark. I'm here to help you find out what happened—"

"Did you hear what I said?" Mustaine lurched forward, putting both elbows on the table, head tilted sideways.

Wolf just stopped himself from flinching.

"Did you hear what I said?" Mustaine repeated.

"I heard what you said. And I hope you heard what I said. I'm here to help. I understand ... check that...I don't understand what it's like to lose a son, and I hope I never know what it's like, but I can imagine, only imagine, and I'm sorry. And I do know what it's like to lose somebody, and with foul play involved. I understand the pain and anger involved."

The booth crackled as Mustaine slid sideways and stood. Without another word he walked out of the restaurant.

The volume of conversation slowly rose, and he was pretty sure the volume of the music rose with it.

Shannon walked into view and Wolf raised his hand, catching her attention with the check gesture.

"Anything else for you?" she asked, still looking shell-shocked.

"No, thanks."

He put a hand on Mustaine's plate, stopping her from picking it up.

"Maybe just a few," he said, grabbing a handful of the fries Mustaine hadn't touched.

She smiled. "Take a few more. I won't tell anybody."

He grabbed another handful. "Take it away."

She laughed, picking up the plate.

"So, you were here Friday night, too, weren't you?" he asked.

"Yeah," she said.

"And what do you think?"

"You mean, do I think Carrie and Valentina left with Bennett?"

Wolf nodded. "Tell me what you saw."

"Honestly? I was serving all of them drinks. I see them here all the time. They don't hang out much. Bennett kind of acts weird with those girls."

"Like how?"

"I don't know. He ignores them. He was a good-looking guy. Big like daddy, but a much gentler soul." She turned her head quickly to the exit, as if things were too late and she'd been caught talking about Mustaine and he was back. "I don't know. I'm just saying, they weren't talking much. If they left together, something must have happened out in the parking lot that I didn't see."

"And did you see anybody else leave at about the same time? Somebody who could have met up with Bennett out there in the parking lot?"

She shook her head. "I've been thinking about that. I really have. And I can't remember. I mean, nobody left at around the same time. Those guys over there were still playing pool until just about closing. They always do that on the weekends."

"Those guys over there?" he asked. "Is there anybody else here now that was here Friday night?"

She looked back toward a group of men playing pool. "Oh, I

was just saying...but, yeah, the guy with the yellow hat on was here."

"What's his name?"

"Travis."

"Thanks."

"Is that it?" She smiled.

"That's it."

She walked away, swinging her hips side to side. Wolf watched for a moment, then looked out the window, the image of Piper in her dressed-up outfit earlier that morning filling his mind.

He pulled out his phone. No missed calls. The lock screen said 7:32. Still early. But the motel bed called his name.

But first he needed to talk to Travis. And, he decided, another word with the bartender wouldn't be a bad idea, and maybe without Mustaine around the guy would open up.

He signed the check and walked to the bar, waiting patiently for Barry to pour a drink and slide it to a customer.

"Can I get you a drink?" he asked Wolf.

"No, I'm all set. I just wanted to thank you for talking with us earlier."

"Yeah." He looked at Wolf's belt, the gun, and the badge. "You're from Rocky Points, eh?"

"Yeah."

"I have a cousin who lives there." Barry gave a name, but Wolf didn't know it.

Wolf cleared his throat. "Listen, so you said Bennett talked with Carrie and Valentina last Friday night."

Barry eyed the door. "Yeah."

"So, what kind of talking?" he asked.

"I don't know what you mean."

"I mean, you know, cracking jokes talking? Or arguing talking? Or maybe Bennett was flirting with them? And they were, I don't know, flirting back?"

Barry smiled and snorted. "No. Not flirting."

"Why are you laughing at that?"

"I don't know. Have you met Valentina?"

"No."

"Well, she's a handful of a woman. If she was talking to Bennett, it would have been calling him names, put downs, that type of stuff. That's just how she is. A real ball-buster."

"And Carrie?"

Barry shrugged. "She talks?"

"Quiet girl, eh?" Wolf asked.

"Yeah." Barry shook his head. "Look, man. They were kind of talking, nothing big. Nothing flashy. No arguments. Just cordial small talk, if anything at all."

"But they left at about the same time."

"Yeah, sure. I mean, according to the receipts I gave over to the sheriff, it was a few minutes apart, but they didn't leave together. At least that's what I saw." He put up his hands. "But I could be wrong."

Wolf nodded.

"Is that all? I have to get back to pouring drinks."

Wolf thanked him and turned around to face the room. He watched the two men play a game of eight-ball, one of them the guy with the yellow hat named Travis, and another guy with a beard that reached halfway down his chest. Neither were particularly good pool players, but Travis was worse.

"Howdy officer," Travis said, not looking at Wolf.

"Hello," Wolf said. "Actually, I'm a detective."

Travis made a shot and lined up another.

"Are you Travis?"

Travis missed and went to the table to sip his beer. "Yeah. Why?"

"My name's David Wolf, like I said, I'm a detective. I'm working with the sheriff's department."

"You looking into Bennett's death?"

"Yeah. You think we could talk privately?"

Travis set his stick against the wall. "Okay, I need a smoke anyway. I'll be back," he told the bearded guy.

Wolf followed Travis outside, and into a puff of cigarette smoke coming out of his mouth.

"What do you need to know?"

"I'm just wondering if you saw Bennett that night."

"Yeah. I was playing pool with him."

"Did you see Valentina Johnson and Carrie Whitlock that night as well?"

"Yeah." Travis pointed at the windows, to a table inside that was near the pool table. "They was sitting down at that table."

"Was Bennett speaking with them?"

Travis sucked a drag, showing he had a missing front tooth as he exhaled. He shook his head slowly. "Not really."

"No?"

"S'what I said."

"What about when the girls left?" he asked.

"What about it?"

"Did they speak at all? Bennett and the two girls?"

Travis thought about it. "Not that I saw."

Wolf studied him. The man said the words with indifference. He saw none of the obvious indications the man was lying, but maybe the guy was a pro poker player. "And then Bennett left?" he asked.

"Yeah, sure."

"Before or after the two women?"

"I dunno."

Wolf folded his arms against the cold. A few snowflakes drifted on a light breeze that burrowed into his bones.

"Did Bennett leave with anybody?" Wolf asked, cutting to the chase.

"No."

"How much time elapsed between Valentina and Carrie leaving and Bennett leaving?"

"I dunno."

Wolf noticed Travis was swaying back and forth.

"How many beers did you have that night?"

"Shit, Friday night?" Travis's lungs rattled as he smiled in recollection. "All of them."

Wolf smiled back. "You threw back a few."

"Always do. Don't affect me much anymore though."

Wolf watched the man's hand quiver as he put the cigarette back into his lips. His face was tough to gauge for age; he was probably in his fifties but looked twenty years older than that. Wolf remembered looking at himself in the mirror during his time lost in the bottle and seeing something similar.

Wolf thanked him for his time, then walked through the parking lot, making his way through the vehicles to the sidewalk, feet crunching again on the ice-covered snow.

The Chicken House next door seemed to have gathered more of a crowd, the sound billowing out of the front entrance. The smell of fried chicken was stronger than ever but had no power over Wolf now, with his stomach filled and his momentum carrying him toward the motel room.

In and out.

As far as Wolf calculated it, the in part was over. He'd spoken with Mustaine, and it could have gone worse, even though he got the distinct feeling he'd screwed up mentioning the possibility of suicide. Maybe answers would come tomorrow with the cellular and GPS records. Maybe tomorrow he'd be able to leave and sleep in his own bed.

In and out.

10

Detective Tom Rachette sucked in a breath through his nose, feeling the clean pine air burning the inside of his nostrils. The snow hadn't reached all the way down into town last night; somehow the warmth had stuck around in the valley, causing it to rain, but the mountains were all blanketed white.

The morning sun had crested the eastern wall of mountains a few minutes ago, illuminating tendrils of steam rising out of the Main Street buildings.

It all pissed him off.

Last night had been a nightmare with the two boys. Tom Junior was sick with something that gave him a fever and a nose packed with mucus, so he spent the night whining and crying about having to mouth breathe, and Davey insisted on sleeping between him and Charlotte, making the few minutes of sleep Rachette had gotten sporadic, interrupted with toddler karate kicks to the back.

He needed more caffeine, the strong stuff found at the coffee shop known as Dead Ground, the place the hippies opened up a few years ago. Until the good stuff hit his veins the beautiful autumn scenery in Rocky Points was lost on him.

"Hey, Rachette, get me a triple-shot almond milk latte while you're at it," Yates had said on his way out, which wasn't helping his mood, either.

As he approached the coffee shop, he knew the boredom of the job lately wasn't helping. He wished he'd been ordered to go to Crow Valley with Wolf. He would have gotten a good night's sleep last night, and he'd be doing something better today than searching through online bicycle advertisements for leads on a case that he couldn't care less was solved or not.

He stepped inside, and on cue the place lived up to its name, playing a seventies live-version of a Grateful Dead song he failed to recognize as any different from the rest of the band's repertoire. Better than the new crap that was on the radio, though, he had to admit.

"Hey Tom, what can I get you?"

Rachette ordered, and Yates's drink order just came out of his mouth, so he went with it.

"You got it. Thanks for keeping us safe out there, man. I got this round for you," the guy said behind the counter.

"Wow." Rachette nodded, putting a five in the tip jar. "Thanks. I appreciate it."

He stepped aside, deciding the place wasn't too bad, but also wondering if these guys behind the counter were kissing up because they were hiding something. They looked like what the Dead's roadies must have looked like back in the day.

Rachette's large regular coffee came over the counter first and he took a sip while he waited for Yates's frou-frou drink to be crafted.

The jolt of caffeine hit like a massage to his neck, calming him down, but also gave him an internal kick. The only thing better would be to have a pinch of Copenhagen, too. But that ship had sailed. He was on his fifty-five-thousandth attempt to quit the stuff, and it had been over two months since his last fix. Pretty good, if he did say so himself.

He turned, eyeing the clientele seated at the tables along the walls, chatting with each other or their electronic equivalents.

A startlingly beautiful woman seated near the entrance caught his eye, and it took a moment to realize it was Piper Cain —the Dredge satellite deputy and Wolf's girlfriend of almost a year. He had seen her yesterday for the first time in a long time, and she'd been similarly dressed. She wore a fitted, sheer-but-not-too-sheer blouse that hugged her curves in just the right way, and as Rachette had noticed, the woman had nice curves.

She was laughing, hard, and he wondered who was sitting across from her that could make her look so radiant with joy. But he couldn't see the other person, as they were blocked by the high back of the booth.

But he did see a shoe underneath the table, leather so shiny and tastefully weathered they could only have been designed that way, surely costing a fortune, the size large enough that it could only be a tall male wearing them. Dark socks. Dark slacks. Definitely a guy.

She twirled her hair with a finger, eyes wide, like she was smitten with this dude and whatever he was saying. What was she up to? And with Wolf down in Crow Valley?

He turned around, snatched up Yates's drink and walked out the door.

Piper gave him a double take and she got that worried jolt look in her eye as he neared the door.

"Hey, how's it going?" he said, cutting into whatever the other guy was saying.

He stopped and looked, immediately recognizing Michael Venus, the former deputy district attorney from the fourth floor.

"Well, hello Thomas Rachette." Venus looked up with a movie-star smile. "I thought that was you who walked in." Venus held out his hand and pulled it back. "Oh, looks like your hands are full."

Rachette nodded, eyeing them both. Piper waved with a wiggle of her fingers.

"How are you two doing?" Rachette asked.

"Not bad," Piper said. "You?"

"Not bad." Rachette saw they both had folders on the table, Piper's manila, Michael's a fancy leather zip-up job. He also saw Michael's hand resting on the table past the halfway point, as if he was horning in as close as he could to her.

What was this, Rachette wondered again. If Piper was having a social coffee with this guy, dating behind Wolf's back, she'd picked quite a scumbag to be with, and quite a bad location. But she wasn't from town, so maybe she didn't know the location would be so close to the sheriff's office...no, that didn't make sense. And how about Michael Venus? She probably didn't know about Venus's unceremonious exit from the district attorney's office, where the guy had been fired for hitting on another of the other deputy DA's wife. Well, hitting on was a gentle term. Rachette had heard Michael Venus exposed himself to said wife, asking, "Are you hungry?"

"Double-fisting," Piper said.

"What?"

"You really like your caffeine." She gestured to his hands.

"Oh, yeah. Got one for Yates. The lazy bum."

They laughed, and it seemed strained.

Rachette nodded. "Well. I'll leave you two. Have a great day. Hey, have you talked to Wolf recently?"

Venus slid his hand back, a fisherman without a license reeling in his lure at the sight of the game warden.

"No, I haven't. Not since yesterday morning at the station," she said. "Why? Is everything okay?"

"Yeah. I mean, I'm not sure. I haven't talked to him. Just wondering if you had."

She drew her lips into a line. "Nope."

He clucked his mouth. "Well. Okay. I'm back to the grind. See you soon. Good seeing you, Michael."

"You too."

Rachette left, his mind going a mile a minute. He wasn't exactly the greatest judge of women's behavior, and he'd probably have to run this past Charlotte when he got back to the office, but the finger-twirling of her hair, the laughing, this was looking like she was shopping around for another guy.

Charlotte was always telling him to mind his own business when it came to other peoples' love lives. That was fine enough when it came to ignoring the disturbing escapades Yates put himself through around the valley, but Wolf...he wasn't so sure he could ignore this.

A pair of young women came at him on bicycles, swerving back and forth as they laughed and chatted.

He stepped aside, letting them pass.

"Excuse us," one of them said, smiling at him.

Rachette smiled back and watched them park in front of the coffee shop and go in, leaving their bikes unattended and unlocked outside.

"Dumbasses," he said.

He was about to walk back and go inside to warn them about a bike thief on the loose, to lock up and care about their possessions, or don't come running to them when they get nabbed, but he noticed the bikes were black with the town logo sticker wrapped around the top tube.

The town of Rocky Points had recently started a community

bicycle program, making bikes available for citizens to use. They were all over the place now, leaning up against buildings, parked outside shops, lying in the parks. They were all spray painted black with the sticker to let people know they were free to use. Personally, Rachette thought it was cool, but he'd never sat on one before.

He stared at one of them, seeing it was strange the crank was a bright blue alloy that looked like it glowed. The front and back brakes were the same color, and so was the sprocket.

Rachette narrowed his eyes and walked toward the bike, transfixed. The closer he got the more excitement built.

He set down Yates's drink on the ground and took out his cell phone. He pulled up the pictures of Jake Morehaus and Theo Anders atop the mountain with their mountain bikes.

"That's it."

He was staring at Jake's bike. The frame was the same shape and everything, with the blue crank shafts and sprockets, and front and rear brakes. He checked the seat, seeing it was the same model. The pedals were different, but that would have been the doing of the city to put pedestrian pedals on instead of the kind that shoes clip into. The picture showed the frame was chrome, and not matte black like it was now painted. He leaned down and ran his hand over the paint, seeing few if any scratches. It looked fresh.

He pulled the bike back and checked the brakes closely against his picture, triple-checking they were the same. They were. He then swiped back and checked the next bike against the photograph of Theo. He was not as lucky this time. They didn't match.

"I'll be damned," he said. But he had no idea what to make of this. Had the town of Rocky Points stolen this bike? Not likely. But...then what?

The two young women came back outside with cups of

coffee in their hand, their smiles fading from their lips as they looked at Rachette.

"Hi," he said.

"Hello?" One of them said with a frown. "Um..." Her eyebrows rose, looking like she'd noticed the badge and gun on his hip.

"Hey, I gotta take this, okay?"

"Leroy! No!" A woman who had passed with a dog pulled hard on a leash. Her black lab had knocked over Yates's drink and was lapping up the liquid off the sidewalk. "Oh my gosh, I'm so sorry."

Rachette stared at it. "No worries. You can just throw it away."

She picked it up, pulling her dog away by the collar. "Listen, I'll buy you a new one."

"Nah." Rachette handed her his coffee. "Listen. You can throw this away for me, too, and we'll call it even."

She fumbled the leash, and the other cup, and took the second cup and stood there looking just as confused as her dog.

Rachette got on the bike and pushed away. Only half the caffeine he needed coursed through his body, but he felt alive with energy, the earlier boredom pushed aside and forgotten. He had been delivered a double shot of purpose for the day.

11

Wolf parked next to two trucks he recognized as Normandy's and Elan's, along with the sedan cruiser he assumed was Garcia's.

The air outside at 7:30 a.m. was still and cold, save a murmur of a breeze. The storm had left overnight, pushed out on winds that had rattled the flimsy windows in Wolf's motel room. His sleep had been fitful, full of strange dreams involving Bennett Mustaine's dead body, Clark Mustaine chasing after Wolf.

The sky was a blue dome overhead, no clouds in sight. The mountains to the west were lit yellow with the rising sun, while the valley here at the station was still in transition.

He walked inside, the glass door squealing behind him as it shut, the floor underneath his feet moaning as he stepped.

Elan, Alvarez, and Normandy were at their desks, Elan on the phone, Alvarez and Normandy looking up from their computer screens.

"Good morning, detective," Elan said, lowering the receiver to his chin.

A noise drew Wolf's eyes to the wall near Mustaine's office, where Deputy Garcia stood making coffee.

His eyes latched onto the steam rising from the mug in Garcia's hands. He had woken up late and still had no food or caffeine in him.

"Good morning," he said.

Elan held up a finger. "Thanks. You have my information. Like I said, please include me with that … Thanks, goodbye."

The undersheriff hung up and sighed, standing up. "How was your first night in Crow County?"

"Not bad."

"What did they say?" Alvarez asked, his tone impatient.

"She told me early afternoon at the latest." Elan popped his eyebrows. "Summit Wireless. I was just giving them a good morning call, making sure they know we're still waiting."

Wolf nodded. "So nothing new."

"Nope," Elan said. "You want some coffee?"

"That would be great, thanks."

Elan chaperoned him over to the coffee station and got him a mug.

Wolf sipped. "Whoa. Strong."

"That's Garcia's fault."

"I like my brew strong," she said, sitting down in front of her computer.

Alvarez had his eyes on his computer, his face a mask of seriousness and concentration, while Normandy sat at his desk, feet up, twirling a pencil, watching Wolf and Elan.

Garcia looked well-rested. Elan's eyes were still ringed black underneath, but he was in a vibrant mood.

"Did you guys get some rest last night?" Wolf asked.

"Yeah," Elan said. "You're going to the coroner this morning."

"That's right," Wolf said.

"I was going to have Normandy keep you company again, if that's all right with you."

"Sounds good."

Elan sat easily behind his desk, motioning to the cracked plastic seat again.

Wolf sat, sipping his coffee, feeling the heat spread within.

"Garcia, can you please email me last week's report from CSP?"

"The Junction Cove stop?"

"That's the one."

"It's already in your inbox," Garcia said, her tone chiding.

"Oh." He checked. "There it is."

"You're welcome."

Elan smiled and Wolf caught a hint of a smile breaking out on Alvarez's face as he pecked at his keyboard.

Wolf cleared his throat. "I went to the Tavern last night."

"Oh, you did?" Elan asked.

"I was hungry. Thought I'd kill two birds with one stone."

"They have a great burger," Garcia said. "Best in town, in my opinion."

"Yeah," he said. "Good food. I talked to the waitress and bartender who were on that night. And a guy named Travis, who was playing pool with Bennett the night he died."

"And?" Elan asked, putting his feet up on his desk.

"As far as I see it, nobody seemed to think the three of them interacted much. At least, not much more than a word or two of conversation. And as far as them leaving? Nobody seemed to think they were together."

"That Travis guy is a major drunk," Alvarez said. "Can't really go off what he says."

Wolf gestured to Elan. "Do you have those receipts?"

Elan upturned his hands. "Mustaine has them."

Wolf ran a hand over his now three-day beard. "I'd like to see everything that Mustaine has."

The front door squealed at that moment, and if the floor had moaned when Wolf had entered, it grunted in pain now.

"What about me?" Mustaine asked, standing in the doorway.

Everyone snapped to attention, Elan and Normandy dropping their legs from the desk, Alvarez sitting straight in his chair.

"Sheriff," Elan said with a nod.

"Sheriff," the other three deputies said.

"Good morning," Wolf said with a nod of his own.

The sheriff's eyes were red with black crescents below. His face looked heavy, like it was being pulled by twice the gravity of the rest of the planet.

Mustaine ignored everyone at once. "Coffee," he said.

Garcia stood up and walked to the table, then slowed to a halt. "Shit," she said under her breath, pulling out the carafe and filling it up in the sink. She worked fast, preparing another pot for brewing.

Wolf watched Mustaine's eyes go from Garcia to the coffee cup in Wolf's hand, the equation solved.

Mustaine walked past them to his office and disappeared inside, the light flicking on. "What are we talking about?" he called out to them.

Wolf sat confused, wondering if Mustaine would be coming back out to speak to them or not. Eventually he did, his face expectant.

"Not much you don't already know," Wolf said.

"I could have told you that."

Mustaine slipped back out of sight into his office.

Wolf stood up and walked over, stopping in the entryway.

Mustaine sat behind his desk, elbows on the surface, hands pressed into his eyes.

"I was just telling them I'd like to see the receipts from the Tavern."

Mustaine remained motionless, apparently not hearing him. Wolf stood patiently in the threshold, eying the space within. One wall was covered in pictures of football players in action, and it took him a second to realize Mustaine himself was in each of the photos. They were all action shots, showcasing Mustaine's raw power mid-tackle, or post-tackle with his triumphant flexing body arched to the sky. The photos seemed to be arranged in chronological order, beginning with high school photographs, his body already large and imposing, growing steadily to monstrous as ones' eyes moved right.

"Got hurt in training camp for the Kansas City Chiefs," Mustaine said.

Wolf nodded. "I'm sorry to hear that."

Mustaine gestured to the wall next to Wolf. Wolf stepped inside the office and saw the same type of shrine, this time displaying photographs that had slightly brighter colors.

Bennett Mustaine in action. The young man was slightly thinner than his father, but still an imposing presence on the field judging by the cultivated pictures.

"We had the same curse," Mustaine said. "Blown out knee. But he never really got to have much of a college career."

Wolf stood silent and motionless, watching Mustaine's eyes well up as he stared at the wall. "I'm sorry."

"You played college, didn't you?" Mustaine asked.

Wolf nodded. "CSU."

"How did that go?"

"I quit after a year. After my father died, I wasn't up for it anymore."

Mustaine blew a pulse of air from his nose, nodded with a faint smile that said, *sounds about right.*

Garcia walked into the office past Wolf and put a cup of coffee in front of Mustaine, then walked out into the front room to her desk.

The sheriff took a sip and set it down. "Ah, shit. That's a good cup of coffee, Garcia!"

Garcia said nothing, and from Wolf's vantage saw she sat with her eyes locked on her computer screen.

Mustaine put the cup down and put his hands together. "What did you learn while I was gone last night? Did Barry tell you anything else I should know about? How about Travis? I never did talk to him."

Wolf nodded. "You were watching."

Mustaine winked.

"Nobody seemed to think Carrie and Valentina were chatting much with Bennett," Wolf said.

"What are you getting at?"

"I'm just wondering if we're missing somebody. And I'd like to see those receipts you took from the bartender."

Mustaine stared at Wolf for a beat, then reached in his drawer and pulled out two pieces of paper. "Bennett paid and left at 11:15. Carrie and Valentina at 11:21. Six minutes apart. Pretty close."

Pretty close, Wolf thought, but a lot can happen in six minutes. A person can get in their car and drive away, getting to the other side of this small town in that span of time.

Mustaine studied him, a smile touching his lips for a second before it disappeared beneath his red, smoky beard. "You think you have the scene down pat, do you? What's it been, one night in town and a few conversations?"

"No, I don't," Wolf said. "I'm far from having this scene down pat."

Mustaine looked like he was strangling Wolf in his mind. "I want you to be respectful when you go see him this morning."

Wolf nodded. "Of course I will, Clark."

"You can call me Sheriff." Mustaine sipped his coffee, staring into nothing over the rim. He set it down. "And then what are you going to do today?"

"Then I'll go talk to Valentina Johnson."

Mustaine's eyes narrowed at the mention of her name. "I already talked to her."

Wolf said nothing.

"So why are you still here?"

Wolf saw it was 7:40 on the wall clock, which was now ticking out a rhythm that sounded like a stick on a garbage can lid in the silence.

He turned and walked out of the office.

"Keep me abreast of the situation," Mustaine called out.

Wolf went to Elan's desk. "Please give me or Normandy a call the minute you get that cell phone data."

"Yep," Elan said, his voice a whisper.

"You ready?"

Normandy got up and put his jacket on.

Wolf left, the young deputy following behind.

12

Wolf hitched a ride in Normandy's truck to the Crow Valley Hospital, and the location of the county morgue, where Bennett Mustaine was still being held in a refrigeration locker.

"How far do we have?" Wolf asked.

"Not far. It's about a mile north on the highway, on the edge of town." Normandy eyed the clock, and then Wolf, and the rearview mirror.

"What's up?" Wolf asked.

"I've been meaning to tell you something."

"Yeah?"

Normandy hooked a left onto Main Street and nodded. "Yeah."

"You know about Bennett's going to Ohio State for football, right?"

"Yeah."

"And he blew out his knee in like the third game he ever played. You know that, right?"

"Mustaine said something. I didn't know the specifics."

"Yeah. Third game. Screwed it up big time. Ended his career.

Anyway, when Bennett came back into town he was in a bad way. And I don't just mean physically. He was ashamed to be back, you could see it. He was beaten down by his trip to the big show out in Ohio, could barely walk, limping with crutches. He was pissed off. Always drinking down in that bar."

"The Tavern?"

"Yeah. And you think he was upset? You should have seen the Sheriff. It was like his son had died. It was exactly like it is right now, I'm not kidding. When he was playing division one, the games on television, the sheriff couldn't have been a happier guy. When Bennett was injured, the sheriff was devastated. Sometimes he didn't show up to work. And if he did show up, some days he wouldn't talk. Or he would yell, and ... hell, I thought I was gonna get killed once when he got mad at me for asking him something."

Normandy stared out the window.

Wolf said nothing, sensing Normandy had more to say. He did.

"He was a rapist."

"What? Who?"

Normandy flicked his eyes to the rearview. "Bennett Mustaine. Everyone knows it, too. Or at least they suspect it, and it's not too big a stretch of the imagination to believe the allegation."

"What allegation, exactly?"

He looked at Wolf with intense eyes. "I could get beat down real good for talking about this right now."

Wolf nodded. "I understand. But I appreciate you filling me in. If there's more to this whole story, I have to know about it." He thought of the way everyone had paused yesterday when he asked whether Bennett had a record.

Normandy exhaled loudly. "About a year after Bennett came home from school, he was drinking a lot, you know, like I said, typical of a guy who had gone through what he had. He was out at nights, sleeping all day. Smoking weed. Maybe some of the harsher stuff, I don't know. But he was a deadbeat twenty-year-old.

"Well, that went on for a while until his dad had enough and kicked his ass into gear. And Bennett cleaned himself up, and Mustaine went and talked to my dad about getting his son a job."

"Your dad?"

Normandy nodded. "My dad has a wood fabrication company in town. Normandy Wood Works. It's a pretty big deal. He employs over a hundred people. It's down on Main to the south."

Wolf had yet to travel to the southern end of the town. "But not you?"

"No, I didn't want to work there. I wanted to break out on my own and do something more adventurous, you know?"

Wolf nodded. He knew, except in his case he had followed his dad's career path for the adventure.

The hospital came up on the right side and Normandy slowed and pulled into the parking lot.

"My dad did the favor and hired Bennett. Bennett was there for about six months, and then he was involved in an incident with a woman named Sadie Moreno.

"Sadie was a year behind Bennett, a few years younger than me. Now listen, I really don't know the extent of what happened, I really don't."

Wolf raised his eyebrows and nodded.

"But one night, the night of the incident in question, Sadie came into the sheriff's office and wrote a report. She was hurt, upset, and she was with a doctor. You know, they have to report that kind of stuff as a medical worker. It was Doctor Traver."

"The forensic guy?"

"Yeah. He's a medical doctor in town, used to work here at this hospital. He made his own report, too."

"Who took her statement?" Wolf asked. "Mustaine?"

"No. He wasn't there that night. Our previous undersheriff took the report."

Wolf looked at him. "There was somebody before Elan?"

"Elan's new. He was brought in after this incident, in fact."

Wolf frowned but remained silent, letting Normandy explain.

"Undersheriff Dexter. Henry Dexter."

"Where is he now?"

"Got himself a job up in Bend, Oregon."

Wolf waved his hand, motioning for Normandy to continue.

"Anyway, I wasn't at work when Sadie came in, but Alvarez was. And he told me that when Sadie Moreno came in, she could barely walk. The doctor had his arm around her, and the undersheriff helped her walk, too."

"Did you see the report?" Wolf asked.

"No, sir."

"Did Alvarez?"

"No."

"Then how do you know it was Bennett that hurt her?"

"Over the next few days, we kind of put the pieces together. First of all, the next day she came back in and retracted her first report and gave another one. That time she was alone, not with the doctor. And this time Mustaine was there."

"Sheriff Mustaine," Wolf said.

"Yes."

"And what did she say in the new report?"

Normandy shook his head. "I didn't read it."

He looked at Normandy. "And what happened next?"

"Nothing in the way of arrests or charges pressed, if that's what you mean. Mustaine never told me, Alvarez, or Garcia anything. He told us to stop asking questions about it, and... he can be persuasive. So, we dropped it, confused about what we were looking at.

"But you know how it is, people around town started talking, and the word was that Bennett had attacked her. And then it all made sense at that point, that Mustaine was sweeping an incident involving his son under the rug. But, of course, I'm a cop and I was in a situation where I could check the facts for myself. I mean, it was my father's business."

"What did your father say?"

Normandy shook his head. "When I asked him, he just looked at me and shook his head. It was like a 'don't you dare ask me about that' kind of shake of the head."

Wolf narrowed his eyes. "And the undersheriff left."

Normandy nodded. "Dexter left right after that. He was definitely upset about whatever Mustaine did, and so he up and quit. Or... maybe he was swept under the rug, too. I don't know the details there. Just what I suspect. But he was a good man. I like to think he quit."

They sat in silence for a beat.

Wolf could scarcely believe the nerve of Sheriff Mustaine if only half of this story was true. "When exactly did this all take place?"

Normandy tilted his head. "Let's see, when Bennett came home, that was his second year in school, his first year on the team. He was twenty years old then, I remember his age, because he was drinking underage. That was another piece of controversy when he came home with his injury and got into the alcohol and drugs. So that means he was twenty when he got the job at my dad's place. He was twenty-three as of his death. So ... three years ago? Two and a half? Yeah. About that. That's when I moved into my new place."

Wolf nodded. "And you've never seen either report from Sadie Moreno? The first one, or the retracted?"

"No, sir." Normandy chuckled without mirth. "But you think I haven't thought about going into that records room and looking? But I'm afraid. He probably has a secret camera in there or something."

"What about Alvarez or Garcia? Or Elan? They haven't read it either?"

"No. We don't really talk about it."

Wolf thought about Doctor Traver and the night before. He'd left hastily under the excuse of having to beat the storm as he drove to Silverton, but it had been right after Wolf had alluded to the possibility of suicide. Was the man threatened back during the Sadie Moreno incident to keep quiet, and now remaining silent due to threat again?

"What about the doctor's report?" Wolf asked. "Didn't that still stand after she retracted it?"

Normandy shrugged. "This was, and is, all above my pay grade." After another brief silence Normandy said, "Mustaine has a way with dealing with people, in case you hadn't noticed. Everything's a threat, even when it's not. He asks you to hand him a pen, there's the threat of death if you don't do it. Or don't do it to his liking."

"You think the doctor was threatened into retracting his statement, too."

Normandy said nothing.

"Sadie, what was her last name again?"

"Moreno."

"Where is she now?"

"She still works at my father's place."

Wolf shook his head, thinking.

"What?" Normandy asked.

"I think that's a big piece of the puzzle I needed to know. Thanks for telling me."

"You think Sadie Moreno might have had something to do with this?" Normandy asked.

"How long ago was this?"

Normandy thought. "It would have been two years."

Wolf shook his head in thought. "Bluthe is new in town, too."

Normandy shrugged. "I'm not sure if that has anything to do with anything. As far as I know, Bluthe won the election and moved in. Lamont retired and went to South Carolina to fish on his boat."

Wolf thought about that, deciding he didn't have enough information to think one way or the other.

"But there's motive for Sadie to hurt Bennett, right?" Normandy said.

"If Bennett really did attack her, then I'd have to agree. Yes."

"The only thing is, I really don't see her being violent like that, though," Normandy said. "She might be upset about what happened, but it's a whole new level to point a gun at his head and pull the trigger. And there would be the threat of the sheriff coming after her."

Wolf nodded. "I'd still like to talk to her."

"We can go talk to her today. She'll be at my dad's factory."

Their day was already stacking up.

The dash clock clicked over to 7:58.

"Let's head inside." Wolf opened his door and got out.

Wolf waited while Normandy dug into the back seat of his truck and came out with a small container. Before he shoved it into his pocket Wolf could see it was mentholated rub.

They walked across the parking lot, Wolf taking in warm, humid air into his lungs that smelled like the high desert foliage.

Given a little more time the snow would begin melting. Sixty-degree weather was not uncommon for a day or two in October up in Rocky Points, and the altitude was lower here. He hadn't checked the weather app on his phone, but his five senses were telling him it was going to be a warm day.

The building was two stories, smallish in size as far as hospitals went. An ambulance sat parked near the emergency room entrance off to one side of the building and there were few vehicles in the lot.

They went into the front entrance, checked in with the front desk, and then descended in an elevator to the basement level.

"You want some?" Normandy put a finger into the mentholated rub and smeared it beneath his nose.

"No, thanks." Wolf didn't go into detail that he didn't mind the smell of the dead in a morgue. It was out in the field where it could get to him.

Normandy fidgeted, his face turning a shade paler.

"You don't have to look with me," Wolf said. "I'll just take a quick look with the coroner. You can stand back."

"I'm fine."

The doors opened and they walked out into the smell of embalming chemicals and nose-searing cleaners.

"This way," Normandy said, taking the lead. Wolf followed behind him down the hallway to a wooden door propped open, the name plate reading MORGUE.

They walked inside, Normandy knocking on the door as they entered. The man behind the desk looked up at them.

"Hi Doc," Normandy said. "This is Detective David Wolf."

"Hi."

"Doctor Hesperus," he said, standing and shaking Wolf's hand.

Dr. Hesperus was a shorter man with a bald head that was a

placid lake of tanned skin. He wore frameless glasses and had kind eyes behind the lenses.

"I hear you're in town to help with the case," Hesperus said.

"That's right."

"I gave my report to the sheriff yesterday. But here's another copy for you." He handed a folder over to Wolf.

Wolf opened it and leafed through the papers, seeing dense typed paragraphs and hard-to-read handwriting. "Do you mind showing me the major details?"

Hesperus nodded. "No problem. In here." He led them into the next room, which was lined with body lockers, and pulled on a handle.

Wolf instinctually took a big breath and moved in as the body slid out on the rack.

Hesperus wasted no time removing the blanket, unveiling Bennett beneath it.

The young man had reddish-brown eyebrows and facial hair like his father, but the shape of his face was less square, more oval compared to his dad. His features had the sunken look of death. His eyes were closed, freckled skin ashen white, mouth slightly parted and slid backward, unnatural looking.

"I've shaved around the entrance wound here," Hesperus said pointing. "And, well, you can see ..."

He gestured toward the flap of skull that had blown open on the other side, exposing brain and bone beneath it.

Wolf noted Normandy was taking Wolf's earlier offer, keeping well away from the body, his eyes focused on something in a parallel universe.

"Tell me about the wound," Wolf said.

"You can see here," Hesperus pointed with a pen, "there are some powder burns on his skull, and there was some burnt hair I removed, which suggests the barrel was pressed to his head at the time of firing. The bullet definitely came from his Glock Model 30, found at the scene. As you know, forty-five caliber. Not hollow point. There's one small thing we can be thankful for. We removed the bullet from the ceiling."

Wolf cut to it. "Do you think this wound was self-inflicted or did somebody else pull the trigger?"

Hesperus straightened, taking a breath, looking at Normandy and then Wolf. "It's tough to tell."

"What about the GSR found on his hand?" Wolf asked.

"What about it?"

"Was there a lot? A little?"

Hesperus shrugged. "Enough to suggest he either fired the gun or his hand was very close at the moment of firing."

"There was stippling on his skull, powder burns," Wolf said. "There would not be any on his hand if he fired the gun, right?"

"Correct. There would be no stippling."

"But if his hand was close to the muzzle, there would be stippling."

"There could be. Yes."

"Was there stippling on his hand?"

"No."

Wolf raised his eyebrows.

"But his hand could have been anywhere but near the muzzle and gotten a good dose of GSR," Hesperus said.

Wolf said nothing.

"There's no way for me to know if he pulled the trigger. There are too many factors at play. Any good doctor would tell you the same."

Wolf nodded. "What does your gut tell you?"

"My gut says a gut feeling isn't enough for the courts," Hesperus said, not blinking or breaking eye contact when he said it.

Wolf returned the stare for a beat, then gestured toward

Bennett's lower half. "I saw the photos of his body, how it was found. Was there any evidence of sexual contact? Fluids?"

"I found a small amount of semen in his underwear, suggesting he was aroused at some point before his death."

"So...if somebody were to suggest the scene was staged to look like he was in the midst of a sexual act, what would you say to that?" Wolf asked.

"I would say it's possible. But he was sexually aroused at some point, which to me points that the scene, his pants being down, his lying face down, suggests he was in the midst of a sexual act, or was about to begin a sexual act. But then again, the car was moved. It was wiped down. The whole thing was staged, right?"

"No fluids found on the seat underneath him?"

"Nothing besides the blood."

"No saliva found on his genitals?" Wolf asked.

"No."

Wolf eyed the body some more, hypnotized by the stillness of death. "Is there anything else you can think of that I need to know?"

"Not particularly." Hesperus lowered the sheet back over Bennett's head.

Wolf stepped away, seeing Normandy was waiting in the other room now. He went out to join him, letting the doctor push the storage locker closed.

Hesperus followed them out into the anteroom, shutting off the lights and locking the door behind him. He gathered his bag off the ground. "I have a private practice a few blocks away. It's my day job," he said with a chuckle.

They left out into the hall, waited for Hesperus to lock the door behind them, and walked to the elevator, which they rode in silence to the ground floor.

Wolf took a deep breath as they got back out into the

sunshine. A breeze had whipped up, blowing in from the south. He closed his eyes, feeling the death wash off him, out of his clothing.

"Feels good to get out of there, eh? Here." Hesperus said, handing a card to Wolf. "Give me a call if you have any other questions."

Wolf handed over one of his own. "Thank you. And you do the same."

The doctor climbed into a vehicle that raised four by four Jeep with all the bells and whistles on it and drove away.

Normandy and Wolf got back into Normandy's SUV.

"Sorry about that," Normandy said, firing up the engine.

"For what?"

"For not being, you know, closer in on the action." Some color had come back into Normandy's face. He pulled out a Copenhagen and put one in. "I mean, I'm fine with the pictures and everything. It's just the in-person stuff. I just need to get used to it."

"Let's hope you never do," Wolf said.

"Yeah. Right, I guess." Normandy fished in his back seat and came back with an empty Red Bull can. He pressed his elbow into the top until it cracked, pushed the pop-top through, and spat into it. "What do you think? Did you learn anything?"

"I don't know." He looked down the highway leading into town.

"Where to?" Normandy asked.

"Which place is closer? The car parts store or your father's factory?"

"Car parts."

"Then we'll go there first," Wolf said. "And go see Valentina Johnson."

13

"That's her car," Normandy said.

Wolf squinted as they turned in the parking lot of Underhill's Auto Parts. Sunlight lanced off the wet asphalt, illuminating tendrils of steam rising around a beat-up silver hatchback.

"She's here."

The clock read almost nine and the sign on the door told them it opened at eight-thirty.

Wolf was still chewing on a breakfast sandwich they'd picked up at a place called Burger Brad's. He reluctantly wrapped up what was left, shoved it in the bag, and followed Normandy into the shop. Inside it smelled of motor oil, rubber, cleaning agents, and stale cigarette smoke.

"Hey, Jake." Normandy waved to a man behind the counter, the source of the stale cigarette smoke smell. "Is Valentina around?"

Jake said nothing, just pointed toward the back.

"Who wants to know?" a female voice called from an open back room off the main shop floor.

"It's John Normandy," Normandy announced.

There was a sound, then some footsteps, then a woman in her early twenties came out of the doorway. Valentina Johnson was heavy set, with dyed jet-black hair pulled back in twin braids that brushed her shoulders. She wore a black shirt and black lipstick and black pants.

"What?" she said, ducking left and right, looking past them. "Is that asshole here?"

"No," Normandy said.

She relaxed and eyed Wolf up and down. "So who's this?"

"This is Detective Wolf. He's down here from Rocky Points, helping us with the case."

"You're not going to choke me out looking for information, too, are you?"

The man known as Jake was watching them with one eye.

"No, I'm not," Wolf said. "That would be illegal and wrong. You know you can press charges against Sheriff Mustaine, right?"

She scoffed. "Have you ever met Sheriff Mustaine?"

"I have."

"Then you'll know picking a fight with that man is bad for your health."

Wolf had no comeback.

She crossed her arms over her chest. "Well?"

"Could we please talk with you a few minutes in private?" Wolf asked.

"I've already told you assholes everything I know. My story's not going to change. A-n-y-thing you say will be used against you. That's what a good lawyer would tell me. He would say never say a flippin' word to the cops."

"I'm just interested in the truth," Wolf said, putting his hands up.

"I've already told the truth."

"Sometimes what people say gets distorted, and from what I've heard that people said you said is not very clear to me."

She looked him hard in the eye. Her irises were pale blue, the white around them clear.

Wolf did his best to not blink. "I just want to hear it from you. I know it's a pain. I'll try to make it quick."

She eyed him again, then shook her head. "Okay, fine. Jake, here." She handed Jake a cordless landline phone. "If Bill calls take the order number and write it down, will you?"

"Yup."

"Back here," she said, walking through the entryway to the back. Wolf followed her into a room where metal shelves were stacked haphazardly with boxes and parts, the place smelling even more strongly of motor lubricants, machined metal, rubber, and plastic.

"What's happening?" A man ducked out from between the shelves at the end of the room, clipboard in hand.

"Cops," she said. "It's okay, they just want to talk more about Bennett or something."

"Hey," he said. "I don't want any more trouble like what happened last time, John."

"We know," Normandy said. "The sheriff's not here."

Valentina flicked her hands towards the man, shooing him away with long black fingernails.

The man stared at them a beat and disappeared amid the shelves.

She sat down at a desk along the wall in a hot-pink roll-chair and crossed her legs. Gum clicked and squished between her teeth as she looked up at them.

"So, seriously. Who the hell are you?" she asked. "Why am I talking to you now?"

"I've taken over this case," Wolf said.

"Isn't this out of your jurisdiction? He said you were from Rocky Points."

"That's true. But the DA has deputized me, giving me authority to investigate and make arrests down here for the time being."

She stared at him for a beat. "Whatever. Okay, fine. Listen, the bottom line is this. Me and Carrie had a couple glasses of wine at the Tavern. We were sitting near the pool table. So what? We weren't with Bennett. The dude's a rapist, did you know that?"

When Wolf said nothing, she looked at Normandy. "Did you tell him about Sadie Moreno?"

"What happened with Sadie Moreno?" Wolf asked.

"Ask your boy here."

Wolf nodded. "I've heard that Carrie and Bennett might have a history."

Valentina frowned.

"Is that not accurate?" Wolf asked.

"What do you mean by history?"

"I don't know," Wolf said, telling the truth. "Were they dating at some point?"

"No. Bennett used to hang out with Carrie's brothers back in the day. I think they used to dirt bike and stuff up there. But no, Carrie and Bennett never dated."

"When is back in the day?"

"High school. Around then."

Wolf nodded. "Got it. So, moving on to Friday night. You two were having a couple of drinks. Then what?"

"Then we left."

"What time?"

"Eleven. Eleven-fifteen, or something like that."

"The receipt we got from The Tavern said 11:21."

"Okay, we left at 11:21 then."

"And then what?"

"Then we went home."

"To Carrie's ranch?"

"That's right. I dropped her off."

"Where do you live?"

"Here in town."

Wolf frowned. "Carrie lives miles away out in the boonies, up a thousand feet or more up that canyon and into those mountains. You went and picked her up that night? And then drove her home after a couple of drinks?"

"I had a glass of wine." She put her wrists together. "Cuff me."

"I'm sure you were sober. I'm just saying it's a far drive."

She shrugged. "I wish I lived up there on that ranch. Place is beautiful. You sit around too long in this shithole of a town, in this back room in an auto parts shop, sucking in this shit air, and you forget the beauty that surrounds you. I go and pick her up because I like to take the drive. It helps me clear my head."

Wolf nodded. "Okay."

"Sometimes I stay up there, too. I'll pick her up, we'll go do something, and I'll take her home and spend the night. I've done that since we were kids. I like it. She's got a family. Land. Horses. I ain't got shit."

"You have me, Valentina." The guy with the clipboard walked past.

She ignored him. "I was the first to turn sixteen and get my driver's license. I used to come pick her up back then. I guess we kept the tradition alive."

"Okay," Wolf said. "But you came back home that night, not stayed up there, correct?"

"Correct."

"I understand."

"Good. Tell that to that gorilla for a sheriff we got down there." She leaned over and spat her gum in the waste basket.

"Did you see when Bennett left the Tavern?"

"Nope."

"He left a few minutes before you."

She said nothing.

"Did you see Bennett outside? Maybe in the parking lot?"

"Yes."

He raised his eyebrows.

She rolled her neck, ultimate impatience pushing a breath out of her. "He was sitting in the front seat of his truck. We were parked next to him. I got into my car, looked over, and he was sitting there, looking at his phone, texting somebody or something."

"Did he look at you?"

"I don't know, yeah I guess."

"Did you interact with him?"

"No. Like I said, he was on the phone. And he's a rapist. I don't like interacting with him."

Wolf nodded. "How long did you stay at Carrie's when you dropped her off?"

"Not long. Just pulled up. We talked for like, maybe a minute or two. But then I left."

Wolf pulled out his phone. "What's the address of Carrie's ranch?"

"What am I, the post office? I don't know."

"What's the name of the ranch?"

"The Whitlock Ranch, I think," Normandy said.

Wolf entered the name in his mapping app. It came up with a pin mark on screen. He measured the distance from where they were to it. "Says here the drive takes twenty-one minutes."

"Yeah? And?"

"So, if you left The Tavern at eleven-twenty...I don't know, say eleven-twenty-three, that puts you at Carrie's house at eleven-forty-four give or take a few minutes."

She said nothing while he studied the map. "Did you pass anybody on the way back down into Crow Valley?"

"No." She seemed to really think about it. "I would have remembered. It's always kind of freaky if I do pass somebody when it's late at night."

She pulled out a fresh piece of gum from a pack sitting on the desk and folded it into her mouth.

"I appreciate your time," Wolf said.

"Is that it? This guy's much better than Mustaine. You can come talk to me anytime," she winked, looking him up and down. "Tell Mustaine I say eat shit for me." She stood up and kicked the chair back under her desk.

"One more thing," Wolf said.

"Yeah?"

"We're going to be getting the GPS data from Bennett's phone later today."

She said nothing, then popped her eyebrows. "So?"

"That data will show exactly where he went Friday night."

"So?"

"It's not going to implicate you in any way, is it?"

"No. It's not."

Wolf nodded. "Okay."

"Yeah. It is okay. I'm done. Bye." She flicked her long fingernails at them. "Out. I have to get to work."

"Thanks for your time," Wolf said again, turning to leave.

Wolf and Normandy left. The air outside was much warmer, the sun higher overhead. Water splashed on the ground off the gutters from the building.

"What do you think?" Normandy asked.

"It seems like she's telling the truth," Wolf said.

"That's what I was thinking."

"But she might be a great liar."

They got to Normandy's truck and climbed inside. The interior was warm, almost hot, smelling of Wolf's food. He perked up at the thought of more breakfast waiting inside the bag for him and dug his hand inside, unwrapped his sandwich and took another bite.

"Where to next?" Normandy asked. "Sadie Moreno?"

"I think it's a good idea. And what about this Paco guy? What's his name?"

"Paco Nez," Normandy said. "He was Bennett's business partner. Co-owner of P and J's Pizza."

"What's he like? Big? Strong like Bennett?"

Normandy laughed. "No. Small. Skinny. Unlike Bennett."

"Were you there when Mustaine questioned him?"

"Yeah," Normandy said. "Like Elan said, he told us Bennett left the restaurant first, and he closed up with another employee."

Normandy squirmed and pulled out his phone. "I got a text from Elan. Ah, I guess they already got the readout from Summit."

Wolf nodded, feeling a jolt of excitement.

In and out.

The radio crackled. "Normandy, you copy?"

"There's Elan." Normandy pulled it off the hook and thumbed it. "Yeah, go ahead."

"Where are you?" The undersheriff's voice was high pitched and excited.

"Down at the auto parts shop. Just got done talking to Valentina—"

"You'd better come back in."

"What's going on?"

"Just make it fast."

14

Elan was waiting outside of the building for their arrival, pacing near the single vehicle that remained in the lot.

Normandy pulled up and Wolf rolled down his window. "What's up?"

Elan shoved a packet of paper at Wolf. "The cell GPS readout."

Wolf flipped through the packet. The top page had a list of phone calls, all phone numbers he didn't recognize, but somebody had written in pencil next to them.

The first number had Paco Nez written next to it. The second a name called Randy Stenger. The third another name Wolf didn't recognize.

"Those are two employees of the pizza shop," Elan said.

The next page was a map with a series of lines drawn on it, along with a date stamped on the top, and Wolf recognized it was the path Bennett's phone took on Friday night.

The line traveled from town to the west, up a snaking line Wolf recognized from just minutes before looking at his own map app, as a route toward the Whitlock Ranch. But it was different. The end veered straight north, whereas the line that showed how to get to Carrie Whitlock's place would have travelled continuously to the west.

"That's High Road," Normandy said, leaning over to see. "He turned up High Road."

There was a mark on the page indicating multiple cellular pings happened at one spot, only a short distance from the turnoff, meaning, his phone had stopped moving for several hours. Then the line led north and stopped at its final destination before shutting off, where there were multiple pings in one spot again, this time over twenty-four hours worth.

"It looks like that's the spot his body was found," Elan said, pointing to the last location.

Wolf flipped back to the other page. "Where's the text messages?"

"On the final page."

Wolf flipped and saw a list of dozens of messages in tiny font.

"They're jumbled. Mostly work related, or if they aren't about work, they're about mundane stuff."

Wolf looked down the list, following the time stamps to Saturday night, searching for eleven-twenty-one p.m., or somewhere about that time, when Valentina Johnson said she saw him staring at his phone.

There was a single message at ten-forty-five. It was to Paco Nez. Wolf recognized the phone number from the previous pages. It read:

I'm bouncing home early. I'll catch you tomorrow.

"Listen. Mustaine's already on his way up," Elan said.

"Up where?"

"Up there." Elan pointed at the map. "That spot there, where Bennett's phone pinged for over three hours. Mustaine thinks he must have died there. He mentioned how close it was to the Whitlock Ranch, and he did this creepy thing. He pulled out his gun and checked the chamber."

"Shit," Normandy said.

"Yeah."

"Where's Alvarez?" Normandy asked.

"He followed after Mustaine. We have to move. Follow me." He walked away, got in his own SUV and fired it up.

They followed the man as he sped through town and out onto the road leading west.

Elan drove fast and Normandy kept up.

They climbed up through the canyon, hitting a few icy patches that clung to the shadows, but mostly the snow had melted, leaving mud flinging up the sides of Normandy's truck, slapping the bottom of the floorboards at Wolf's feet.

Soon they exited the canyon and were up on the high plateau. Up here the snow was more plentiful than down in the valley, white clinging to the north side of the pine trees, carpeting the meadows between, and smearing across the road every few hundred yards.

Wolf eyed the papers again. "There was a ping right around here. The time stamp reads twelve thirty-one a.m."

"Valentina would have been leaving the Whitlock Ranch by...what did we say?"

"We said she probably got up there at eleven-forty-four. Call it eleven-fifty by the time she left." Wolf checked his watch. "What are we, ten minutes from the ranch if we were driving the speed limit?"

"Probably, yeah," Normandy said.

"She would have been driving here at around twelve, give or take a few minutes. Her story checks out, and if she drove when she said she did she wouldn't have passed him. Bennett drove up here a good thirty minutes later."

Normandy spat in his can. "We need to get Carrie and Valentina's GPS readouts for any of this to make sense."

Either Valentina was telling the truth, or she was very calculating, Wolf thought. Either way, Normandy was right.

Wolf stared at the next dot on the map, where Bennett Mustaine had pinged once at 12:59 a.m., and then a few more times, the final one being at 4:10 a.m. before moving north.

Elan slowed ahead, then hung a right onto High Road.

It wasn't long before they were bouncing in their seats, the road wrapping up to the right and left as it gained altitude over the valley below.

The road was covered in an inch or so of snow, sliced by Mustaine's and Alvarez's vehicles that had passed minutes before. Rocks jutted from the white blanket, some that Normandy could avoid, others that Normandy had no choice but to hit head out, sending the truck popping up and down.

Wolf gripped the ceiling handle, flexing his arm, as they made their way for another ten minutes until the road leveled out on the ridge line above.

Here the trees thinned out and Wolf recognized this had been the stretch of road where he and Normandy had stopped the day before to relieve themselves and look out at the Whitlock Ranch.

Wolf looked left, past Normandy, down on the valley below. Steam rose from the melting snow, pooling in the valley, veiling the Ranch with a slight mist.

"There they are."

Two vehicles were parked ahead. Elan's vehicle bucked to a stop and Normandy pulled behind him, shutting off the engine.

Mustaine and Deputy Alvarez were standing outside, both studying the ground.

The sun was higher still now, but the temperature up here had yet to reach anything near what it had been down in town.

Wolf got out and shut his door, then zipped his jacket all the way up. A cold breeze tickled his three-day beard, smelling of pine, minty sage, and the faint whiff of animal dung.

His boots creaked on the snow. Mustaine and Alvarez were hypnotized by something in the snow, but Wolf saw nothing but deer tracks.

"You find anything?" Wolf asked.

Mustaine put his hands on his hips and stood straight, sucking in a breath. "This is the spot my son died." The sheriff turned his back to them, staring out into the distance.

They all stood in silence for more than a minute.

Here there was a rise to the west, covered in low brush, blocking out the view of the Whitlock Ranch below.

"Did you see the readout?" Mustaine said, turning to Wolf.

Wolf nodded.

"The time stamps say his phone was here for at least three hours."

"I saw that."

Mustaine gestured to the ground. "This snow's making it impossible to see anything. But this was the spot. I know it." He shook his head. "I can feel it."

Barbed wire lined the road on either side, and here the wire widened, the brush non-existent in a half-circle off the west of the road, indicating a vehicle turn off underneath the snow.

"Did you call a forensic team?" Wolf asked.

"Not yet."

Wolf and Elan exchanged a glance.

Elan nodded. "I'll call Traver."

"It would be good to get a K9 unit up here, too," Wolf said. "There might be something under this snow."

Elan looked at his screen and pointed it at the sky, fishing for a signal. "Got one bar."

"If you follow this north, you get right to the spot he was found," Mustaine said.

Wolf nodded. "Yeah, we took this road back yesterday."

Mustaine's boots crunch through dry grass and snow as he walked around the edge of the turnout. "So, he was up here. With somebody. They shot him. They drove him up to Dry Wash. We know they shot him here, because the blood was smeared all over the back seat because he was moved. He was shot, then he sat for hours. Then he was moved."

Wolf watched as Mustaine paced back and forth, his hands flexing and relaxing, like a predator pacing along a zoo enclosure window.

Elan held up his phone. "I just spoke to Traver. He's still in Silverton. He's working his way back today. He says he'll get Eddie and Lucy ... uh, Lucy's the dog, Eddie's the handler, and they'll get up here asap. But he says Eddie's out of town, too."

"Where?" Mustaine's voice was a cannon shot in the still air.

"I don't know, sir."

"God damn it. These back woods..." Mustaine murmured to himself, turning away from them.

"When can Traver get up here?" Wolf asked.

"He says he's shooting for later today. He'll keep me posted."

The fence wobbled, and they turned to see Mustaine had stepped over it and was marching toward the peaks to the west, weaving between the low brush.

"What's he doing?" Alvarez asked.

"You guys take a look around for anything else." Wolf walked along the fence to where Mustaine had stepped over and followed him.

Wolf's strides were three-quarters as long as Mustaine's scratched into the snow. Again, he noticed the hitch in the gait, every left footstep dragging before it hit the ground. The NFL training camp career-stopper.

Mustaine stood ahead, hands on hips, and as Wolf neared, more of the valley below came into view, along with the Whitlock Ranch.

Wolf turned and saw the view extended all the way down to Crow Valley, the long flat zone that cradled the town, and then the peaks behind it to the east.

He blinked out of the reverie and followed Mustaine's gaze, which was locked on the Whitlock Ranch below.

"They're behind this." Mustaine's voice was quiet.

They stared down at the ranch. It was maybe two miles away, or three, by Wolf's best guess, a vast distance that could be covered on foot in about an hour. Cattle dotted the grounds north of the house, near the edge of the pine trees. The barn shone bright red in the mid-morning sun, the tan outbuilding gleaming with reflection that cut through the mist.

Far below a vehicle drove into view, drawing both their attention. It was a dark blue pickup Wolf recognized from the day before as the Whitlocks'. It drove in on the road leading from Crow Valley, slowed, came to a stop, and somebody got out, a small black dot of a form, pushed open the gate in front, drove in, and pushed it back closed.

Mustaine turned and walked away.

"Where are you going?"

Mustaine didn't respond, stepping straight through a bush as he made his way back toward the vehicles at a pace considerably faster than before.

"Shit." He jogged, catching up. "What are you going to do?"

Mustaine stepped over the fence, and Wolf saw his eyes

were that creepy half-closed version he'd seen once behind a football mask, and then the night before at The Tavern.

Mustaine opened his door. The SUV sagged hard as he sat down.

Wolf inserted himself between the truck and the door. "The proximity of this spot to the Whitlock Ranch is suspicious. We'll be able to get Carrie's phone GPS records now, too."

"And wait another three days for them?" Mustaine made a noise like a bull exhaling before a charge. "Move."

"But what we have is not enough to go in there right now, if that's what you're thinking."

"Move," he said again, his voice dropping to a growl.

Wolf remained where he was.

Mustaine pushed the start button and the truck roared to life. The truck lurched forward, the window frame knocking hard against Wolf's elbow.

The wheels spun while the engine revved, and the vehicle turned a half-circle, grinding through the previously untouched turn-out. It bounced through a rut and the door slammed shut, and then it sped down the hill.

15

They never did catch up to Mustaine until the Whitlock ranch gate.

"What is he doing?" Normandy gripped the wheel with both hands as he began slowing down.

Wolf leaned into the windshield, squinting to see through the mud-covered windshield. They had been behind Alvarez on the drive and had caught a lot of spatter.

Mustaine was gripping the gate with both hands, pulling and pushing, the gate lurching back and forth, waves rippling out on either side of the game fence.

Normandy skidded to a stop, and they got out.

"—Now! Come out you bitches! I want to talk to you!"

Elan and Alvarez were already out, yelling at the sheriff, their words ignored, or not heard.

"Come out murderers!" Mustaine yelled.

Wolf eyed the house and saw Nola Whitlock standing in the doorway, half in and half out, a shotgun in her hands aimed at the ground.

"Hey! Get that bitch daughter of yours out here right now!"

Nola stepped back into the house and shut the door. The

drapes parted, revealing Cruz's face against the glass, the muzzle of a hunting rifle in plain sight.

"Shit, what do we do?" Alvarez asked, looking at Wolf.

Elan looked at him, too. "We have to...what? Arrest him?"

"Sheriff!" Wolf screamed the word, barely getting above the volume of Mustaine's voice.

Mustaine grabbed both hands on the bars and shook the gates again. There was a creaking noise in one of the wooden posts, which seemed to give him more encouragement. He thrashed, animalistic.

"Sheriff." Wolf put a hand on Mustaine's shoulder, feeling the muscles rippling beneath. "Hey, sheriff." He tried the voice of a guy trying to calm down a rabid dog.

Eyes still on the house inside, Mustaine reached back with one arm and pushed, connecting against Wolf's chest like a horse kick.

Wolf stumbled back, rubbing the deep pain out of his pectoral.

Mustaine grabbed the bars again. "Get out here! I want to talk to you!"

Wolf turned around and saw Elan was standing closest. The undersheriff's hand was resting on his gun. His eyes were wide, skin pale, mouth moving like he was sucking on a chunk of lemon.

"Either you guys get out here and talk to me, or I start shooting!" Mustaine put a hand on his gun. "I'm going to shoot this lock! And then I'm coming in!"

"Sheriff," Wolf said, making a decision. "I'm afraid I'm going to have to place you under arrest."

The words coming out sounded weak to his own ears, but he put a hand on the big boulder of Mustaine's shoulder and pulled him around. He had his cuffs pulled and slapped them down on Mustaine's forearm, but the opening loop for the cuff was too small where he'd connected on the flesh, and it didn't slam closed on the other side.

Mustaine pulled the cuffs off and threw them aside, squaring at Wolf. "What the hell are you doing?"

"I said I'm sorry, but you're under arrest." He tried to use a matter-of-fact tone, no fight in it. He put his hand back toward Elan, or one of the other two deputies, Wolf didn't dare take his eyes off the big man. "Hand me your cuffs. Turn around. Put your hands behind your back."

Mustaine got closer, his breath hot and putrid landing on Wolf's nose. "You remember what I told you last night."

Wolf held his ground, letting hot saliva fleck his face.

"I said you mess with my investigation, and I'll put my fist through your face."

"You can't do this, sheriff. And you know it."

"I can do whatever I want!"

Mustaine jerked in place, and in the same instant Wolf felt like he'd been shot in the stomach by a cannon ball.

Wolf fell to the ground, spilling over the fist and arm that was still buried in his abdomen. He landed on the ground, cold wetness pressing into the side of his face.

"—with my investigation! I told you!" The words were loud as gunfire in his ear.

Wolf fought to take a breath, but nothing came. He'd been punched in the stomach before and knew the wind would return at some point, but then again, he'd never been punched this hard. Maybe this was it, he thought, rolling to his side in agony.

The world darkened at the edges, and he heard more yelling, and more of Mustaine's face in his, this time with a finger poking the top of his head. His body jerked as hot wires of pain lanced up and down, emanating from his guts.

And then, just as he thought he was going to pass out,

slowly his diaphragm released, and air filled his lungs again. And slowly the world brightened, his vision righting itself as the oxygen starved cells of his body drank.

"You okay?" Normandy and Alvarez were kneeling next to him.

"Sir!" Elan stood behind them, inching his way toward the fence and Mustaine, who had turned his attention back to the house. "Please stand down!"

Mustaine gripped both hands again, ignoring his undersheriff.

Wolf rolled onto his hands and knees, feeling the cold wetness soaking through the legs of his jeans. Drool streamed from his mouth, reaching the ground. He heaved and his breakfast tumbled onto the wet earth, sparking even more pain in his stomach as he grunted involuntarily.

But he got up, Normandy and Alvarez helping him to his feet.

"Be ready," he said.

Alvarez and Normandy exchanged a glance.

"For what?" Alvarez asked.

Mustaine had begun climbing the fence, and he was a few feet off the ground, reaching up for a handhold.

Wolf walked up fast behind him and wrenched the gun out of the sheriff's holster.

"What the fuck?" Mustaine twisted and kicked out.

Wolf easily stepped to the side and threw the gun back towards Normandy.

Normandy caught it, eyeing it in his outstretched hands like it was a grenade.

The ground shook as Mustaine jumped down from the fence, in almost one movement landing and throwing a vicious right hand at Wolf.

Wolf ducked, getting only a glancing blow on the side of his head, but it was enough to feel like he'd been scalped.

Mustaine threw another punch and Wolf lunged back, almost colliding with Elan.

"Move!" Wolf said. "Get back!"

Mustaine had stopped talking, the angry rant silenced by rage.

"You're dead." Mustaine cocked a fist, his entire mass twisting sideways, loading force behind it.

Wolf jumped forward, twisting to avoid the blow while punching as hard as he could into Mustaine's jaw. He connected squarely but hadn't made a hard enough fist, and his knuckles crunched against the rock-hard horseshoe-shaped bone underneath the big man's beard.

But Wolf's quick move caused Mustaine to miss completely. The sheriff stumbled forward, his eyes going blank for a moment from the force of the blow. It was short lived, though, and the rage came back, multiplied.

Wolf punched again, this time with his left, connecting with Mustaine's ear, and then he followed with a right, hitting the back of his head.

Mustaine was bent at the waist, and when he clawed at Wolf with his hand Wolf slammed down with an elbow, hitting the sheriff hard in the meat of his forearm.

Wolf reared up and slammed down again on his shoulder with the same elbow, then the back of his head, punching the side of his face once, twice, and then a third and fourth time, ending with another hard upturned elbow that landed square in Mustaine's upper face.

Then Mustaine hit the ground face first without putting his arms out for bracing. His head wrenched back as the hundreds of pounds of body weight behind it rammed it straight into the rocky mud.

And then the man slowly rolled to his side.

"Holy shit," Normandy said.

Wolf searched the ground for his cuffs and saw them beneath Mustaine's legs.

The stunning effect of Wolf's blows was short-lived, and a roar came from Mustaine first, then he put his hands on the ground to get up.

Wolf forgot the cuffs and backed away just in time to miss another twirling back hand punch as Mustaine got to his feet, followed by another punch that caught air.

Mustaine kept swinging, lunging toward Wolf with fists, turning Wolf's shock and awe tactic back on him with double the ferocity.

Wolf backed up and slammed into the fence, then used the momentum to push off, going toward the punches again, this time even faster. He ignored a slam into his shoulder and delivered another fast punch square into Mustaine's nose.

Mustaine's head jolted back and his hands flailed out to his sides. Wolf punched him three more times in the jaw and then once in the stomach. Mustaine fell over, landing on his side, his head whiplashing hard into the ground.

Wolf picked up the cuffs and put them on the narrowest part of one of his wrists, just getting them closed, then yanked the other arm down and into position, managed to get them both cuffed, then backed away, collapsing into the fence and landing hard on his backside.

His lungs burned, chest heaving for air as he sat, watching through tear filled eyes as Normandy and Alvarez stood over their boss with shocked expressions. He grunted, doubling over as his stomach seared hot, but just as quickly as it had come the pain was gone.

"Are you alright?" Elan put a hand on his shoulder.

Wolf nodded, taking the offered hand and stood up. "Yeah."

Alvarez walked up to Mustaine, his eyes wide.

The front door of the house on the other side of the fence opened and Nola Whitlock came out, along with her youngest son, Cruz, Carrie trailing behind. They were all carrying guns, taking unsure steps out onto the covered porch.

"What did you do?" Alvarez asked.

"Get him up, put him in a vehicle, bring him to the station, and put him in a cell," Wolf said. "And read him his rights."

Alvarez and Normandy stood over their boss. Mustaine was beginning to squirm and fight against the restraints.

"Let's go," Elan moved in and put a hand under one of Mustaine's arms, spurring his other two deputies into action.

With considerable effort the three of them got the sheriff to his feet. Mustaine was conscious, but slow moving, his legs shaky under him. He grumbled and spit on the ground, blood oozing out of his nose over his mouth and down his chin, staining the front of his uniform.

"Wait," Wolf said.

They stopped and Wolf went to Mustaine and felt the front pockets of his jeans. He felt a lump and dug out a set of keys, which included a key fob for Mustaine's truck.

Wolf watched as they loaded the sheriff into the back of Elan's SUV and shut the door. Wolf flexed his right hand and felt pain between his knuckles, sure that he'd broken at least one bone.

"Shit," Wolf said under his breath.

"What do you want to do?" Elan asked, walking up to Wolf.

Wolf looked back at the Whitlocks' house. They were still on the porch, watching in silence.

"Why don't you take him down. Take everybody. You'll need the help putting him in that cell."

"What are you going to do?"

Wolf held up Mustaine's set of keys. "I'll drive Mustaine's

truck down. I'm going to try and talk to them," he flicked his chin at the Whitlocks. "And then I'll meet you at the station."

"Yes sir."

The vehicles drove off, Alvarez's first, Elan's vehicle next, followed by Normandy. For a moment he wondered if Elan was safe, but there would be a cage between him and the back seat. Would the sheriff be able to influence him otherwise? Perhaps a threat or two making him pull over and let him go?

Wolf looked down at his hands and saw a lot of blood. He couldn't find cuts of his own, but the adrenaline was still coursing through his veins, dulling any pain in his body.

When the engine noise of the SUVs dissipated, he noticed another sound emerge from the silence. He turned to see a green tractor far in the field to the west, outside the enclosed fence surrounding the house, out in the snow-covered cattle fields.

Nola, Carrie, and Cruz had gone back inside but left the front door open, suggesting they might come back out, so Wolf stood patiently by the gate. He turned to the tractor and watched it come in high gear, the trailer behind it an empty flat-bed trailer, save a few strands of hay still clinging.

Wolf saw piles of hay out in the fields, and cattle gathered around them, and realized Kent, the oldest son, must have been out there all along.

The sun was blazing now, and Wolf was sweating. He unzipped his jacket, letting the southerly breeze caress his undershirt with cool air. He ran a hand over his hair and wiped his temples.

His body shook from the adrenaline wearing off, and he took some deep breaths through his nose to calm himself down.

Footsteps approached and he turned to see Nola walking down the muddy drive towards the gate, Carrie and Cruz flanking her sides. They had lost their guns.

"Thank you," she said. "I'm pretty sure if you weren't here, we'd be shooting at each other right now."

Wolf nodded.

The tractor grew louder, approaching the western fence, then slowed to a stop and went quiet, sending the property into dead silence.

The pilot door opened and Kent, the eldest son, stood up from the seat.

"What's going on?" he asked.

"Everything's okay!" Nola said. "You can stay there!"

But Kent was already down off the tractor and opening a side gate, pushing it inward.

"Just stay!"

Kent stopped in his tracks, letting the gate swing in lazily until it hit the interior wall of wire and bounced on its hinges.

"I'm not going to hurt you guys," Wolf said.

She looked at him. "What the hell was he screaming about? Cell phone GPS records? He said they showed Bennett came here. Bullshit. He didn't come here."

Wolf shook his head. "They showed that he was up High Road. Close to here."

"High Road," she said. "Well, that's not here."

They stared at each other for a few moments.

Nola's eyes were wide with excitement, her mouth pursed with determination. She crossed her arms, her daughter mirroring her body language.

Wolf moved his gaze to Kent again. The eldest son watched, standing still and quiet.

"Sheriff Mustaine really seems to think you had something to do with this, Carrie," Wolf said. "He says you and Bennett have a history. What does he mean by that?"

Nola looked over her shoulder and mumbled something Wolf couldn't hear.

Carrie made no attempt to speak.

"What's that?" he asked.

"We don't have a history," Carrie said.

Wolf was shocked to hear her voice. Given how little she spoke, he thought she'd sound timid, but she spoke with fierce articulation.

He waited for more explanation, but none came. "Then why does he think you two have a history?"

"I don't know." She shrugged.

"Bennett used to hang out up here, right? Back in high school?"

A clank came from the tractor, and they turned to see Kent had fallen somehow while climbing up the ladder to the pilot seat. He was lying on the floorboards, and, gingerly, he picked himself up and sat down in the seat.

It looked to Wolf like he had injured himself badly, his face a mask of pain suppressed under a false calm. A country boy taught to never show pain or weakness.

"You okay?" Wolf called out.

Kent said nothing, just stared out the open door of the tractor.

"There's no history," Nola said.

"Right." Wolf rubbed his stubble, another reminder of pain flaring between his pinkie and ring finger. "Listen, Carrie. There's ways I can find out if there is history between you two. I can interview people you went to school with. Valentina, for one. And I'm sure there are other people who can give me the information I need to know."

She said nothing.

"Hearing it from you would be best."

She said nothing.

He exhaled. "Carrie. I'm going to lay out a scenario for you. And I want you to—"

"My daughter doesn't need to speak with you."

Wolf nodded. "I know. You've said that before. And you're right. She doesn't. Not at all. But...maybe you could just hear me out. I would hate for all that just happened between me and the sheriff to be for nothing. I'm sure there's going to be hell to pay on my end for that."

He chuckled. They didn't seem to find anything funny.

"My point is, can you humor me? Just hear me out."

Again, she said nothing.

It wasn't a no, so Wolf continued. "I'm wondering if you did end up hooking up with Bennett that night."

Nola un-crossed her arms, and Wolf put his hands up in a defenseless gesture. "I'm not saying you two hooked up. I'm just saying, that maybe you two drove home together."

"Valentina drove me home," Carrie said.

Wolf waited a beat, then continued, choosing to ignore Carrie's words. He had to push through, to get his theory out to them. "Maybe there was some sort of spark in the Tavern that night, and you two ended up talking outside in the parking lot. And one thing led to another, and you got in the truck with him, and you told Valentina, 'Hey, I'll go home with him.' Or he said, 'I'll take her home.' Maybe Valentina protested, and you told her, 'Don't worry about it. I'll be fine.'"

Wolf watched their expressions. He'd seen more movement staring at mountains.

"So, maybe you got into Bennett's truck, and he drove you home," Wolf continued, "But, the night was young for you two, so you turned onto High Road and parked up there. Up where the stars were bright and...well...I was a young person doing that kind of stuff at one time, too. It's just out of sight from your ranch. A perfect spot for young lovers."

Carrie shook her head and looked at the ground, then snapped her attention back to him.

"Am I wrong?" he asked.

She said nothing.

"Then I'll go on. So, you're up there with Bennett. And, well...I've heard about the kind of guy he can be. I've heard about...what was her name? I'm new in town. It's only been a day or two. Sadie? Sarah? What's her name?"

"Sadie," Nola said.

"Sadie Moreno," Wolf said. "That's it."

They stood in silence for a beat, Wolf watching them some more. He looked at Cruz. The kid averted his eyes. Carrie was shaking her head, looking into the distance.

"I've heard about Sadie Moreno, and I wonder if he got physical with you also that night. And if he did maybe you had to defend yourself. He was shot with his own gun. Maybe, I don't know, you two had a struggle, and that's what happened. He was attacking you, and you grabbed the gun, and you defended yourself."

She shook her head.

Wolf walked sideways, eyeing them through the fence. "But if that's the case, if he attacked you and you defended yourself, then why not just come out with the truth?" He looked at Carrie, then Nola. "Are you two afraid of what Mustaine would do or something? People around here seem to think that Mustaine covered up whatever happened with Sadie Moreno. That he made her recant her statements against his son. Are you afraid he would do the same with you?"

Nola turned her head and said something Wolf couldn't hear.

"I'm not Mustaine," Wolf said. "All I want to know is the truth. The real truth."

"Let's go," Nola said. "Kent! Get back to work!"

Kent reached over and shut the door. The engine fired up and he drove away.

He stood watching the other three turn and walk into the house, none of them glancing toward him as the door shut, this time the drapes never parting.

With a sigh he fished the keys out of his pocket, the memories of his fist slamming into Mustaine's face. He twisted his arm and saw a squished star of blood painting his elbow.

"Shit," he said, wondering just how much hell he'd unleashed.

16

Wolf lurched into the parking spot at the Crow Sheriff's office, accidentally riding up onto the curb when he shifted Mustaine's truck into park.

None of the deputies had called him in the twenty-minute drive back down to town, and he wondered if that was good news or bad news. It would have been both a physical and psychological feat to put Mustaine behind bars.

He had spent the whole drive going over the memories of what had happened, and he was convinced more than ever that he had been the luckiest man on earth to not be sitting in the hospital now, or dead. If there was a second time, and Wolf had a feeling that Mustaine would live the rest of his life making sure there was a second time, then Wolf would not get off so unscathed.

The door squealed as he entered, and he found the squad room inside empty.

He walked past the desks toward the back hallway, first stopping to look inside the sheriff's office. The door stood propped open, light inside spilling out.

There was nobody home, thankfully.

He heard a conversation coming from down the hallway between Deputy Garcia and one of the men.

Wolf walked down to an open door on the right and found Garcia and Alvarez talking inside a small conference room.

"What's happening?" Wolf asked.

The two of them stepped apart.

"I was just telling her about what happened," Alvarez said. "We put him in the cell."

Elan and Normandy came out of a doorway and walked towards him.

"How did it go?" Wolf asked.

"Difficult," Elan said. "How about you?"

"Same."

"You have blood on your arm," Normandy said.

Wolf nodded. "So do you. I'd like to see him."

Elan nodded. "Garcia, can you please bring in some rags and water to clean him up with?"

Garcia nodded and walked out of the room.

"Follow me."

"Count me out," Normandy said. "I'll wait out front."

Wolf followed Elan down the hallway, past a closed door that read *Records Room*, to the end of the hallway and to another door with a sign reading *Cell Room*. The undersheriff pulled it open and let Wolf in first.

The room smelled of sweat. There was an empty cell on the right and Mustaine in another on the left. Inside Mustaine's huge mass rested on a cement cot that had been built into the brown-painted cinder-block wall, sticking out as a shelf, testing the limits of its construction.

Mustaine sat up, his elbows on his knees. His face was a mess, with one swollen eye, a swollen fat lip, and a stream of dried blood smeared on his chin, turning into a dark red lightning bolt that went down his neck and disappeared into his shirt.

The big man stared at Wolf, a new expression that promised retribution.

Garcia came in with two bottles of water laying atop a folded towel. She handed them to Elan and left.

Elan knelt and put the two bottles through the bottom row of bars, then threaded the towel through.

Mustaine's eyes remained on Wolf's.

"I didn't mean to do this," Wolf said. "You gave me no choice."

Mustaine stared.

Wolf felt like an idiot for even trying to speak. Nothing could be said to help this situation. Nothing could be done. It was as expected: impossible. Except maybe finding out what happened to Bennett Mustaine, but even then, this situation was FUBAR, as they used to say in the army.

He nodded to Elan and moved toward the door. "Let's go."

"I want my phone call," Mustaine said.

Wolf paused, then ushered Elan outside.

Wolf shut the door behind him, and they went out into the main room and sat in silence for a long beat.

Staring at the foreign landscape art on the walls, and the downtrodden deputies of the Crow County Sheriff's Department, Wolf felt compelled to explain himself.

"Look, I didn't mean for this to happen," he said, repeating what he'd said to Mustaine, because it was the truth. "I was asked to take over this case, and now I've taken it over. I never expected a father to step aside and let the death of his son be investigated by somebody else. But the sheriff was putting innocent lives at risk."

"You did what you had to do," Normandy said.

"Yeah," Elan said. "Shit. It looked to me like he was about to take some innocent lives."

Alvarez cleared his throat. "What if he was right? What if they're not innocent lives?"

Wolf nodded. "Innocent until proven guilty. We don't do the opposite in this job. We don't do what Mustaine was doing up there."

The room descended into silence again.

"He was right to suspect the Whitlocks," Wolf said. "I don't dispute that. Something's going on with them. They're not talking, which is within their rights, but I think they're hiding something."

"We need to get a warrant to search the ranch," Normandy said.

Wolf nodded. "I agree wholeheartedly."

"What are we looking for?" Elan asked.

"Clothing with GSR on it. We have the yellow microfibers found inside Bennett's truck. Maybe we can find those rags they belong to. And we have the cleaning agents the truck was cleaned with. We have the time they left the Tavern. We have the ranch being in the vicinity of the body," Wolf said, using his fingers to tick off each item.

He stood up and began pacing. "And we're going to need Carrie's and Valentina's cell records. The proximity of Bennett's GPS data to their location is enough to get her records, too."

"And hopefully they'll be faster this time," Garcia said.

"I'll get on it," Elan said.

Wolf looked toward the back hallway.

"What's up?" Elan asked.

"I want to see every record you have on Sadie Moreno."

They all reacted, all of them trying not to react, Garcia leaning into her computer screen, Alvarez looking down at his hands, and Normandy looking over at Elan.

And Elan? He looked confused. "Who's Sadie Moreno."

Wolf eyed them in turn. "None of you have spoken to him about this?"

"About what?" Elan asked.

"It was before your time. Do you have digital copies of all your reports?"

Elan nodded and gestured to Garcia.

Garcia shook her head. "The records aren't in there."

"How do you know?" Wolf asked.

"I've checked."

"And what about your records room? Where are the keys?"

"We don't keep it locked."

Wolf began walking.

"It's not in there, either." Garcia looked up from her computer. "I've checked before there, too. He's gotten rid of all of it: Sadie Moreno's reports, and Dr. Traver's."

"And the updated, retracted report she came in and made later?" Wolf asked.

"He got rid of that, too. Don't you see?" She smiled, sadness in her eyes. "That never happened."

Wolf eyed Elan, and saw the undersheriff he was now quiet, staring at the carpet.

"Do you know about this incident?" Wolf asked.

Elan blinked. "No. I mean, I've heard some rumors, too. And I can confirm there are no reports in there, or in the computer system. I've also looked."

"Not that I don't trust you all...but please show me." Wolf walked to Garcia's desk.

Garcia clicked a few buttons on the screen, then clicked her mouse. "Here. I'll type in a search...Sa-die-Moreno. See? Nothing."

"And what about Dr. Traver?"

"Tra-ver...nothing."

"Try his first name."

"Donald...Traver. Nothing."

Wolf shook his head. "I want to see the paper records."

Elan led him to the records room door and pushed inside. He flicked on a light, revealing neat rows of hanging folders lined along wall-mounted shelves.

"The M's are here," Elan said.

Wolf flicked through the folders and found no file for Moreno.

He checked the S section for Sadie, and when he didn't find her there, he tried T for Traver, came up empty, then tried D for Donald. Nothing.

Satisfied there was no trace of the reports, Wolf went back out into the main room with Elan trailing behind.

After a brief silence Normandy cleared his throat. "We can talk to Sadie today. I know she's there."

The clock on the wall read just after noon.

"What do you think?" Normandy asked.

The phone vibrated and chimed, and Wolf read the screen. He looked at the deputies in turn. "Do any of you know what happened to Sadie Moreno?"

They all shook their heads, looking like they were telling the truth.

"I think she's been threatened into silence," Wolf said. "I think she's not going to talk if we show up there asking what happened."

"So ... what are you going to do?" Alvarez asked. "Who was that?"

"I'm going to hopefully get some more information. And then two or three hours from now Normandy and I will go have a talk with her."

"And us?"

"Get that warrant going for the Whitlock Ranch, and the

cell records for Carrie and Valentina. Maybe go get some lunch. Take a breath, it's been a rough morning."

"What are we doing with Mustaine?" Alvarez asked.

"We have seventy-two hours to charge him with something," Wolf said. "I intend to use as much of that as possible without him around, so we can get some real work done."

"He asked for his phone call," Elan said.

Wolf nodded. "Give it to him."

"And if he gets out?" Alvarez asked. "He has some powerful friends he could call."

"Then we'll cross that bridge when we get there."

Alvarez chuckled. "You mean jump off that bridge?"

Wolf left, Patterson's words echoing in his mind once again as he left the building.

In and out.

If he wasn't in on this action before, he was in deep now. As for an out, a clean exit from this situation had been locked, the key flushed down the drain.

One thing was for certain, if he could get back home unscathed, Patterson was going to owe him big time.

17

Wolf sat on a country road east of town eating a cheeseburger and fries from Burger Brad's, washing it down with a watery Coke.

The wind outside had picked up, stacking tumble weeds up against the barbed wire fence, whipping dust across the dirt road, painting a rust-colored streak across a strip of snow on the shoulder that had yet to melt.

He took another bite, and a dagger of pain stabbed his abdomen for the second time, so he stopped chewing and opened the door, letting in a blast of wind as he bent over and spat onto the dirt.

He shut the door and leaned back, the pain dissipating to a background discomfort. Eating could wait, he decided.

He jolted as a loud ring tone blared through his speakers. He picked up the phone, cursing whatever setting he needed to change to go back to old fashioned phone to ear conversations.

The screen read Piper Cain. He hovered his finger over the button, considering whether he had the energy to have a conversation about new jobs and new houses and new lives.

He pressed talk. "Hello?"

"Hey, how's it going?"

"Good. How are you?"

"I'm good. How's the case going?"

"It's...interesting."

"That great, huh?"

He skimmed over the details of what had happened so far, only vaguely touching on the morning's incident by telling her he had to get physical with the sheriff.

"You had to get physical?" She asked. "Like, how physical? Pushing?"

"More like punching. I had to place him under arrest."

"Isn't he huge?" She asked. "I heard he's like seven feet tall. Three hundred fifty pounds."

Wolf smiled. "That's exactly what he was. Tell everyone that."

She chuckled. "Geez. So, he's sitting in jail right now?"

"Yeah."

He flagged some more exasperated clarifying questions, and then he sat with her in silence.

"So, I have to tell you something."

"Okay." He felt his chest constrict. Something about her tone told him the next sentence was going to change things.

"We sold the house in Dredge."

She owes you guys. She's getting a ton of money from the sale of that house. He had been right reading into Patterson's comment.

"Hello? Can you hear me?"

"Yeah. Sorry, wow, that's great! Was it a good offer?"

"It was more than we would have ever thought of listing it for."

"I never even knew you listed it," Wolf said.

"I know. I know what it must seem like. But we didn't even list it. I met Margaret out in town the other week, and she told me about a client she had, and how he was looking for a place, and how ours might just be perfect. Well, anyway, one thing led to another, and the guy ended up making us an offer."

"That's amazing."

"Yeah. It is."

"And your father's okay with everything?"

"Surprisingly so, yes. He was very into moving to Rocky Points."

"Wow. Great. So, how far along are you in the process? Have you done inspection, and all that?"

"It's done. The guy gave us the money. We closed in a matter of days. It was all cash. Well, we have to move out, of course. We're renting it back for two weeks. It's going to be a whirlwind, but I've hired a packing and moving company already."

"Wow."

"Dad, can you put that in the boxes down in the basement?" Her father said something in the background. "Yes. Thank you."

"I thought you just said you were hiring a packing company."

"Yeah, well, I figured we may as well get a head start," she said.

"Where are you going to stay in Rocky Points?" Wolf asked. "You can stay with me."

Silence.

"You there?"

"Yeah," she said. "Thank you. I really appreciate the offer. Seriously."

"But, hell, no?"

She laughed. "The places to buy may be few and far between, but there are some rentals available. I've already found one that would be perfect for us while we look to buy a house. Margaret's getting the rental agreement together today or tomorrow."

"Oh, okay," Wolf said. "And how about the job? How did your meeting with Patterson go?"

"It went well. She offered me a position."

"Wow that's amazing."

It's great rolling over at night, seeing them sleeping next to you, then seeing them in the kitchen at breakfast, then in the squad room, then in the hall every time you're going to take a piss.

"Hello?"

"Yeah, sorry. I'm here."

"I said what do you think?"

"I think it's great." But he cringed, hearing the fake-sounding enthusiasm in his own tone. "I mean, if that's...that's awesome. When do you start?" He put a hand to his forehead.

Hissing silence came out of the speakers.

"You there?" he asked.

"Yeah."

"I said when—"

"I'm not sure yet. We still have to iron out the details. And, frankly, I'm not sure if I'm taking it or not."

"Why not?"

When she said nothing, he said, "Piper?"

"Yes."

"What's the matter?"

"Nothing," she said. "We'll talk about everything later. I'd rather be talking to you in person."

"Yeah. Okay."

"So, what are you going to do now?"

"About what?" Wolf asked.

"About the case?"

"Oh right. I'll figure it out. I'm going to talk to the DA right now. I'm checking on a lead that might be important."

More silence.

"Be careful," she said.

"I will." He thought of Mustaine sitting in that cell, of him making a phone call, of a lawyer showing up with threats, Elan letting him out, and then he thought of Mustaine's fist pushing through his skull.

"David?"

"Yes."

"I said keep me posted."

"Sorry, yeah. I will."

"Bye," she said.

"Bye," he said to the empty car, because she'd already hung up.

He stared outside for a good minute, the wind rocking the SUV, thinking about their conversation and how for everything said there were a dozen left unsaid. She'd just sold her house in Dredge, she'd been offered her dream job, and yet she was clearly unhappy.

And what about him? Moving to Rocky Points was what she wanted, working in Rocky Points was also what she wanted, and he wanted what she wanted. It was a pain in the ass to drive back and forth to Dredge, but he'd done it for months because, whether he liked it or not, he was smitten with this woman.

But he was clearly unhappy, too. Or maybe that wasn't it. Maybe he was...uneasy.

What would Dr. Hawkwood, his former therapist turned friend, tell him? What would he tell Hawkwood? That he was worried about being cramped, at work and at home. That he was worried about getting close with another woman and screwing it up again.

So, you want her to have a more complicated life so yours might be easier?

Selfish bastard.

He snapped out of it and got out to relieve his bladder,

shielding himself with the car, feeling the warmth of the sun baking the back of his neck.

The road stretched left to right, desolate out here in the far eastern portion of the valley. To his left sat Crow Valley, a dark spot with twinkling reflections, to his right, the smooth dirt road cutting into rolling hills that flanked the larger mountains behind it.

The breeze came from the southwest, bringing hot air from the desert. In between gusts he could hear the melt water running across the land, snaking over the dirt into the drainage ditch alongside the county road.

He zipped himself up and stretched his arms overhead, feeling a new twinge in his back. Add that to the painful swelling in his right hand, and the dull ache in his stomach, and...well, he still wasn't as bad as Mustaine had looked, slumped in that cell.

He pulled out his phone and pressed the address he'd been texted before lunch. The map came up, showing his destination was a few miles ahead.

18

District Attorney Gabriel Bluthe lived square in the middle of nowhere, Colorado.

Wolf had been driving twenty minutes east before he'd stopped to eat, and it had been another fifteen minutes since, but he had finally reached the man's property.

He pulled off the county road at a mailbox, a rusted iron sculpture complete with a wagon wheel as a post, then followed a long drive towards a low-slung house and a red barn, a flagpole standing between them, the American and Colorado flags quivering horizontal in the wind. The scent of pinion pine and juniper flowed into Wolf's open windows.

He parked in front of the barn, next to a super-duty pickup, in between a hay trailer and a tractor. Outside the wind roared harder than ever, appearing to gather speed up the flat southern portion of his property, which was a series of green cattle fields that stretched out to the valley.

"In here!"

Bluthe was inside the barn, brushing a horse inside a stall. Wolf waited at the threshold of the outbuilding and watched the man pat the horse and approach him. Bluthe was old but strong, his bowlegged gait fast and sure. He wore jeans, a flannel shirt, and a trucker snap-back hat pulled low on his head, eyes squinting pleasantly underneath the bill.

"How are you doing? Thanks for coming all the way out. I could have met you in town."

"It was no problem," Wolf said. The truth was, he enjoyed the solitude after the morning's action.

Bluthe eyed him seriously. "You didn't tell me you beat him up and put him in jail in your texts."

"You heard."

"Word gets around pretty quick around here. You probably know all about that. Small towns and all."

"I'm not sure I'd call Rocky Points a small town anymore."

Bluthe smiled.

Wolf looked around. "And you don't exactly live in town."

"I've always lived on the land. I was the same over in Ridgway." Bluthe looked hard into Wolf's eyes. "Are you okay?"

Wolf nodded. "I'm not sure I'm too proud of what I did."

"From what I heard, you did what you had to." He slapped Wolf on the shoulder as a gust of wind blew straws of hay across their face. "Geez. Let's get inside."

The house was a modest and plain looking ranch, two rectangle wings jutting out from a central A-frame. Clean and meticulously maintained, with a fresh off-white paint job that gleamed in the afternoon sun, shrubs sculpted into cubes, a dirt driveway wrapping a half-circle in front with a flagpole in the middle, it was an all-American home that bordered on looking like a government building.

"Bought the place from a cattle rancher who moved to Arizona to get away from the cold weather. His loss. Shoes off please." Bluthe removed his boots at the front porch and carried them inside.

Wolf followed suit, leaving his boots on the porch.

Bluthe shut the door behind him, and in contrast to the hurricane-like winds outside, the silence inside felt like being dunked into a tank of warm water.

They stood in a tall arching entryway, the A-frame of the house arching high above, with a wood-floor living room spread out before them. The wall opposite was nearly all windows, framing the vast landscape outside, the slope to the south giving onto the flat valley, a serrated horizon of jagged mountains beyond.

"That's better," Bluthe said.

"What's that?" a woman's voice called out from down one of the wing hallways.

"Nothing! I have a guest!"

"Guess what?"

"I said I have a guest! A guest is here!"

"Oh." A woman about Bluthe's age came into view wearing sweatpants and a sweater. "How are you?"

"My wife, Winnie. Winnie, this is the detective from Rocky Points I told you about. David Wolf."

"Oh." She walked toward him, her mouth drawn in an O. She stopped, staring intently into his eyes. "I heard what you did this morning."

"Oh," Wolf said, not sure how else to react.

She shook her head, slowly. "I know he's going through a tough time with the death of his son. But it was only a matter of time that asshole got what was coming to him. He's a menace. Somebody has to run him out of this town, or I told Gabe we're going back to Ridgway."

"Winnie."

"What? You're the first to tell me that—"

"Winnie. Can you please…just…?"

She smiled. "It's nice to meet you, David." She walked away and disappeared into a back room.

"You want a cup of coffee or something?"

Wolf thought of stomach spasms. "No. Thanks."

"Please, have a seat." Bluthe sat in a lounge chair and Wolf took the couch next to it.

"Nice view," Wolf said.

"Yeah, isn't it?"

"I thought I lived in the middle of nowhere," Wolf said. "I think you have me beat."

"Like I said, I like to keep out in the wilderness. I work with people all day, I'm not sure why I'd want to live near them. Know what I mean?"

Wolf nodded, knowing exactly what he meant.

"So." Bluthe said. "Tell me what happened."

Wolf told him what happened, starting with the GPS data from Bennett's phone they received that morning, the spot where Bennett's phone stayed in place for over three hours, the proximity to the Whitlock Ranch, and Mustaine going haywire, ultimately leading to the big man sitting in jail.

They sat in silence for a beat. "Well." Bluthe scratched his head, looking out the window. "I have a call in to my prosecutor. Who happens to be a guy who elk hunts with Mustaine."

Bluthe made a gesture like he wasn't sure what he could do about the situation.

"I couldn't care less about charges being brought against Mustaine," Wolf said. "You brought me here to solve this case, and we knew from the start that the biggest obstacle would be my presence here, trying to take over the case from him. I thought we could deal with it like civilized adults, but things changed. He was threatening innocent lives. At least, innocent until proven guilty. The obstacle is removed as long as he's in jail, and I'd like to keep it that way as long as possible."

"Mustaine made a phone call from the jail to one of the judges. The judge is not happy." He paused a moment. "But don't you worry about that. I'll work on quelling the powers that be."

"I've heard that before."

Bluthe said nothing.

"And we're working on getting a warrant for the Whitlock Ranch, and Carrie and Valentina's phone records."

Bluthe nodded. "Good. I didn't talk to the judge about that, but I'm sure you'll have your warrant soon if it means figuring out what happened to Bennett."

Wolf crossed a leg, feeling stiffness in his hamstring that pulled on his back.

"So it's been slow going so far?" Bluthe stood up and went to the kitchen, opened the refrigerator door, and held up a can of flavored seltzer. "Want one?"

"No, thank you."

Bluthe opened the can, took a sip, sighed, and sat down again.

"Mustaine told me that Carrie Whitlock and Bennett had a history," Wolf said. "Do you know anything about this history?"

Bluthe shook his head. "I've only been around for...what is it? Almost two years. I'm not privy to the personal information of the youth of this town yet. Not that I was any better in Ridgway. You'll have to ask somebody else. What about that kid who owns the pizza place with Bennett?"

"Paco Nez," Wolf said.

"That's right. He may know."

"I'm working on it. And what about Sadie Moreno?"

Bluthe stared at him for a beat, then his lips curled into a toothless resigned-looking smile. "Sadie Moreno. I don't know much about her."

"Why are you here? In Crow County?" Wolf asked. "You've got to be close to retirement age, and you're taking a new job? Uprooting yourself for this job down here?"

Bluthe shrugged. "This place is cheaper than Ridgway. Over there you have the Telluride spillovers. I sold my place for a hundred times what I bought it for twenty years ago. We have a few friends who live over here, Winnie's brother lives just south of here. It was a good move."

"So you being here has nothing to do with the previous DA leaving because of Sadie Moreno?"

"Lamont? No. That old fart wanted to fish for the rest of his life on the ocean, so he left. It was a perfect windfall for me and Winnie that the job opened up."

"But Undersheriff Dexter," Wolf said. "He left right after the Sadie Moreno incident, didn't he?"

Bluthe took a sip of his drink.

Wolf shook his head impatiently. "It seems Mustaine has quite a hold on the people around here. Has he gotten to you, too?"

"Hell no." Bluthe's eyes flashed. "The Sadie Moreno incident was before my time. I was in Ridgway."

Wolf shook his head. "You know nothing about it."

"Well, funnily enough, even though it was before my time, I do know something about it. I spent a couple weeks with Lamont before he left, getting the lay of the land, and he told me about Sadie Moreno. He was pretty upset about it. You could tell it was the one thing he regretted about his career. You think she had something to do with this?"

"I couldn't answer that question. I've only heard rumors about what happened, and vague ones at that. I'd appreciate it if you'd fill me in on the details so I can start working this case with all the pieces necessary."

"Okay, okay." Bluthe set down his drink on the coffee table and sat back, his eyes unfocused. "Apparently, two years ago, Lamont got a call from a doctor in town."

"Doctor Traver," Wolf said. "The forensic guy working this

case."

Bluthe nodded. "He used to work at the hospital back then, and he was the doctor on duty in the ER that night. He was the one who saw Sadie when she came in. Traver supposedly called Lamont at home and told him he'd just finished giving Sadie stitches. And where the stitches were. And that it was looking like she may have been sexually assaulted, and not only that, but it had been Bennett Mustaine, and she was afraid to go to the sheriff's office to report it.

"Dr. Traver was calling the DA so he'd come down to the station, for moral support, you know. Apparently Mustaine wasn't even there that night. Undersheriff Dexter was on duty."

"What happened to Sadie? Do you have a copy of that report on file at the DA's office?"

Bluthe shook his head, turning his hands up. "The sheriff's office never turned it over to Lamont."

"Did Lamont ever read the reports?"

Bluthe shook his head.

"How is that possible?"

"The DA's office only gets what the sheriff's department gives them."

"They can launch their own investigation," Wolf said.

"But he didn't," Bluthe said. "And I gather that's why Lamont was pounding his liquor when he was telling me about this."

Wolf said nothing.

"Think how I felt learning about this incident, right after I'd taken the job down here? And then learning that the undersheriff had left, too?" Bluthe shook his head and sipped his drink.

"What happened?"

"Lamont said he never spoke to Dr. Traver or Sadie Moreno at the sheriff's office that night. He wasn't present in the room while they gave the reports, because he ended up leaving."

"Why?" Wolf asked.

"Because Mustaine got wind of what was going on and called him on his cell phone and told the DA to leave."

"Why?"

"I don't know. Lamont never told me. But obviously he either had something on him or just plain threatened him and told him to get out of there, to turn a blind eye. And he did."

"Lamont never learned what happened?" Wolf asked.

"No."

Wolf shook his head. "And what about Dr. Traver? Doesn't he have a record of what happened? Medical records?"

Bluthe shrugged. "I'm not sure."

"You haven't looked?"

"No."

"So you're turning a blind eye, too."

"No, I'm not!" Bluthe's voice echoed through the house.

"Honey?" Winnie's voice came from down the hall. "Is everything okay?"

"It's okay, Win. We're fine."

A door closed. Bluthe brushed the front of his shirt. "I talked to Dr. Traver, after my conversation with Lamont, when I took over in the office. I decided I wanted to start looking into Mustaine, and that I wasn't going to be like Lamont when I took over. Anyway...I spoke to Traver.

"Traver said she was hurt, and when she came into the ER she needed five stitches, you know, in her vaginal region. She didn't tell him she'd been attacked, but he suspected it. He did a rape kit and told her she needed to go to the sheriff's department to report whoever did it. Traver said she was afraid to go to the sheriff, afraid to say who did it, but it was clear she knew who it was. That it was not a stranger, but somebody she knew.

"Anyway, Traver called the DA to come down and witness the statements."

"What did Traver say happened?"

Bluthe shook his head. "What I just said."

"He never found out who did it?"

"According to him, no."

Wolf frowned. "And then she recanted her statement."

"Lamont told me she went to the sheriff's office the next day and recanted her original report, then gave a revised statement of how the rolling wheels of a stepladder were not locked properly, causing her to fall awkwardly, landing in a straddle position, which caused the injury."

"And Traver?" Wolf asked. "What did he say about that?"

"The rape kit had come up clean, no semen, so, although the injuries didn't look consistent to him, what was he going to do? She'd recanted her statement and called it an accident. Anything he said would be moot at that point. He gave his expert opinion, but there were no allegations. No charges filed."

Wolf exhaled, closing his eyes. The wind outside whistled softly over the tiny holes in the house, buffeting the window.

"What did Mustaine do to Sadie to make her change her mind?"

Bluthe shook his head, held up his hands again. Wolf wished he was back in time, given another chance to land one more punch square into Mustaine's nose.

"Have you asked Mustaine about what happened?"

Bluthe swallowed. "No."

"How about your prosecutor, the one who's Mustaine's hunting buddy."

"Craig Purvis? No."

"What's the story on the undersheriff that took the report?"

"He left."

"He left? Or he was fired?"

"He left. He went up to Deschutes County, Oregon. I did call and speak to Undersheriff Dexter. I'm not a complete coward." He looked at Wolf.

"And what did Undersheriff Dexter say?"

"He said she gave a report that she fell on the rolling stairs. And he didn't want to talk about the recanted statement. I asked why he never sent anything to the DA's office, and he told me there were no charges to be filed. And that was that."

"So Mustaine has something on him, too."

Bluthe shrugged.

"Have you spoken to Sadie Moreno?"

"I tried. She wouldn't talk to me." Bluthe smiled, joy not reaching his eyes. "I haven't been around here very long. I'm not sure people trust me much yet."

Wolf stared at him, then stood up. "Thanks, I guess, for the talk."

Bluthe stood with him. "What are you going to do now?"

"I'll go talk to Sadie. Maybe she won't talk about what happened that night, but I still have questions about where she was last weekend. And then I'll go talk to Paco Nez and follow the clues as they come."

Bluthe led him to the front door and opened it, letting a blast of wind inside. Wolf went out into the breeze and put his boots on the front porch with Bluthe standing next to him.

"Listen," Bluthe said. "Maybe it's about time you headed back to Rocky Points. I don't want you to get hurt. I can call in the feds to finish this up."

Wolf stood up and looked out into the distance.

"He's in jail now, but he's not going to be in there forever," Bluthe said. "And then it's not going to be good for you."

Wolf thought of his father stepping in between him and Mustaine that night in the parking lot.

"There's only one way through this," he said. "And that's finding out what happened to Bennett Mustaine."

19

"He's balking at signing the warrant."

Wolf turned onto the main highway leading back into Crow Valley. "Why's that?"

Elan sighed, which sounded like static in Wolf's SUV speakers. "The Judge is a good friend of Mustaine's."

"So I heard."

"Yeah. And he doesn't like that Mustaine's being held without charge."

"And if we charge him with assault of a law enforcement officer?"

"He's not going to like that, either."

"And ... so what?"

"So, he'll sign it the second Mustaine's out of that cell."

Wolf snorted. "So we're not getting inside the Whitlocks' property until Mustaine's out."

"Yep."

Wolf drove in silence down the highway as it slowed and became Main Street.

"Well?" Elan asked.

"I think the second he's out things are going to be more difficult." And most likely painful, Wolf thought.

"I agree," Elan said.

"We need to get into that ranch, but I think Carrie's and Valentina's GPS data is going to tell a better story."

"And that's not going to be for at least another day or two according to Summit," Elan said.

Wolf sighed inwardly.

"They're still not any faster with that?" He asked.

"No, sir. I gave them an earful, but you know where that gets you. Where are you now?"

"On my way to talk to Sadie Moreno at the Normandy wood place."

"It's called Normandy Woodworks," Elan said. "You know how to get there?"

"Yeah, I have it pulled up on my map." Wolf had been back to following the red line since he'd reached Crow Valley.

"So what about Mustaine?" Elan said.

"Don't let him out."

"Understood."

"Have you spoken to Normandy?" Wolf asked.

"He went to lunch a while ago. And then he said he was going to hook up with you."

"Okay, I'll be back in later," Wolf said.

He hung up and dialed Normandy. As it rang his motel came up on the left side, then the Chicken House, then the Tavern, and beyond that the auto parts shop on the right.

"Hello?" Normandy said.

"Hey, I'm back. I'd like to hook up at your father's factory and talk to Sadie Moreno."

"I'm already here," Normandy said. "I ended up having lunch with my dad. How far out are you?"

"A few minutes."

"See you in a bit."

He hung up and rubbed his temple, trying to soothe the headache pulsing in his skull. He'd been thinking about the case all the way back from Bluthe's and it was getting to him. He knew he was missing something, but following these threads ended at frayed sever points.

It looked like the Whitlocks were involved. That much was clear to Wolf. They looked like they were hiding something, and when somebody looked that way they usually were. Mustaine seemed to think Bennett and Carrie had a history of hooking up, and maybe the sheriff was right about everything. But there was no evidence pointing to their involvement, at least not yet.

What about this Nola Whitlock? She was the matriarch of the family. Where was the father? What was that story?

Was Valentina Johnson lying? She wore her disdain for cops as boldly as her black lipstick. Had she not taken Carrie home? And Carrie? She had said three or four words to him through a wire fence, and no more.

Was that theory he proposed anything close to the truth?

One thing Wolf knew for sure, Sheriff Mustaine had a way of shutting people up with his mere presence. It looked like he'd already shoved this Sadie Moreno assault under the rug, erasing his son's first terrible deed. His son could do no wrong, and it seemed Mustaine would do anything to keep it that way.

What would the sheriff do if Carrie Whitlock had killed his son out of self-defense?

The answer came to Wolf effortlessly. Mustaine would spin it that his son was murdered in cold blood. Carrie Whitlock would be sacrificed to preserve the Mustaine family name.

Wolf put his thoughts to rest and followed the red line on the computer screen.

After a half-mile he slowed and took a right and parked in a large parking lot surrounding a tall boxy structure with plenty of windows lining the front of the building.

He spotted Normandy's SUV among a few dozen other vehicles in the lot and parked next to it. As he shut off his engine his phone vibrated in his pocket, telling him he'd received a text message. It was Rachette.

Hey, so I've been wondering if I should butt my nose in this or not, but we're friends and I would hope you would do the same for me. I saw Piper having coffee with Michael Venus this morning. She was dressed nicely. I'm not sure what was going on there, but he looked like he was putting the moves on her. There. I said it. I'll butt out now.

Wolf read the text again, his blood pressure spiking and a twinge in his stomach as he re-read the name Michael Venus. The man had worked for DA White's office for a short time, but in that short time had been caught having multiple affairs with women that had been deemed inappropriate—one with a defendant in a case out of Ashland, and another simultaneous sexual relationship with a deputy DA's wife in the Rocky Points office. When the deputy DA had learned about it there were punches thrown, and threats to do more than that.

It was probably a professional coffee situation. He hoped. Piper was probably...what? What was Venus doing these days after his unceremonious firing? Maybe it was something to do with the real estate transaction, or a rental property. It could have been a thousand things.

He shook his head and put the phone in his pocket, walking toward the front entrance of Normandy Woodworks. There was a sign that hung over the door made of huge wooden letters, so detailed and well-carved that just reading the sign would make him want to hire these people.

His mind travelled back to the conversation he'd had a

couple hours ago with Piper. She had been strangely distant, hadn't she?

"Damn it," he said under his breath, rubbing his temple again.

He needed some Advil.

20

"You sent him the message?" Yates asked.

"Yeah."

Yates shook his head.

"What? I'd do the same for you."

"I'm not so sure that was a good idea."

"Whatever. Drive." Rachette opened back up the mapping app. "Turn here."

Yates turned onto a washboard dirt road and slowed his speed.

Rachette checked his phone and saw the map showed exactly what was outside the windshield: a road gently curving right, dense forest on either side, houses set back in the trees, some space between them.

"I wonder how these guys afford a place up here," Rachette said.

"It's gotta be affordable housing for resort employees. And it's not a good idea to get into other peoples' business like that. It always backfires."

Rachette looked at him. "So, what's with this Trisha woman anyway?"

Yates shook his head. "You're annoying as shit."

"You're still gonna keep your mouth shut about that, huh? Fine. I'll keep my nose out of your business."

They rode in silence for a beat.

"We square danced together, okay?" Yates said.

Rachette squinted, then squinted some more. "Did you just say you square danced together?"

"Yeah. I took a few square-dancing lessons. You know."

Rachette struggled mightily but managed to keep his face blank. "No. I do not know."

"Whatever." Yates flipped his hand. "You're an asshole."

"No. Okay. Tell me. You did square dancing lessons. Sorry, I've just...that's never occurred to me that you, John Yates, pumper of iron and all things masculine, would square dance, is all."

"Which house?" Yates asked.

"The blue one with the white pickup in front. Looks like somebody's home. We know they didn't ride their bikes to work." Rachette smiled.

Yates ignored him, pulling the vehicle up fast, skidding the tires on the dirt as he stopped in front of the house. He shifted in park and got out in one motion, shutting the door and leaving Rachette sitting by himself.

Rachette rolled his eyes, pocketed his phone, and got out.

The air was surprisingly warm. The wind pushed the trees back and forth, sounding like the snowmakers up on the mountain as it whooshed through the pine forest.

Yates was standing at the back bumper, looking like he wanted to say something, but he remained silent.

"Dude," Rachette said. "I think it's great you're taking square dancing lessons. I really do. I always wondered if you ever did anything besides bench press, and now I know."

"I don't," Yates said. "That's the problem."

Rachette was surprised to hear a response at all, much less one laced with so much emotion. He eyed the house. There was movement in one of the windows. Theo's face appeared, eyes wide, and then vanished.

Rachette turned his back to the house and eyed his partner. "What's the problem?"

"Like you said. I never do anything but work out and go to work. That's pretty much my life. You're spot on."

Rachette said nothing.

"So, I took some square-dancing lessons. And I met her the first night. She was...I don't know, she was kind of latching on to me from the beginning."

"She's pretty," Rachette said.

Yates looked at him suspiciously.

"I'm serious. She's fit, and her eyes? I was thinking she was cute." He slapped Yates's shoulder. "She's so obviously into you. Did you not see that?"

Yates eyed the house. "No. I got that. And I have to admit I'm glad she chose me as a partner. They're looking out at us."

Rachette turned and saw Jake peeking out of the window now. He waved. Rachette nodded back.

"What are you going to do about it?" Rachette asked.

Yates shrugged. "I don't know. It's just been so long since I've dated anybody."

Rachette smiled and shook his head.

Yates's eyes darkened. "You're such an asshole."

"No, wait. I'm not making fun of you. I'm just thinking."

"What are you thinking?"

"I'm thinking, My God, if I can get a woman like Charlotte?" Rachette shook his head, reached down and patted his gut, then gestured to Yates's non-existent gut. "If I can do it? I'm short and fat."

"Yeah, you should do something about that," Yates said.

"You're becoming quite the fat-ass. You weren't that huge when you got Charlotte, though."

"Thanks. Yes. I'm going to start working on it one day soon, my point is, you'll be just fine."

The door behind them opened. "Hello officers!" Jake said.

Rachette ignored him, keeping his back turned to the house. "She is into you."

Yates walked past him toward the house.

Rachette turned, joining his partner on the driveway a few paces away from the front door.

"How's it going, detectives?" Jake asked.

"Hey Jake," Yates said. "Good news. We found your bikes."

"Oh wow." Jake seemed semi-enthused. "Really? Wh...where?"

"Somebody dropped them off the other night at the Town of Rocky Points building," Rachette said. "There was a sign taped to both of them reading 'Donation'."

Jake frowned. "Somebody donated them?"

"Yeah," Yates said. "Where's Theo?"

Jake's eyes were blank.

"Jake." Rachette snapped in the air.

"Yes. Hey! Theo!"

Theo emerged in the doorway, nodding but avoiding eye contact.

"Hey, Theo," Rachette said. "Can I see your shoes?"

Theo looked at him. "Excuse me?"

"The shoes you were wearing yesterday."

Theo looked like he'd been punched in the crotch.

"The shoes you were wearing yesterday," Yates said again.

They waited. Theo thought about it, then nodded and disappeared.

"What's this all about?" Jake asked.

"This is about us finding your bikes." Rachette nodded enthusiastically.

"Right." Jake looked behind them. "Um...where are they?"

"They're still down at the Town of Rocky Points building, where they were donated. Didn't you hear us?"

Jake went silent. His cool demeanor cracked for the first time, a hint of fear making his chest rise and fall.

Theo came back into view and reached his long arm out, presenting the shoes.

Rachette walked up and grabbed one of them. "Thanks." He turned back to Yates, and they huddled over the shoe, studying the toe where Rachette had seen Theo trying to rub off a smudge with his other foot the day before. It was clean, with fresh scrape marks that revealed rubber a brighter white than the surrounding area.

"You got it off," Rachette said.

"Got what off?" Jake asked.

"There was a dark smudge here yesterday," Rachette said. "I saw you trying to rub it off. You did some good scraping."

He handed the shoe back to Theo.

Jake put up his hands. "I don't understand what's going on here."

Yates walked away from the conversation toward the side of the house, where a rickety gate hung loosely on its hinges. "May I?"

Jake's mouth opened, but no sound came out.

Yates opened the gate and disappeared alongside the house.

Rachette smiled and crossed his arms. Jake's skin was looking pale. Theo stared at the ground.

Rachette winked. "He's probably just taking a leak or something."

Yates came back out and craned his finger.

"What are you guys doing?" Jake asked. "You can't really go back there."

"Why not?" Rachette asked. "Are you hiding something back there?"

"No. Of course not."

"You don't mind then?"

"N...no."

"Good." Rachette walked to the gate and followed Yates down the side of the house.

Yates pointed to a spot on the ground, and then another. Rachette nodded and went back to the front door. "Why don't you guys slip those shoes on and come outside?"

Jake's voice went high pitched. "You still haven't—"

"You can slip your shoes on and come talk to us outside, or you can come down to the station and talk to us. You understand?"

Jake swallowed and nodded, and they hurriedly put their shoes on in the doorway and came out.

Rachette waved them over, leading them through the gate to the side of the house. Yates stood near the markings on the ground, arms folded, looking like a nightclub bouncer.

Rachette said, "I saw your bike being ridden around town, Jake. It was lucky I saw it, but I did. It was spray-painted black, you know, like they do with the bikes in the community bike share program, or whatever they're calling it? But the sprocket and the brakes were unpainted, so I recognized the bright blue color."

They said nothing.

"We spoke to the guy who runs the bike program, the Bike Fleet Manager I think he called himself. Anyway, he said it was the strangest thing about the bike donations—he said somebody had already gone through all the trouble of removing all the parts and spray painting the frames, then putting them back together. Usually that's what he does, and he says it takes a while. He also said it was strange that the bikes were donated overnight, left with those signs on them. Usually people come up and do it in person. He just figured it was a good Samaritan, you know, who didn't want to take any credit."

They remained silent.

Rachette pointed at the ground, where blotches of black spray paint on the rocks and dirt had been revealed by the melting snow. He pointed at the side of the house. "There's even droplets on the side of the house. Must have been windy. That's the problem with spray paint. It gets everywhere, even when you think you're being careful."

Jake shook his head.

"We did it," Theo said. "It was us. You're right. We pretended like the bikes were stolen. We weren't trying to hurt anyone. We were just trying to get the insurance to pay us for new bikes. We have this friend who did the same thing up in Steamboat. He was telling us about it, and we thought we could pull it off. But it was freaking stupid. It was dumb. We shouldn't have done anything like this. And...and we haven't done anything yet! We haven't even done anything. The insurance company sent us a link to make the claim and we haven't submitted it. So, really, it's like, you know...we haven't done anything yet."

Jake stared at his friend and roommate, his mouth agape.

"What?" Theo said. "We haven't done anything."

Rachette and Yates exchanged a look. "Wow," Rachette said. "That was...thank you for telling us all of that, Theo."

Jake squatted down on his heels, covering his face with both hands. "Damn it. I knew this was a stupid idea." He lowered his hands. "But he's right, right? I mean, we haven't done anything wrong yet?"

"You made up a crime and reported it to the sheriff's

department," Yates said. "So that you could commit insurance fraud."

"But there are no real crimes yet, right?"

Rachette ticked off their transgressions on his fingers. "Making a false statement to a law enforcement officer. Obstruction of justice for not telling us about each other's false statements, accessory after the fact. Should I go on?" Rachette couldn't think of anything else, so he looked at Yates.

Yates pulled his cuffs off his belt.

Rachette put up a hand to his partner, the good cop holding back the bad. "You have that claim link the insurance company sent you?"

Jake nodded, standing back up. "Yeah." He reached in his pocket and pulled out his phone.

"Text it to my partner," Rachette said. "The same number you sent the pictures to."

"Okay. Yeah."

They watched as Jake frantically searched his phone, swiping, swiping, cursing, and then finally poking the screen. "There."

Yates's phone chimed and with a bored expression he pulled it out and tapped the screen. A few seconds later he nodded.

Rachette looked at the two men. "I'm going to talk to my partner for a moment."

Jake nodded. Theo nodded. And when Rachette and Yates didn't move they hurried out of the gate again and disappeared around to the front of the house.

"What do you think?" Rachette asked, keeping his voice low.

"I think I don't want to deal with any paperwork."

"What about Trisha?"

Yates didn't blink. "What about her?"

"Do you like her?"

His partner thought about it for a long while, then nodded almost imperceptibly.

"Good. Then you'll ask her out. And I'll be there. Right next to you when you call her and do it. Because I'm your partner."

"You will not be there when I call her. I'll do it myself."

Rachette stared at him.

Yates stared back.

"Okay then."

"Okay then."

Rachette patted his belly. "Let's go get some food. I'm hungry as crap. And don't say of course you are, or I'll punch you in the face."

21

The air inside the front office room of Normandy Woodworks smelled like sawdust and turpentine.

Wolf stood inside the glass enclosure of the building's entryway and looked around for Normandy. There were half a dozen desks covering a wood-stained floor. Three people —an older man, a woman in her fifties, and a young woman in her mid-twenties—sat at the desks while the other desks sat vacant.

"Can I help you?" the woman in her fifties asked.

"Hi." Wolf locked eyes with the younger woman for a moment, and Wolf saw a name plate on her desk that read Sadie.

"Wolf," a voice came from Wolf's left.

Deputy Normandy stood inside a glass office doorway, beckoning him inside.

"Hey."

"This is my father. Dad, this is Detective Wolf."

A man stood on the other side of a paper-strewn desk. He was the same short and squat build as his son, had the same creases at the corners of his eyes as he smiled.

"Nice to meet you," Wolf said.

Deputy Normandy glanced past Wolf. "Yeah, so, I was just telling my dad here that we'd like to speak to Sadie."

Ted spoke in a low voice. "And I'll ask you what I asked my son. Do you really think that Sadie Moreno had anything to do with Bennett's death?"

"I'm not exactly saying that. But I think she can tell us something that might help us," Wolf said.

Ted Normandy shook his head. "Don't you think she would have done something about it by now if she was going to?"

Wolf said nothing.

"And I'll tell you what, she's not capable of anything like that. She's anti-gun, for one. She ribs me all the time about my hunting and shooting." Ted leaned, sneaking a glance beyond Wolf. "Bennett Mustaine was shot in the head point blank? No. There's no way she did that. She works her ass off here, takes a pittance for herself, and chips the rest in to take care of her family down in Alamosa. Her aunt and uncle are having trouble getting work, and she foots the bill. She has a heart of gold." Ted sat back heavily, face red, chair clanking against the wall behind him.

Wolf looked at Deputy Normandy, then his father. "I would just like to speak to her."

Ted stared at him, then looked at his son.

"It's important, Dad," Normandy said.

Ted took a deep breath and nodded in resignation. "You guys can use the conference room over there. I'll get her. John, you know where to go."

Normandy led Wolf out of the office, down a hallway, and into a glass-enclosed conference room. Light streamed into a window, boasting a view of the town and distant, snow-covered mountains.

Wolf heard a noise and watched through the interior glass

and saw that Ted Normandy hadn't left his office, but Sadie had walked up into his doorway with a "What's up?" or something to that effect. She turned to them, her expression turning serious, and walked to the conference room.

"Hi," she said to Normandy, entering.

"Hi," Normandy said. "Sadie, this is Detective David Wolf."

"Hi."

Wolf shook her hand, a warm, unenthusiastic appendage.

Sadie Moreno was Latina with large brown eyes and long black hair pulled into a ponytail. She wore jeans and a sweater, and white tennis shoes strung with bright green laces.

"Please, have a seat Ms. Moreno." Wolf motioned. "Can I call you Sadie?"

"Yeah, sure."

"I just wanted to ask you a few questions."

She remained half in the doorway. "About what?"

Wolf pulled back a chair and took a seat while Normandy closed the door. Sadie eyed the door as it shut, looking trapped.

"I've been called down from Rocky Points to help look into the death of Bennett Mustaine," Wolf said. "You've heard about that, of course, haven't you?"

"Yeah."

"Please, Sadie. Have a seat."

She sat, timid as a cat testing bath water, but she sat.

Normandy took a seat a few spots from them both at the head of the table.

"I just came here from District Attorney Bluthe's house."

She went red in the face, but she said nothing.

"And he told me about how the incident that happened a couple years ago here in this building involving you and Bennett Mustaine."

"Bennett didn't do anything to me."

Wolf stared at her for a moment. "I said an incident, I didn't say that he'd done anything to you."

She didn't skip a beat. "But I know what you're getting at. And you heard what I just said. He didn't do anything to me. I fell off the step ladder." Her face was blank, emotionless.

Wolf nodded slowly. "I heard that you changed your initial report."

"Then you heard wrong. Is that what you wanted to know?" She stood up.

Wolf stood with her. "I also wanted to know where you were last Friday night, from around ten-thirty, to, say, midnight?"

She looked like she'd been struck. "Where was I?"

Wolf nodded.

She broke into a nervous laugh, looking at Normandy. "Me?"

Normandy looked at the tabletop.

"I...I was home."

"And where's that?" Wolf asked. "Where do you live?"

"Here. In town."

"Where?"

"Other side of the highway. In the northeast corner, basically. Seventh and Orca."

"Can you confirm your whereabouts?" Wolf asked. "Was there somebody else with you?"

"My cat."

Wolf nodded.

"I mean, what do you want from me? I live alone." Her face gained its earlier confidence and she shook her head. "I have to go back to work." She opened the door and marched down the hallway.

Outside Ted Normandy tried to speak to her but she pushed past him.

Ted came in, staring at them with fatherly disappointment. "What the hell?"

"I didn't mean to upset her," Wolf said. "I'm sorry."

Ted turned to get a better look down the hallway, rubbing his face with his hand.

"Mr. Normandy, did she ever talk to you about what happened with Bennett?"

"What does that have to do with anything?" He looked at them in turn. "What's the sense in digging up her past?"

Wolf shook his head, thinking that was a good question. What was his point? Was he following a dead-end lead? Or no lead at all? His gut told him she had insight into Bennett Mustaine that might be helpful. Then again, his gut was probably leaking blood into the rest of his insides.

"Well?" Ted put his hands on his hips.

"Sorry," Wolf said. "I didn't mean to disturb your workday. Deputy, we have other places we need to go. We can let ourselves out."

Normandy hugged his father and followed Wolf down the hallway.

When they passed the office on the way out, Sadie's desk was vacant, with the other two workers eyeing them with disdain.

"Damn." Normandy rubbed his hands together as they stepped outside. "Getting cold. Where did that come from?"

The sun was low in the west and had ducked behind a cloud, plunging the air around them into arctic temperatures.

"My dad can be a bit..."

Your dad didn't do anything wrong. He was right."

They walked in silence for a few yards.

"How was Bluthe's house?"

"Not very fruitful." Wolf stopped at his SUV. "The judge isn't signing the search warrant for the Whitlock Ranch."

"What? Why?"

"He doesn't like that we're holding Mustaine."

"He can't do that."

"Well, I'm sure he would cite a different reason that the warrant doesn't hold up. So, yeah, he can do that."

"So, what are we going to do?"

"I want to talk to Paco Nez."

"P and J's Pizza," Normandy said. "Let's do it."

Wolf nodded. "You lead the way."

22

P and J's Pizza was once the home of a chain restaurant, but Wolf couldn't put his finger on which one. It was updated with paint and pictures that said it was modern and hip, but it still had that front counter with a winding line, a side door leading into the kitchen behind it, and a fizzy drink station on the far wall like every fast-food joint Wolf had ever been in.

It wasn't busy by city standards, with just three people eating at different booths while another waited at the register for service.

Three more people worked furiously behind the counter, none of them seeming to notice the customer in line, or the arrival of a cop in uniform and a man with a badge and a gun on his hip as anything special.

One worker, a young man with long hair and ratty clothes, shuttled a dough tray from a back walk-in and slapped it down next to a man making pizza and gestured to Wolf and Normandy.

"Paco," Normandy said, bypassing the customer and stepping up to the counter.

Paco was thin and much shorter than his two employees, dark skinned with straight jet-black hair that reached his shoulders, tucked behind his ears. His name had suggested Navajo descent and Wolf thought his appearance backed that up.

"Yeah?"

"We need to talk to you for a few minutes," Normandy said.

Paco exhaled. "Give me a few minutes. I got a big order." He turned back to his pizza, shoved the peel underneath, and put it into the conveyor oven.

Another kid, much younger-looking and dressed in baggy clothes with a face full of acne, was taking the pizzas off the oven and putting them in boxes. Quite a stack was piling up.

Wolf and Normandy stood patiently, and Wolf found himself staring at the pizza coming out of the oven, noting the way the smell made his mouth water. He'd been perpetually hungry all day after losing his breakfast in the fight and not finishing lunch. Suddenly he knew what he'd be attempting for dinner tonight.

Five minutes later Paco slapped his hands on his jeans in a puff of flour and came out the side door to meet them. His face was somber, as if he knew what topic of conversation was coming.

"This is Detective David Wolf," Normandy said when Paco came out and shook their hands. "He's here from Rocky Points working Bennett's case."

"Where's a good spot to talk?" Normandy asked.

"Not out here. Let's go out back."

They followed Paco through the swinging door and through the back of the restaurant. He pushed open the exit door with both hands, then waited for Wolf and Normandy to exit past him.

Outside, Paco pulled out a pack of Marlboro Reds and lit one up.

"You want?" He pointed the pack at Normandy and Wolf, who both waved it off.

"How's the investigation going?" Paco asked. "I've been hearing all sorts of shit. Like, he was tied up, taken up to Dry Wash, and they shot him. And that he was left out for the animals. They're saying all sorts of shit, man."

"We can't really discuss the exact details of what we've figured out so far, Paco," Wolf said.

"But," Paco said, eyes wide, "it's foul play, right? Otherwise you'd just tell me, right? I mean, shit, it sure ain't natural causes, otherwise we wouldn't be talking."

"You're right," Wolf said, conceding the point to establish some rapport with Paco. "It wasn't natural causes."

"Gaw-damn." Paco inhaled, his eyes sad, lost in thought.

"Were you working with him Friday night?" Wolf asked.

"Yeah. Friday's the biggest night. Gotta have everyone on board, you know?"

"You two were co-owners of this place, huh?"

"Yeah. Fifty-fifty." Paco shook his head. "I'm screwed now," he said as if to himself.

"Why's that?"

"I don't know." He took his time, another drag. "We're not doing so great, you know? This pizza place isn't exactly a profit machine. And now with Bennett gone I'm in over my head, man. It's a lot to deal with."

Paco turned his back and walked a few paces away, looking to the sky. When he turned back Wolf saw he was genuinely upset.

"When did he leave work Friday night?" Wolf asked.

"He got off first, left early while Manny and I closed up."

"Manny?"

"Manny in there—the kid cutting the pizzas. He's our main delivery guy."

"How late do you guys stay open Fridays?"

"Eh, it's different every time. Depends on if we get a big order late or not. After midnight for sure. Usually about one o'clock we close up. But earlier if it's dead."

"And last Friday night? What time did he leave? And then what time did you and Manny stay behind until?"

"He left at like ten. Me and him switch being the first off Friday nights. It was his turn to be cut early. Me and Manny? I'm not sure exactly." He blinked a few times. "It was like twelve-thirty that night. We had a couple orders before midnight, I remember. Then we shut it down."

Wolf nodded. "Got it. And what did Bennett say he was going to do after work?"

"He said he was going to throw back a few at the Tavern. I was going to meet him there."

"You were?"

"Yeah. But when I got there, he wasn't there anymore."

"You said you closed this place down at about twelve-thirty. What time did you get to the Tavern?"

"A few minutes later. Just went straight there. What's it, like five minutes' drive?"

"And was he there?" Wolf asked.

"No. He was already gone."

"Did you ask about him? Ask others where he'd gone?"

"Yeah."

"And what did people say?"

"They just said he left." Paco shrugged. "I figured he was just tired. Went home."

Wolf eyed him.

Paco took another drag, lost in his own thoughts again.

Wolf eyed the mountains to the east, bright with an orange

tint in the final blaze of the late afternoon light. The wind eddied around the corner and blasted Paco's cigarette smoke in a swirl across Wolf's face. The smell was strangely satisfying, Wolf's long-kicked habit rearing up with a cocked ear.

"Did Bennett carry a gun in his truck?" Wolf asked.

Paco shrugged. "Yeah."

"What kind of gun did he have?"

"That Glock thirty."

Wolf nodded. "Why did he carry a gun in his truck? Did he have reason to fear for his life?"

"What? No. I mean, I don't think so. I don't know. It's just what some guys do. Just in case the other guy has a gun, you know?"

Wolf shifted the subject again. "What about Carrie and Valentina? Did you see them Friday night?"

"No. I never saw Carrie or Valentina at the bar. They were gone, too. Bennett's dad was asking me about that. I never even knew they were there. We ain't exactly best friends, you know?"

"You don't ever hang out with them?"

"Yeah, I mean, I know them. We all went to high school together. Me, Bennett, Valentina, and Carrie were all in the same class. But that was years ago, you know? Now I hang out with Bennett, and Carrie and Valentina got their own thing going on. When I see them, I say hi, you know? But other than that…" He finished his sentence by taking another drag.

"And what about Carrie and Bennett? I hear they have a history."

"They do?"

Wolf eyed Normandy. "That's what I hear. Do you know anything about that?"

Paco's face scrunched up. "I mean, I guess maybe?"

"Why maybe?"

Paco seemed to be thinking of what to say, and the implications of what might be said. "I don't know."

Wolf raised his eyebrows. Paco looked at his cigarette.

"Did he used to hang out at the Whitlocks' ranch?" Wolf asked. "I heard he used to go up there a lot and hang out with the boys. They used to ride dirt bikes or something like that."

Paco nodded, his eyes absent looking. "Yeah."

"How about you? Did you used to go up there, too?"

"No." Paco dropped his cigarette and stepped on it. "I never dirt biked. Wasn't my thing."

Wolf shifted directions. "Is there anybody you can think of that would want to harm Bennett?"

Paco shook his head, slowly at first, then faster. "No."

"How about Bennett's mood lately," Wolf asked.

Paco laughed. "Shit. Yeah, not good."

"He's been in a bad mood lately?"

"Always."

"Always," Wolf repeated the word. "And why do you think that is?"

"I don't know. Just everything. Starting with the football injury back in college, and now the numbers for our business weren't exactly helping. But I guess even before the football thing, he's just always kind of been dark and moody, you know? And his dad. You met his dad?" He blew air from his lips, then looked up at Normandy and Wolf and swallowed, like he'd said too much.

"I have met his dad," Wolf said. "Pretty strict guy. It was probably pretty tough to be his son."

Paco nodded. "Yeah. He comes in and picks apart the place, makes... or ...used to make Bennett feel like shit for owning a pizza place. Just everything he did, it was never good enough for Mr. Mustaine."

They stood in silence for a beat. Wolf thought Paco was ready to say more.

"You know..." Paco shook his head. "He really was depressed."

"Yeah?"

"Yeah." Paco nodded, his eyes sharpening as a thought solidified in his brain.

"Tell me," Wolf said.

"Somebody came into the place yesterday and said it looked like he shot himself."

"Who said that?" Wolf asked.

Paco shook his head. "Just a friend."

"Like you said," Wolf said, "he was really depressed, huh?"

"He once told me that he tried to get injured that day."

"On the football field?"

"Yeah. We got drunk one night and he was telling me about it. He said that he remembered that play like it was yesterday. That he saw the football, where it was, and knew that he was going to get messed up, that his leg would get completely crushed if he stepped over this guy and went for it, but he did it anyway. Like, he wanted to get messed up. He didn't want to play anymore."

"Wow," Wolf said.

"He was sick of playing for daddy," Paco said.

Wolf folded his arms and nodded. "I can imagine it was tough for him."

"It was real tough for him that he was actually hurt, though," Paco said. "He came back, limping around town. Everybody had seen the play online a thousand times by then. We all pussy-footed around him for a while. He was kind of ..."

"Kind of what?"

"He was smoking a lot of weed. Drinking a lot. You know, doing anything to run away from the problem."

"He was?"

Paco nodded. "That was for a while. But he sobered up, I mean, he wasn't sober with alcohol. But he stopped getting so drunk all the time and he stopped smoking weed."

"And then?"

"And then...he was yeah, he was back in town. Then he got that job at Normandy Woodworks, and..."

"What happened there, Paco?"

Paco's eyes went suddenly wide, like he was accessing a file in his brain and the file was called *How to answer the Normandy Woodworks question*.

"And then he left the job there," Paco said.

"He left? Or he got fired?"

"I think he got fired."

"And how did that affect him?"

Paco's voice was quiet. "I don't know."

"Were you good friends with Bennett?"

Paco's eyes glistened. "He was my best friend."

"Did he ever tell you about what happened at Normandy Woodworks?"

Paco sucked a drag, flicking his eyes between Wolf and Normandy. "One time he did. When we were drunk. I mean, I don't know what happened. But I had heard the rumors going around. That he was, like, groping her, or...I mean, I don't think he full on raped her. I don't think he was like, a freakin' rapist. I mean...I know it's bad no matter what he did, if he did anything to her, that it was bad, but..." He took another drag, then scratched his face.

"What did Bennett say to you?" Wolf asked.

Paco took his time, then said, "He was real drunk one night and he started talking about it. I finally got the guts to ask him what happened. And he just told me that he was 'proving a point.'"

Wolf narrowed his eyes. "Proving a point? And what point was that?"

"That was my question. And then he said that 'she found out the secret.'"

"She found out the secret?" Normandy asked.

"Yeah. I don't know what it meant. I didn't want to press him. Didn't want to press my luck. I mean, I don't want to make it seem like he was anything like his old man. He's not the bully like his dad. He was nice. Gentle. I mean, yeah, he was amazing and bad ass on the football field, but off it he wasn't like that."

Paco stared at the ground. "There was this one time these two guys were pushing me around outside the bar. I was trashed and accidentally flicked some cigarette ash on one of their girlfriends or something, and they were pissed off as hell, about to kick the crap out of me. But then Bennett came outside. And, he was big, you know, he was strong and could have just pummeled these guys, but somehow he befriended everyone instead. He had them laughing and joking. Shaking hands. And that's how he solved the situation. He didn't use his size like his dad did. He used his heart, you know?" Paco laughed heartily. "I shit you not, those two dudes and their girlfriends ended up buying us drinks all night."

Wolf and Normandy smiled.

Paco flicked his cigarette. "Listen. I really do have to get back in there. I saw four cars come up in the time we were talking, and these two kids can't keep this place running with a map and a compass, you know what I'm saying?"

Wolf gave him his card. "If you can think of anything else, any thoughts you may have forgot but you want to share, you can call me anytime, okay?"

"Yeah. Sure. You want to go back through the building?"

"That's okay, we'll stay out here," Wolf said.

Paco went back inside.

"The secret?" Normandy asked. "What the hell does that mean?"

Wolf shook his head. "I was going to ask you the same thing."

Normandy stifled a yawn, then gave in and let his mouth stretch wide.

They walked around the building and out into the parking lot. Just as Paco said, there were a few more cars parked there.

The sun was on the brink of ducking behind the western wall of mountains in the distance. The air sliced cold on the breeze.

"Let's call it a day," Wolf said. "It's been a long one."

"What about Mustaine?"

Wolf eyed the pizza building again. He was hungrier than he could remember being in a long time. His stomach felt fine; maybe whatever injury he had in there had healed. Or maybe it felt fine because it was empty.

"I'm going to bring him dinner," he said. "Keep your phone on in case I need you, but otherwise I'll see you in the morning."

"You sure you don't want me in the cell room with you? I'm pretty sure Mustaine could bend those bars if he just gave it a try. That cell has to be sixty years old. No. Seventy."

"I'll be okay. You go home. Get some rest."

23

The Crow Valley Sheriff's Office building glowed incandescent yellow while the sky above it blazed blood red.

Wolf parked next to Mustaine's truck, still sitting where Wolf had parked it earlier that morning. My God, he thought, his body was tired. That morning felt like it had been a month ago.

He eyed his hand, swollen twice it's normal size, with blue streaking on the outer edge between the final two knuckles.

He opened his rear door and pulled out two pizza boxes and a stack of napkins, using his left hand to avoid pain, and left the third pizza in the truck for his own dinner. He fantasized he'd eat it sitting on the motel bed, a soda cracked open next to him, while watching Thursday Night Football.

The air was cold, his breath clouding. As he walked inside, he saw Elan was alone at his desk.

"You hungry?" He walked over and put a box on the desk.

"Oh wow. Yeah, you could say that."

"Have at it." Wolf opened the box, revealing a pepperoni and sausage.

"Damn straight." Elan pulled out a piece and ate. "Aren't you going to have any?"

"No, I'm good."

"Is that for our guest?" Nodding to the box in Wolf's hand.

"Yeah. How's he doing?"

"I think Garcia fed him a bunch of food this afternoon. But he's...shit...I've been keeping my distance if I'm being honest. I haven't seen him since this morning."

"Where's Alvarez and Garcia?"

"I sent them home. It's my shift Friday nights."

"Again?"

Elan took a bite and shrugged.

"I'm going to go deliver this." Wolf turned and walked.

"Good luck. Don't get too close to those bars."

That's exactly what Wolf had been thinking as he walked out of the room and down the hallway to the cell. His hand flared with pain as he gripped the box using his index finger and thumb, keeping his other fingers limp and straight. He wasn't sure he could have bent them if he wanted to.

The door swung open with a high-pitched squeal, giving away his entrance to the cell's occupant.

Wolf turned, slightly shocked to see Mustaine sitting upright, staring directly at him.

The overhead lights were on but dimmed. It was warm, the air reeking of sweat and overgrown man.

"Look who it is," Mustaine said.

"Brought you some food." Wolf dropped the box on the floor in front of the cell door and scooted it with his foot. It was a little too high to fit, but that didn't stop him. He pulled it back, mashed the corners down with his heel and tried again. It went in a few inches, then got stuck again.

"Why don't you open the door and hand it to me?" Mustaine said.

Wolf had been keeping an eye on the sheriff the whole time. The big man hadn't moved a millimeter, but still reminded Wolf of a coiled snake.

Failing to push it under again, he pulled the box out and sat down crossed-legged in the middle of the floor. He opened it up, ripped off the lid, slid the pizza onto it, then shoved it under the iron door.

"I'm not hungry."

"For when you get hungry."

"I hate that pizza. Always have."

"So I hear."

Wolf scooted back, remaining seated in the middle of the room.

"You figure out who killed my son?"

"Not yet."

"Garcia says Trex is not giving you the warrant to search the Whitlocks'."

"I take it Trex is the judge?" Wolf said. "No, he's not. Not until we release you."

Mustaine smiled. "We."

"What's that?"

"You're not part of a team down here in Crow Valley."

"Neither are you."

Mustaine's face went slack. He folded his arms, his biceps spreading, chest muscles pushing together into a formidable sight in the shadows cast by the overhead lights.

The ground underneath the Rocky Points High School football stadium field had been hard, grass planted on bedrock, or something close to it if not, and at least twice Wolf had been smothered under Mustaine's full weight.

Wolf must have connected just perfectly on Mustaine's jaw this morning with that first blow and thank God he had never let up until he was in cuffs, or no doubt Wolf would have been lying next to Bennett Mustaine right now.

"What are you thinking about?" Mustaine asked.

"I'm thinking about where we go from here."

"Like I said. There is no we."

Wolf shook his head. "I can't put Carrie at that spot up on the road, not until I get GPS records that say otherwise. I can't match the microfibers to rags inside the Whitlock property. Or the cleaner used to wipe Bennett's car. Or find anything else that might be waiting inside that house that we don't know about."

"Then let me out."

"I can't guarantee that you'll be calm if I let you out."

"I'll be calm." Mustaine smiled.

"You punched me first."

"I know. It was me. I started it. I was upset. You let me out and I'll let everything slide between you and me. I don't care about that. I care about getting that warrant and going up to Carrie Whitlock's place, so we can find what we need to put those people behind bars."

The light overhead dimmed and brightened.

"What if I give you the phone and you call Judge Trex? And you tell him to sign that warrant, and you let us go up to Carrie Whitlock's and find what we need to prove they had anything to do with it?"

Mustaine scooted back and crossed his legs, the fabric of his pants sounding like it was on the verge of ripping. "What do you think happened to my son? You've been out there, presumably gathering all the facts today. Presumably not lazing on your ass like you used to do in the pocket. What do you think happened to my son? You think a gun took itself out from under his seat, put itself to his head, and pulled its own trigger? Then the gun drove his truck up to Dry Wash and wipe itself down? And then dropped to the floorboards and went back to sleep?"

"I think he was shot in the head," Wolf said. "Point blank. I think somebody else touched that gun, or they wouldn't have wiped it down. I think somebody was with him. Moved his body. I think maybe the Whitlocks have something to do with it."

Mustaine nodded.

"But I'm not sure what your son was capable of."

Mustaine remained silent.

"I'm talking about Sadie Moreno. I'm not sure if what he was doing Friday night wasn't the same type of thing he had already done to her two and a half years ago."

Mustaine said nothing.

"His pants were down."

"You'd better watch what you're saying now."

They stared at each other.

Wolf continued, ignoring the death glare. "What if it was Carrie? What if she shot him? Then we have to ask why."

"Because he wasn't interested in her," Mustaine said. "And she was upset about it."

"Okay. Or what if she was being attacked by Bennett and she had to kill him to defend herself? Which is the more plausible scenario there?"

Mustaine glared.

"And what would she do then?" Wolf continued. "She'd know you were going to act like this, making up your own version of truth and sticking to it with fierce determination. She'd be scared shitless. So would her mother. They would try and hide the fact that she was with him at all that night, for fear of the wrath of Clark Mustaine."

Mustaine's arms rippled under the light.

"Or what if we follow what the forensic evidence is really

telling us?" Wolf asked. "What if there's so much GSR on your son's hand because...and I'm sorry, Clark, I really am...but what if he fired the weapon himself?"

"No." Mustaine shook his head. "No, it looks like a person shot my son in the head. It looks like my son put his hand up to block it and that's where the GSR came from. Those tests are unreliable, they can be interpreted a million different ways by a million different forensic scientists."

Wolf put up his hands. "So, there are a couple—or three, was it? — versions of truth right there, all perfectly plausible. Just because you favor one over the others doesn't make it truer."

"It does to me."

Wolf sucked in a breath and let it out slowly.

"Here's what I think," Mustaine said. "Carrie knew the gun was under the seat. For some reason she lured him up to that road, they were getting intimate, and she pulled it out and shot him. Then she freaked out, couldn't believe what she'd done, and she walked home, told mommy, or her brothers, or all of them...and they came back and started cleaning it up. Making it look like a suicide.

"Or Valentina was there, too. She and her lured him in, promising of a two-on-one situation, and they shot him. One of them kept him busy while the other shot. Maybe it was Valentina. She's a class-A hooker, that girl there."

Mustaine upturned his hands. *Ta-da.*

"Why?" Wolf asked. "What's the motive?"

Mustaine made a motion like that was the least of his worries.

"You can't beat a *why* out of them."

"I beg to differ."

Wolf blew an exasperated breath.

"Maybe you need to get into the Whitlock house and do

some GSR tests on Carrie's clothing. That stuff washes off the skin easy enough, but it can stay in clothing for a good while, you know that."

"I can't lawfully get onto their property without a warrant, as you know."

They stared at each other for some time, the lights above flickering again.

"Was Bennett depressed?" Wolf asked.

Mustaine jumped to his feet and gripped the bars. "You piece of shit! My son didn't kill himself and if you suggest that again I'll rip these bars down and beat you dead! Fucking bloody pulp dead!" He stepped to the side and kicked the pizza.

Wolf shut his eyes as warm sauce splattered his face. When he opened them, he saw a piece stuck to the wall inside the cell, another hanging from between the bars.

"My son..." Mustaine sat heavily and sobbed, his head lowered, tears streaming onto his lap, shoulders racking up and down.

Wolf wiped some sauce from his face and smeared it onto his pant leg, a new streak of color that looked like blood added to his already muddied jeans.

"I'm sorry," Wolf said. "I was out of line. I shouldn't be talking to you about this. It's too much for a father who loves his son with all his heart. It's too much to handle."

They sat for a few minutes, Wolf remaining where he was, Mustaine letting out what Wolf suspected was the first wave of real emotion since his son's death.

And then Mustaine wiped his nose and eyes, and he sat straight, completely composed.

"What happened with Sadie Moreno?" Wolf asked.

Mustaine said nothing.

"What happened with her?"

"Sadie Moreno fell down and hit her crotch on a step ladder.

My son was there to spot her, knowing what she was doing was dangerous. She was embarrassed after it had happened and blamed it on Bennett."

"And her initial complaint that she had been sexually assaulted by Bennett?"

"No. She never said that."

"Then she blamed him for pushing her off the ladder?"

"Yeah."

"Where's the report? I can't find it in the records room."

"You can't? I don't know. Learn how to find things in alphabetical order."

"It was my understanding that Dr. Traver came with her to the station. Why would he be here making a statement unless he saw that there was evidence of sexual assault? And that DA Lamont was here, called in by Traver, because he wanted to give her moral support, because she was afraid to come in and face you alone with that information, knowing that she was accusing your son of assaulting her."

"Nah."

They stared at each other again.

"I noticed Traver's report was gone, too," Wolf said.

Mustaine shrugged.

"Your explanation is that Sadie hurt herself, and blamed Bennett in her first statement. And then she came back in and changed her statement."

"I don't know," Mustaine said. "Maybe she came in here thinking she could get away with lying like that. But then when she got here? Maybe she didn't want to cross that border."

"That border?"

"The border...you know, between being a liar and a truth-teller." Mustaine smiled.

Wolf shook his head, wondering what kind of drugs this

guy was on. "I'm trying to be sympathetic with your situation here but you're making it very difficult."

When Mustaine said nothing, Wolf shook his head. He stood up, feeling a crick in his back.

"I remember your girlfriend."

Wolf looked at him. "Good for you."

"What was her name?"

Wolf didn't answer.

Mustaine smiled. "Sarah, that was her name."

Wolf wondered how he would have known that.

"Damn she was a hot piece of ass back in the day, wasn't she? You know, there was this one moment during that game that I remember so vividly, and I will remember so for the rest of my life. It was right after I'd gotten done smothering your ass into the ground for the fifth or sixth time. I went to the sidelines and took my helmet off, looked over, and saw her cheering. But she was, you know, kind of looking at me. And she gave me this knowing smile, and then she turned right to me and kicked her leg up over her head. Just for me, she showed me her world for a second."

Wolf looked at the torn pizza box at Mustaine's feet, the piece inside the cell that had now fallen off the wall and lay on the floor, the piece still stuck in the bars, and the man now staring back.

"Oh yeah, sorry about her dying and everything."

Wolf left the room and shut the door. With weary legs that felt like he'd ran a half-marathon, he walked back into the squad room.

"How was it?" Elan asked, putting his feet down from his desk.

"Could have been better," Wolf said. He went to the pizza box on the undersheriff's desk and saw it was half-gone. "You mind?"

"You bought it. Take as much as you want."

Wolf picked up a piece and took a bite. It was a good pizza. Some of the best he'd ever tasted.

"When are you going to rest?" Wolf asked.

"I'll get some sleep."

"I'd like to go meet the forensic team when they show up."

"Last Carl told me, he and Lucy will be there by nine a.m. at the latest. And Traver will be there soon after."

Wolf nodded. "Get some rest. I'm going to go do the same." He started to leave, then stopped before the door.

"What's up?" Elan asked.

"When I showed up yesterday, I saw a sheriff's office running on all cylinders."

"Yeah? How's that?"

"When Mustaine was gone I saw everyone free and easy, and you running the show with no effort. And when Mustaine showed up? I saw the opposite of all that. And it wasn't just because his son's sitting in that morgue. It's because Mustaine is Mustaine."

Elan said nothing.

"You know this isn't going to end well," Wolf said. "The way I see it, it's already over. But that's only if somebody steps up to fill his place."

Wolf turned to leave.

"You stepped down from being sheriff," Elan said.

Wolf turned back around. "Yeah, I did. Because there was a much more qualified candidate for the job than me in waiting. Have a good night."

He went outside, got in his SUV and left. The drive over to the motel felt like ten miles but it only took two minutes.

He parked in front of the motel room and went inside, his legs sore, back aching, his right hand a balloon.

Once inside he undressed and took a shower, the water

coming out of the head like needles burrowing into his skin, but it was warm and it was steamy, and his bones felt better for it.

The moment he'd been waiting for arrived as he sat on the bed and leaned against the pillows, an ice-cold Sprite from the vending machine cracked and on the bed stand, the pizza box open in front of him, television flickering. But two losing teams were going at it on the TV, struggling mightily to score three points apiece, and the pizza hit his stomach like a ball of lead, somehow conglomerating with the piece he'd eaten at the station earlier, making his insides cringe so much he had to put down the slice and close the box.

His phone vibrated with a call from Rachette. "Hey."

"What's up? How are you doing down there? How's the case going?"

"It's going. Still going."

Rachette paused. "I'm sorry for the text message. Charlotte's telling me that I should have kept my nose out of that. That I shouldn't have texted you."

"No. It's okay. Thanks for the heads up."

"Have you talked to her?"

"No, I haven't," Wolf said. "At least, not about that. He paused, then changed the subject., "How's the case of the stolen bikes coming?"

"We figured it all out today."

Wolf popped his eyebrows. "Wow. What happened?"

Rachette spoke quickly, recapping his detective work, starting with the smudge he'd seen on Theo Anders's shoe, then seeing one of the bikes at the coffee shop freshly painted, their trip to talk to the county bicycle fleet manager to learn about the bikes being donated, and finally how he and Yates visited the two young men and got them to confess to their scam.

"Long story short," Rachette said, "the dumbasses were pretending their bikes got stolen, so they could get new ones from the insurance company. I guess they donated their bikes, you know, I guess to counteract the karma of attempting insurance fraud."

"So what charges are we pressing?"

"I'm pushing for none. Patterson's thinking about it, but I think she agrees. But Yates and I told them we'd contact the insurance company, and they would in turn keep an eye out for any incoming claims. And if they did file a claim then we'd come back and hit them with the full arm of the law."

"Did you contact the insurance company?'

"Not yet."

Wolf smiled. "Okay. It's probably a good idea to actually do that."

"Yeah, okay. So, listen," Rachette said. "Sorry about the whole Michael Venus news. People are telling me I shouldn't have said anything to you."

"No. It's fine. I appreciate you telling me."

"You appreciate it? Ah, imagine that Charlotte, he appreciates it. You're welcome."

Rachette said some more words, but Wolf heard none of them.

"I'll talk to you later," Wolf said.

"Yeah, okay."

Wolf hung up, and then he crawled in between the sheets and laid down.

He thought about Piper, and her living in Rocky Points, her working in the sheriff's office. He thought about Michael Venus taking an interest in her, and soon his thoughts took a sharp turn, and he began wondering how well he really knew Piper Cain. They had grown close over the last few months, but was he looking at the situation there all wrong? Had she been toying with him?

And then he thought about Dr. Hawkwood again, and how

he would have smiled kindly at Wolf and said, "Why don't you ask her?"

It would be easier when he was home to talk to Piper. The phone conversations weren't good enough. In the meantime, he needed to concentrate on getting back there, which meant he needed to concentrate on solving this case. He was close. He could feel it. But a piece of the puzzle was missing, he could feel that, too.

His thoughts shifted to Sadie Moreno, and how Mustaine must have threatened her to keep quiet.

"Maybe she came in here thinking she could get away with lying like that. But then when she got here? Maybe she didn't want to cross that border."

"That border?"

"The border...you know, between being a liar and a truth-teller."

He sat up on the edge of the bed and stared at the dirty motel curtains, his thoughts following a new line of logic. And suddenly he knew why Sadie Moreno was keeping her mouth shut.

Like Rachette and Yates and the two would-be bike fraudsters: If you make the claim, we will come down on you with the consequences. Mustaine was doing the same to her. Sadie Moreno was not just being threatened to keep her mouth shut, she was being blackmailed.

The more he thought about it, the more it made sense. She could have just told the truth, with the backing of a doctor and a district attorney, and the full extent of the law protecting her. But she didn't.

A heavy fatigue descended on him. He was tired of thinking. And right now, he needed to sleep.

24

The sun rose above the Sangre De Cristo mountain range in the east, slicing the sky with rays that hit Wolf square in the face as he sat in the parking lot of Normandy Woodworks.

He sipped his coffee, which was surprisingly, and thankfully, gentle on his stomach, the tiny spheres in the steam rising in the light.

His dash clock read 7:58 when the first vehicle pulled into the lot, a full-sized pickup, brand new, silver in color. It turned towards the spots near the front entrance, then slowed and came toward his vehicle.

Wolf saw through the windshield it was Ted Normandy. He pulled up next to Wolf's Explorer and rocked to a stop.

Wolf opened his door and got out, zipping his jacket all the way to block out the icy fingers of air trying to get in.

"Good morning." Ted climbed down from his truck, his breath billowing.

"Morning."

They greeted one another at the bumpers, Wolf presenting his left hand to shake. "Sorry, my good hand's a bit busted up."

Ted nodded, eyeing him with suspicion. "What is it now?"

"I'd like to talk to Sadie one more time."

Ted rolled his eyes, then narrowed them. "Your conversation didn't go over very well yesterday."

"Why did you fire Bennett Mustaine?"

Ted said nothing.

"Because you know what he did, and you knew you needed him out of here."

"I didn't fire him. He quit when I asked him what happened. Why do you need to talk to her again?"

"I just need to talk to her," he said. "I know you don't know me, but trust that if I didn't have a reason I wouldn't be here."

Another car pulled into the lot, an old red sedan.

Ted stared at the vehicle, then turned back to Wolf. "That's her right there."

Ted went to his truck and reached inside, then came out with a travel mug and shut the door. Wolf followed as they walked toward the front of the building, and past Sadie Moreno's still idling vehicle.

"It's up to her, not to me," Ted said, pulling out his keys.

Sadie shut off her car and got out as Ted opened the door.

"Sadie," Wolf said.

She ignored him as she walked inside as Ted held open the door. Wolf followed.

"I'll be in my office if you need me," Ted said to Sadie as he entered his office.

Sadie flicked on a set of lights on the wall, then weaved through the desks to her own and set down her purse as the sound of saws and other whining machines erupted from the back of the building.

"What do you want now?" Sadie asked as she sat down and flicked on her computer.

"Mornin' boss. Mornin' girl," a woman called out as she entered and walked to her own desk near the windows.

Sadie stared up at him, expectantly.

"I'd like to speak to you in private again, please. It's important."

"You said that yesterday. And I said all I'm going to say."

"I know why you changed your mind." He lowered his voice. "Why you decided to not tell the truth about Bennett."

She flicked her eyes to the other woman, who was keeping a close eye on Wolf.

Wolf played his hand, hoping he was right. "I know about the threat of deportation."

Her eyes went dark. She stared at him, her lips tightening. "So what? You gonna threaten me now too?"

"No. I'm not."

"Is everything okay?" the other woman asked.

Wolf stood back a step from Sadie's desk. "Everything's okay. I'm just having a word with Sadie." He pointed to his badge, twisting his hips to show her while he tried to use his most disarming smile.

"Follow me," Sadie said. "If you're going to threaten me, I want somebody else in the room with us."

Wolf followed as she made a direct line to Ted's office. She knocked and went inside, sitting down in front of Ted's desk. Ted sat with crossed legs, hands folded in his lap, eyes on Wolf.

"May I?" Wolf asked.

Ted waved him inside, Wolf closing the door gently behind him.

"Close the blinds, please," Ted said.

Wolf twisted them shut as he was told, blocking out the sight of more employees entering the building.

"Have a seat," Ted said.

Wolf pulled the chair away from Sadie and angled it toward them both, then sat.

Somebody knocked on the door and a woman opened it, poking her head inside. "Hey, I need to ... oh, hey."

"I'll talk to you in a bit, Carla," Ted said.

The woman shut the door, leaving them in silence.

"Well?" Ted said.

"I put Sheriff Mustaine in jail yesterday," Wolf said, directing the sentence to Sadie.

Sadie eyed him skeptically. "You put him in jail?"

"He was interfering with the investigation. He was intimidating people. Threatening them. And I threw him in jail for it."

She said nothing.

"I'm not here to intimidate you, Sadie. I'm here, and I'm here alone, because I want you to know that I'm not going to act on anything I learn about you or your family today. Do you understand? I was given power to arrest people in connection with the Bennett Mustaine case, and that's it. I'm not allowed to..."

He paused, looking at Ted Normandy, wondering if he could divulge the information he was about to or not.

"It's a fuzzy line whether or not we, as law enforcement, have a duty to arrest people who we know to be in the country illegally."

A tear streaked down Sadie's cheek, but she continued to stare at him, unmoving.

"Your family matters have nothing to do with the case I'm working, so I'm not going to make any arrests, or speak to anybody about the aspect of the case we're discussing now."

"What are you talking about, Wolf?" Ted asked.

Wolf nodded. "That's what's going on, right? Sheriff Mustaine found out that a relative of yours is in the country illegally, and he threatened to have them deported if you reported the truth about Bennett Mustaine."

She didn't want to cross that border. Mustaine's words echoed in his mind. The man could never resist taunting on the field, and he'd done the same last night, deliberately dangling the word in front of Wolf's nose.

Ted sat forward and put both elbows on his desk, intensely interested. "Is that true, Sadie?"

Sadie looked down at her hands, letting loose a barrage of tears.

Ted stood up, sending his chair twisting behind him into the wall. "That son of a bitch. Your aunt and uncle?"

She said nothing.

"That son of a bitch," he said again. "I knew he was threatening you with something. Sadie, you could have come to me with this earlier."

"For what?" Sadie all but screamed the words. "What would you have done?"

Ted shook his head. "I don't know. We could have gotten a lawyer to help them."

"He would have found out. There's nothing you can do to go against that man," she said. "He's too... big."

Wolf put up a hand. "Sadie, the truth is out now about why you're not talking. But, like I said, I'm not interested in that."

"Then what are you interested in, Wolf?" Ted asked. "You know what she's going to say. You know what Bennett did to her, we all know. Why do you want her to say it?"

"Because I talked to Paco Nez yesterday," Wolf said, keeping his conversation directed to Sadie. "And he told me he was drinking one night with Bennett, and Bennett came out and told him why he'd done it. He said that he did it...that he assaulted you...because he wanted to make a point. And that you had figured out the secret."

Sadie blinked rapidly, looking like she was computing information she'd never heard before.

"What does that mean to you?"

She paused, like those computations were now complete.

"What?" Wolf spoke low. "What secret? What happened that day? I know it's hard, but can you tell me? Your knowledge might help with what's happening right now."

"My knowledge might help you catch whoever killed Bennett Mustaine?" Her mouth twisted in disgust. "I figure that person did a service to humanity. I'd rather not speak, then."

"I think he may have killed himself."

Her face dropped. "Are you serious?"

"What happened that day back there on the factory floor, Sadie?"

She looked sad again, the rage gone. She spoke with a soft voice. "I was working late, trying to line up a big order that was supposed to be picked up the next morning. There was all sorts of trouble with the way I took the order and stuff...it was my first couple weeks on the job.

"Bennett had just started, too. He'd been hired a week or so earlier than me, but for a shop floor position. I was front office. Anyway, we were kind of drawn together because of it, both learning the ropes at the same time and helping each other out. We became friends."

She looked at Wolf, unsure. "He was good-looking. Funny. I don't know, I guess I kind of liked him. And I thought he liked me. We'd been in different grades in school growing up, and I never knew him really. I always thought he was this big dumb jock, but he turned out to be kind of...cute and funny."

She shook her head and grabbed a tissue off the desk, blew her nose and threw it in the trash can next to her.

"Anyway, so that night, I had to go back into the shop to see if we even had some of the stuff I had included in the order. But it was way up in the rafters, third level. I went back there and saw Bennett was listening to his headphones and cleaning, so I didn't bother him. I just took the rolling ladder, you know, the stairs on wheels?"

"Yeah, sure," Wolf said.

"I was up on that, checking the inventory, and he came over. He asked what I was doing? He seemed kind of upset. Like, something bad had happened to him that day or something. I stopped what I was doing and came down a few steps, and I sat down and asked him what was wrong.

"He didn't tell me. But I knew that his father had been in that day earlier, I'd seen him checking out the place, walking around with Ted. I wondered if it was something to do with that, so I asked him."

"And what did he say?" Wolf asked.

"He wouldn't tell me what was wrong. And so," she snorted, shaking her head, "naturally I asked him out on a date. It was weird, I know that now. But I felt bad for him. I felt like we had been really connecting and thought he might want to talk. It's probably something I shouldn't have done. If I hadn't, then what happened wouldn't have happened." She stared at her hands.

"What did happen?" Wolf asked, keeping his voice low.

"I asked him if he wanted to go get dinner with me after work, and we could talk it out. I tried to make it seem like, you know, just a friendly thing, but he saw through me and knew I wanted it to be something more. He saw I liked him. I guess it was pretty obvious the way I always laughed at his jokes and stuff."

She looked at Wolf and shrugged.

"He was like, 'No thanks.' I know it's not right what I said next, but his answer was like a slap in the face. And so I was like, 'What are you, gay or something?' I know…it was terrible. I shouldn't have said it, but I was just so hurt." She stopped talking and looked at Wolf. "Is that what you were talking about? Is that the secret?"

Wolf's heart was beating, thoughts were racing in his brain, elements of the case rearranging.

"What happened next," Wolf asked, shaking the thoughts out of his mind. He needed to know everything.

"He went crazy. He, like, just got so mad. He reached out and grabbed my crotch through my jeans, really hard, and before I could even scream or make a noise he grabbed me by the leg and pulled me off the ladder. I somehow landed with my arms like, wrapped around his neck. And then he ripped open my pants and..." she closed her eyes "... and then he shoved his hand down my underwear and started, you know."

She plucked another tissue from the box, clutching it in her hand.

"I told him to stop, that he was hurting me, but he just didn't listen. He was like, in this trance. I don't know how long that went on for, but I started yelling for help, and then I started screaming, and finally ..." she shook her head, another stream of tears falling. "...he stopped. Just like that. And he pulled out his hand and saw blood on his fingers, and that's when I could see he really regretted what he'd done. He stood there looking over me, and I saw whatever demon had possessed him completely disappear. He told me he was sorry." She shrugged. "He started crying, and then he left."

Wolf nodded.

"And then I went to the hospital, because I was bleeding. And that's when I saw Dr. Traver. He was my family's doctor when I was in middle school. I told him Bennett had attacked me, and he called the DA, and they took me to make the report at the sheriff's office that night."

"And then Sheriff Mustaine threatened you?" Wolf asked.

She nodded. "He came and saw me the next day? No, it was two days later. He showed up to my house, and that's when he told me that I had fallen off the rolling stairs, and that if I hadn't fallen, then my aunt and uncle down in Alamosa would be getting a visit from ICE."

Wolf let out a breath, feeling like he'd been holding it for quite some time.

Ted sat dumbfounded, tears welling in his eyes.

"Thank you for telling me that story, Sadie," Wolf said.

She nodded and sniffed.

Wolf eyed the clock, seeing it was almost 9:30. "I have to go," he said. "Again, thank you, Sadie. I know it was hard. I'm sorry. I have to go."

25

Wolf jogged out to his SUV and fired it up.

He drove at speed through the parking lot and headed north on the highway into town. He pressed his foot on the accelerator, feeling excited by the new door opened.

What if Bennett Mustaine had been gay? He let the implications roll around in his mind.

What did that mean? It meant everything.

He passed the Tavern, now surrounded by an empty parking lot on a Friday morning. He pictured Bennett sitting there Friday night, contemplating, zoning out, staring at his phone, just like Valentina had reported.

Wolf's eyes slid past and to the restaurant next door—the Chicken House.

He jammed the brakes and turned into the parking lot. Just like the Tavern it was empty, but there was a single vehicle in the lot: a pickup truck with a Chicken House Restaurant and Brewery sticker stuck across the tail gate.

He parked next to it and got out, eyeing the windows of the

place. They were mirrors, reflecting the mountains and traffic behind him. He eyed the Tavern and saw much of the same.

"Can I help you?"

Wolf turned to see the front door of the Chicken House open, a man with a bald pate and closely shorn beard eyeing Wolf suspiciously.

Wolf flashed his badge. "My name's David Wolf. I'm a detective with the sheriff's department."

Wolf walked closer, keeping his badge out and presented.

"Not here. I know all the cops here."

"I'm from up north in Rocky Points, helping out with the Bennett Mustaine case."

"Is that right."

"Yes sir. And what can I call you?"

"Landon."

"You work here, or..."

"I own the place."

"Ah. And you work here as well? Or just collect the money?" Wolf chuckled.

"Psh. I wish. I eat, shit, sleep, do everything but shower at this place."

Wolf smiled. "How about last Friday night?"

"Of course."

Wolf cut right to it. "Was Bennett Mustaine here that night?"

His eyes turned upwards. "Yep."

"Really."

"Yeah. Came in for a few seconds. I remember seeing him."

"Did you see him leave?"

"Yep."

"Was he with somebody?"

"Nope."

Wolf deflated. "So, you saw him come in, though."

"That's right. I usually work the full gamut on weekends, a little serving the tables, a little bartending, I make it a habit of paying attention to everyone who comes and goes. I've been burned a few times with people who leave without paying. Just good business to keep track. Keep your house in order and all that."

"You say he came in for a couple of seconds. Why so quick?"

"I don't know. It could have been five or ten minutes. I just remember it being a short time, because I saw him come in, and then I happened to be at the door when he left. I told him, 'Hey! Where you goin'? You just got here!' I used to watch him play football. The boy was NFL material before that injury of his. It's a damn shame about his death. He was a good kid."

Wolf nodded impatiently. "What did he say to you as he left?"

"Nothing. He just said he had to go and he left."

"How many people were here at that point?" Wolf asked. "A lot?"

"Yeah, probably thirty or so. It's pretty busy Friday nights."

"How about Carrie Whitlock and Valentina Johnson? Were they here?"

"Nope. But Kent was."

"Kent Whitlock?"

"Yes, sir."

Wolf stared at him.

"What?" Landon asked.

"Thanks for your time, sir."

"Wait a minute," Landon said. "You're asking about Kent Whitlock, that night when I left the place after closing I saw Kent Whitlock's motorcycle still parked in the lot."

"You did?"

"Yeah. Can't miss it. He's got a Yamaha dirt bike with a

number 3 pasted all over it. I remember thinking he must have gotten a ride home from somebody."

"What time did you close up?"

"Two a.m."

Wolf nodded. "Thanks for your time."

"You think he's got something to do with Bennett Mustaine's death?" Landon asked.

Wolf turned and walked back to his SUV.

Yes, I do, he thought.

26

"I'm headed up to High Road now. Dr. Traver's there and the K9 unit should be arriving soon." Normandy's voice sounded far away in Wolf's speakers, no matter how much he turned them up.

"Okay," Wolf said. "I'm going to swing by the office to talk to Elan. Then I'll see you up there."

"Yeah, good. Tell him to turn on his ringer. Nobody's answering at the station and he's not answering his phone."

"Where's Alvarez?"

"I talked to him earlier. He's on his... office..." Half his words were garbled.

"What's that?" Wolf said. "You broke up."

"The suspense is killing me," Normandy said, ignoring Wolf's interjection. "What did Sadie Moreno say?"

Wolf turned into the parking lot of the sheriff's office and parked. "I'll talk to you in a few minutes."

"—she didn't sound like she was going to talk again at all," Normandy said, having a completely different conversation. "Hello?"

Wolf pressed the call end button and shut off the engine. He got out and raised his arms overhead, stretching and yawning wide.

Walking to the entrance he eyed the window but saw only the glare from the morning sun and himself staring back. As he reached for the front door he froze.

Eyeing the window reflection again, the skin on his body prickled.

Mustaine's truck was gone.

He pulled on the door and it rattled in the jamb, locked. He put his face to the glass and saw all the ceiling lights were still on.

He stepped back and walked around the building, to the back side where there was an alley with a dumpster and a few empty parking spots.

He rounded the building to the other side, stepping through some crispy snow that had survived yesterday's afternoon melt, and back to the front. Nothing was out of the ordinary with the building as far as he could see, except Mustaine's truck was nowhere to be found.

He pulled his phone and dialed Elan's phone number. It went straight to voicemail.

A vehicle turned into the lot, shooting Wolf's pulse sky high. It was Alvarez arriving, and he pulled into the parking spot next to Wolf's SUV and shut off his engine.

"Morning," he said, shutting his door. He looked at Wolf. "What's up?"

Wolf stood and gestured to the empty parking spot. "Mustaine's truck is gone."

Alvarez looked at it.

"Did you move his truck?" Wolf asked.

"No. Did you ask Elan?"

"He's not answering his phone."

"He's inside."

"It's locked."

"Locked?"

"I take it that's rare?" Wolf asked.

"We never lock it." Alvarez pulled out his keys as he walked briskly to the front door, then twisted the lock open and pushed inside.

Wolf followed behind him.

"Hello?" Alvarez called out.

There was a faint noise of somebody calling out from the rear of the building.

"Did you hear that?" Alvarez asked.

They moved toward the back, slowing at Garcia's desk, which had a reusable lunch bag sitting atop it, unzipped open, a meal of a sandwich and apple, both half-eaten, a wadded napkin next to it.

There was another noise. A loud grunt or call.

Wolf passed Alvarez and reached the back hallway at a jog, his gun pulled.

"What the hell is going on?" Alvarez was on his heels.

There was another call, much louder now, coming from the cell block.

"Careful," Wolf said as they reached the door. Alvarez put his back to the wall and pulled his gun. Wolf opened the door, then kicked it wide, aiming inside. An empty room came into view, and Wolf stepped inside to see Elan sitting on the cot inside the cell. Dried blood streamed down his face as he pressed a hand to the side of his head.

"What the hell?" Alvarez came in behind him, swinging his gun to the empty cell behind them. "Where's Mustaine?"

"He escaped," Elan said.

"Do you have the key?" Wolf asked, pointing to the cell door.

"Yeah," Alvarez said, pulling out his keys. "I mean, I think."

"No, you don't." Elan croaked the words, eyes expressionless, as if facial movement was too painful. "They're in my drawer. Bottom left, in the lock box. The code is 467."

Alvarez nodded and ran out.

Wolf studied the scene. The state of the cell had been bad when Wolf had left it last, with pizza slices stuck to the wall and hanging from the bars. Now it had been tidied up, but there was a much larger red smear on the ground.

"Got it!" Alvarez called out on his way down the hallway. He came in and unlocked the cell. The door screamed in protest as they pulled it open.

They helped Elan up and escorted him into the main room.

"Where's Garcia?" Alvarez asked.

Elan sat down, eyeing her desk warily. "I...I don't know. I was knocked unconscious. She was here when I went back into the cells. She was right here. About to eat her dinner."

"Shit." Alvarez pulled out his cell phone and poked the screen, putting the phone to his ear. He shook his head. "She's not answering. Voicemail. I'm trying again."

For the first time Wolf noticed Alvarez might have had a closer relationship with Garcia than he'd realized.

"What happened?" Wolf asked Elan.

"I heard him whimpering back here, like an hour after you left. I went inside, and he was laid out..." Elan shook his head. "I'm an idiot. Now I know he was painted in pizza sauce, holding his head, but he looked like he was bloody. I asked him if he was okay, but he was unresponsive. It looked like he had a real injury. I mean, he did really have a cut on his face, I swear... he must have put it there. So, it threw me off, he was covered in sauce, and in blood, and I thought he was hurt."

"And then he attacked you when you came in," Wolf said. "We need to know where he is. Do you guys have GPS trackers on your vehicles?"

"No," Alvarez said. "Mustaine didn't want that."

Wolf pulled out his phone. "What's Nola Whitlock's phone number?"

Elan reached in a drawer and pulled out a manila folder, then read off the number.

Wolf dialed and it went straight to voicemail. He tried again, still no answer. "What about Carrie's number? Or Kent's? You guys have it?"

"No, sir," Elan said, standing up.

"Do you have Carrie's number?" Wolf asked Alvarez.

"No."

Elan put a hand on the edge of the desk then sat on it.

"Are you okay?" Wolf asked.

"I'm okay."

Wolf raised his phone. "What's Mustaine's phone number?"

Alvarez poked his screen and handed Wolf the phone.

It too went straight to voicemail.

"No answer." Wolf handed the phone back to Alvarez.

"Well? Where is he?" Alvarez asked.

Both men stared at Wolf expectantly.

"He didn't visit me at the motel last night. If I had to bet, I'd say he's at the Whitlocks' ranch right now."

"And if I had to bet," Alvarez said, "It's not a polite house call."

27

"Just meet us at the bottom!" Elan sat in Wolf's passenger seat, screaming into the phone. "Where it meets County 27! I said, where it meets County 27!" Elan lowered his cell and shook his head. "He heard me. I hope. He's going to meet us on the way up."

Wolf kept his eyes on the road ahead as it swept a tight corner, the slope beside the vehicle dropping off precipitously. He saw Alvarez was keeping close to his bumper, despite the snake of dust he was leaving behind and the winding canyon road.

"So, what did you want to tell me?" Elan asked.

Wolf told him about the conversation with Sadie Moreno, and what she told him happened that evening two years ago in Normandy Woodworks, about her suggesting Bennett was gay for refusing her, and the attack that followed.

"Geez," Elan said, shaking his head. "That's terrible. So, it's true. What everyone thinks happened, really happened. And Mustaine covered it up."

Wolf nodded. "Listen, I never knew Bennett, but it seems to

me that Sheriff Mustaine was an overbearing father. Am I right there?"

"I think that's fair to say," Elan said. "I've witnessed Mustaine talking to Bennett, overheard phone conversations coming out of his office. Bennett may have been an inch taller than his father, but he was like a timid boy when he was with his dad. At least, that's the sense I've always gotten."

"Would Mustaine be the kind of man that would support his son being gay?"

Elan shook his head. "I'm going to go with no on that one."

"When Normandy and I talked to Paco Nez, Paco told us about once he spoke to Bennett about what happened with Sadie. And Bennett told him that Sadie had, quote, 'figured out the secret'."

Elan looked at him. "And Sadie Moreno asked if he was gay. You think that was the secret? And that's why he attacked her?"

"I think so," Wolf said. "And listen, I stopped by the Chicken House after talking to Sadie, and I spoke to the owner. He says Bennett Mustaine stopped by his bar Friday night. Late. *After* he was at the Tavern."

"You're shitting me."

Wolf continued. "Kent Whitlock was also at the Chicken House. The owner said Kent left his motorcycle there that night, that he saw it still parked next to the building as he was closing the place up at two a.m."

Elan held up a hand. "Okay. So, what are we saying here? Kent was with Bennett? Because they were lovers?"

"It fits, and it might explain some things," Wolf said. "Mustaine told me Bennett was hanging out with Carrie's little brother to get close to Carrie back in high school, and then again when he came back from Ohio. I'm wondering if Mustaine was mistaken, and there was no history with Carrie, but rather a history with Kent.

"Mustaine told me how he would tell Bennett he was being soft, that he needed to be more direct, to ask out Carrie rather than hang out with her little brother to get close to her. That tells me Bennett was keeping his sexuality a secret."

"If he really was gay," Elan said. "But what if Kent and Bennett were just friends? Just from an evidence-based point of view, I'm not seeing the proof there. And who cares if he was gay or not?"

"Bennett did. And his father would have. Listen, I'm no psychologist ... but after hearing Sadie's account of what happened that night at Normandy's Woodworks, clearly Bennett was a deeply troubled young man. He was conflicted, he had to hide who he really was from his father. That's a traumatic thing. And the mention of being gay triggered him. Triggered his shame. Triggered something in him that wanted to be straight."

They drove in silence for a while.

"Or I don't know," Wolf said. "Like I said, I'm no psychologist."

"No, I think it fits," Elan said. "He was troubled. He was conflicted. Like you said, he was triggered. So, if he snapped back then and attacked Sadie Moreno, what are we saying about Bennett's death? Did Kent kill him? Was Bennett triggered again, and he attacked Kent? And Kent had to defend himself? That would make sense. The crime scene was wiped down. The gun was wiped down. Why would that be the case unless somebody else handled it? And maybe Mustaine is coming at the Whitlocks the wrong way, but you know they're hiding something."

Wolf shook his head. Even with such a revelation there were still so many questions to be answered.

Elan sat back putting a hand to his temple, touching an

oozing wound. He looked improved, but still weak, slow-moving, and lacking color in his face.

"You think Mustaine's up there?" Elan asked.

"I don't know where else he would be." Wolf would have bet on it. Why hadn't Mustaine broken out and come straight after Wolf? Because revenge for his son's death would come first. Wolf's heart was beating fast, and he took a deep breath to calm his nerves.

Elan wiped his hands on his pants, eyes locked forward. "What do you think he's doing up there?"

"I think he's doing what Mustaine does."

"That's not good."

"No. It's not."

A few minutes later they were out of the canyon and speeding across the flats toward the forested land ahead, and the High Road intersection.

"It's around the next corner," Elan said.

Wolf slowed as they rounded the next corner, the rear of his vehicle sliding on the washboard surface. A Crow Valley SUV came into view, parked alongside the road in a stripe of sun, Deputy Normandy standing at the rear bumper, hands shoved into his pockets.

Wolf slowed and Elan rolled down his window.

"Hey." Normandy stepped close.

"Have you seen or heard anything?" Wolf asked.

"No, sir." He looked down the road, and they all did. The Whitlocks' place was still a mile or so up the valley, inside the trees. A cloud of dust washed over them as Alvarez parked behind.

Alvarez got out, jogged up, and stood next to Normandy. "What's the plan?"

"Follow us."

Wolf drove away slowly, letting Alvarez and Normandy get into their vehicles to follow, then punched the gas.

Elan sat forward, fear making him lick his lips and swallow saliva that clearly wasn't there.

"Take some more water," Wolf said.

They rode in silence while Wolf drove fast through the dense forest.

"How much further after that bend up ahead?"

"Just beyond it. That's where the ranch is."

He jammed the brakes and slowed to the side of the road. Alvarez and Normandy parked behind him.

They all got out and met at Wolf's front bumper, the three other men standing in a semi-circle, looking at Wolf, waiting. For a moment he had a flashback of being on the football field, his teammates looking at him in the huddle, fear on their faces, and for the same exact reason: Mustaine.

He eyed the forest. The lodgepole pines were spaced out, the underbrush sparse.

"We'll stick to the trees the rest of the way," he said. "Elan, you can take the rear if you don't feel up for it, but I say we go fast." He pointed. "The forest is going to end at their property, and then we'll be in sight, so when we reach the edge of the woods keep behind cover and we'll see what we're looking at."

Wolf went over to the barbed wire fence and made a gap for them to crawl through. Normandy got on the other side and did the same for Wolf.

Alvarez was already running, and they followed. A few minutes later they were all huffing air. Wolf's boots thumped and crunched on the pine needles with hypnotic rhythm, his chest wheezed with exertion.

The undersheriff fell behind from the beginning but waved them on. Normandy and Alvarez seemed to be slowing down for Wolf, keeping just a few paces ahead.

Lungs burning, his mouth tasting faintly of blood, Wolf pushed harder.

A few minutes later Alvarez and Normandy slowed to a halt, putting up their hands for them to stop. Ahead of them the forest ended at a vast meadow, all green grass and low native shrubs, cattle, and the Whitlock house and its outbuildings.

Breathing heavily, Wolf ducked behind an oak bush next to Alvarez and Normandy and looked back to see where Elan was. For a moment the undersheriff was completely out of sight, then he came into view, walking with a hand on his side, teeth bared, skin pale.

"Shit, he doesn't look good," Normandy said.

"You see anything?" Alvarez asked, his eyes on the property ahead.

Normandy pointed across to their left, through the trees a vehicle reflected patches of light. "I see Mustaine's truck. Through there."

The truck sat, just visible through the trees, parked inside the tree line, before the foliage thinned out and gave way to the meadows surrounding the ranch.

Wolf glanced back to the front gate, which was still closed. He eyed the fence line from the gate toward the vehicle and spotted a part of the wire fencing that hung open, a slash of the wire pattern missing.

"There," Wolf said, pointing. "He cut his way in."

"Shit," Normandy said. "What's he doing in there?"

They stood in silence, watching. There was no noise, save for a cow mooing in the field and a couple of crows cawing above.

They were to the east of the property, with a field between them and the house. Surrounding the house lay a few acres of property, some of it dotted with cattle on grass, other parts of it carpeted with rabbitbrush, sage, and other native foliage.

The ten-foot game fence circled the house, one entry point now opened up by Mustaine's wire cutters, and the other the swinging gate on the opposite side of the property where he'd seen Kent Whitlock sitting in the tractor.

"I've never been inside of that place," Alvarez said, snapping him out of his thoughts. "Have you?"

"No," Normandy said.

Wolf shook his head.

The house had a wall of east-facing windows pointed straight towards them.

Elan came up behind them. "What's up?" he asked, his voice hoarse.

Wolf pointed out Mustaine's truck and the opening in the fence.

"How are you doing?" Wolf asked.

"That's the living room," Elan said, gesturing. "Those are the living room windows."

"You've been inside?"

"Nola put on a charity thing last year. I attended, yeah, I've been inside. I think our best bet is to approach from the other side of the house, from the rear. They have a garage there without many windows, and that outbuilding next to it can give us some cover."

Wolf nodded, seeing what he meant. Behind the house stood the tan building made of corrugated metal Wolf had seen they kept an antique tractor inside.

He eyed Elan again. The cut on his head was beginning to ooze blood.

"Don't worry about me." Elan said. "We need to get in there."

"Are we thinking of going through that gate?" Alvarez asked. "The one to their cattle pasture? Because I think we'll be completely exposed if we do that."

"Elan's right, we have to come in taking that outbuilding for cover," Wolf said.

"And climb the fence?" Normandy looked at Elan.

Wolf pulled out his multi-tool. "We do like Mustaine did. I can cut us through. Let's move."

They kept to the trees, circling the property to the right. The going was slow, but ten minutes later they had the rear of the house straight across the clearing from them.

Normandy sat down hard, looking back at them with wide eyes, his hand gesturing for them to get down.

Wolf ducked behind a bush near a thick tree and looked out.

There was the slap of a door closing and then somebody stepped out from the side of the house and into view. The person's gait was slow and unsure.

It was Deputy Garcia. Her arms were crossed over her chest, and she looked like she was upset. It also looked like she was covered in blood.

28

"Is that blood?" Alvarez hissed. "That's blood."

Wolf agreed, but he wasn't so sure it was her blood. She walked slow, crying and clearly upset, but she looked uninjured.

She stopped at a white door that led into the side of the outbuilding, fumbled with a key, and stepped inside, leaving it swung wide. They could see multiple tractors parked in the structure, the roll doors pulled open, light streaming in.

"Move!" Wolf whispered to Normandy and Alvarez.

They darted fast, Alvarez taking a commanding lead, weaving between the trees, keeping inside the shadows, until the outbuilding blocked their view of the house behind it.

Wolf caught up to the deputy, feeling a second, adrenaline-fueled wind, and led the way across an expanse of natural meadow, slaloming between the bushes.

They got to the fence and Wolf had his multi-tool out, already with the wire-cutters flipped open. With quick movements he snipped a vertical line in the wire, then cut another slice ninety degrees to the side. Silently Normandy peeled back the wire and Alvarez and Wolf jumped through. Surprisingly, Elan was close behind Wolf.

All four of them moved along the edge of the tan corrugated metal building, keeping out of view of the house. Dogs barked somewhere inside, and Wolf thanked God they weren't outdoors, or their approach would have been blown.

There was a noise on the other side of the metal wall, a loud clank, that spiked Wolf's adrenaline.

They slowed at the corner of the building. Alvarez was in the lead, and there seemed to be no discussing that he would stay there. Wolf, Normandy, and Elan watched as he peeked around the corner, looking ready to pounce.

"Alvarez," Wolf whispered coming up behind him.

Alvarez kept his eyes around the corner. "What?"

Wolf looked past Alvarez at the house and saw two windows—one of them covered with drapes, the other small and square.

"Looks clear," he said, pushing Alvarez's back. "Move."

Alvarez didn't need any more coaxing. He sprinted around the corner and down the exposed length of the building to the open door. One by one they followed, Wolf pushing as fast and as silently as he could.

Alvarez disappeared inside first, but Wolf was quick on his rear and saw Garcia jumping at the sight of them. Alvarez went straight to her while Wolf swept his gun across the interior of the space. He saw nothing but farm machinery, Garcia the only person inside.

"Are you hurt?" Alvarez asked, putting his hands on her with gentle pressure, his eyes sweeping her body for injuries. "Are you hurt?"

She shook her head, but she remained silent.

"What happened?" Alvarez asked.

Wolf pointed at the door and looked at Normandy. "Keep an eye out."

Normandy nodded and put his back to the door, peeking out toward the house.

"He shot one of the kids." Garcia's voice shook, barely above a whisper. "He shot Kent. I've been trying to keep him alive. He's bleeding bad. I'm out here to get a first aid kit. They have one for the animals. I can't find it! I can't stop the bleeding! I need gauze!"

"Shh," Alvarez wrapped her in a hug. "We'll find it." He began helping her look for the first aid.

"Call an ambulance," Wolf said to Elan.

"I'm on it." Elan pulled out his phone and dialed.

"Wait," Garcia said. "What about the sirens? That might spook him. He's really not in his right mind."

"Don't hang up," Wolf said. "Tell them to hurry." He turned to Garcia. "I need you to tell me what's happening in there. And here." He plucked three boxes off the shelf labeled non-adherent dressing and gave them to her.

She took the boxes absently. "He has everyone else tied up. He took my phone, or I would have called you. He took my gun, or ..."

"Where does he have them?" Wolf asked.

"In the living room."

"Does he have his gun drawn? What's he using to make them stay put?"

"He has them tied up. But he takes out his gun when he's asking questions or when he's close to me."

"Ambulance is on its way," Elan said, pocketing his phone.

"I have to go back in. He's going to come out and check what I'm doing."

Wolf said nothing, considering this as a plan. They could

simply make her wait out here until he came out, which would separate him from the others and they could ambush him.

"I have to get back in there and push on the wound. He's bleeding out."

"Okay," Wolf nodded, wiping that idea. "What's the layout like? When you go back in that door, where is he?"

She gestured with her free hand. "He's straight ahead, down the hall, through the kitchen, and to the left. In the living room."

"Where are the dogs?"

"They're locked in the garage."

"Did he see us coming?" Alvarez asked.

"No, I don't think so."

They all looked at Wolf, ready for another play call. "Okay. He's already expecting you to return, so we'll use that. Go back in. Get back to Kent and keep him alive as best you can. We'll follow you in when you open the door. I want you all on my ass when I go in. We pile in behind her as fast and silently as we can."

"What if he's there?" Garcia asked. "What if he's in the kitchen or something?"

"Then get on the ground and plug your ears."

She blinked, Wolf's implication hardening her expression. "Okay."

Wolf nodded. "Let's go."

Garcia walked quickly, wiping the tears from her face with her forearm.

Wolf gestured for everyone to stay to the side, out of sight as they followed her to the door. Leaning out barely, he studied the two windows as she began walking from the outbuilding to the house.

"Move fast," he reminded them, but it turned out they

didn't need reminding. Within seconds they were all crammed behind Garcia, ushering her forward.

The next few seconds were excruciating, waiting for her to cover the remaining dozen steps to the house, all of them exposed as they followed.

"When you go in, keep walking. Give us space to come in without running into you."

She nodded but kept her eyes forward.

Wolf gestured them to the side as she grabbed the knob. The door swung wide and he caught it at its apex. He looked inside, seeing nothing because of the sharp contrast of light, gave her two seconds to disappear inside, then followed her.

The house was cool, smelling of old cooking and dog hair. The floor creaked loudly as Wolf took his second and third step inside. Somebody came in behind him, their rubber soles chirping on the linoleum floor, like a sharp whistle piercing the dead silence.

Garcia turned around, still walking forward, horror in her eyes as she looked down.

Then somebody kicked the door hard as they shuffled in, and there was the accompanying squeal of wood beneath the weight and more chirping of shoe rubber. They all froze.

Wolf gestured forward to Garcia.

She continued walking and coughed loudly, and to Wolf it sounded exactly like a woman trying to fake a cough to cover up the sound of four cops entering the house behind her.

"Shit." Somebody breathed the word behind him.

Wolf held up his left hand, keeping his gun raised and ready, letting his eyes adjust to the light.

Just then a door next to Wolf rattled, claws raking the other side of the wood, and two dogs began barking on the other side.

The rear door clanked shut behind them and the noise squeezed his adrenal gland once more, putting his senses on overload, evaporating any patience for a slow entry he may have had into a distant memory.

"That you Garcia?" Mustaine called from the other room.

Wolf stepped quickly and quietly, ignoring the shock on Garcia's face as he pushed her aside.

"Yeah!" Garcia said as he passed her into the kitchen.

Mustaine said nothing as Wolf stepped through the kitchen and into a short hallway, where the floor turned to carpet. The floorboards underneath were just as squeaky, Wolf's rapid steps clearly audible. As he rounded the corner with his gun raised, he hoped speed would help.

Help him do what?

The question went unanswered as he rounded the corner and took in the scene, his finger tensing on the trigger.

The living room was spacious and bright, with two walls of floor-to-ceiling windows letting in the full morning sun. Two couches made an L-shape, Carrie and her mother on one, both tied up and staring straight ahead out the windows, Cruz on the other, facing Wolf. Mustaine was behind the second couch, ducking behind Cruz, his gun aimed at the side of his head.

"I knew it was you," the sheriff said. "Come join the party."

29

"I can hear the others, too. Come out! Come in this room or I splatter this kid's brains on the couch!"

Wolf stepped further into the room, making space for the others to enter, keeping his eyes on Mustaine. Kent then came into view, on the carpet in a fetal position in front of the two couches, the floor underneath him a smear of blood staining the brown carpet black.

"Put your weapons down," Mustaine said.

Wolf hesitated, wondering if he should take the shot, if Mustaine would have the motor skills and reflexes to pull the trigger if a bullet was traveling through his brain.

Mustaine read his mind and ducked down further. "Three-two-one!"

"Okay!" Wolf put his gun out to the side. "Okay."

"Drop it!"

Wolf dropped it. "Mustaine. You don't want to do this."

Mustaine waited while Elan, Normandy, and Alvarez put their guns down.

"I need to attend to Kent," Garcia said, pushing to the front.

Mustaine nodded. "Yeah, do it."

Garcia hurried to Kent and knelt next to the young man. Kent had his back to them, but from the semi-conscious groan that came out of his mouth as Garcia arrived it was clear he was in a very bad way.

Carrie and Nola had cattle rope tied around their waists, their hands bound behind them. Both had wounds on their faces, blood streaming down their necks, disappearing underneath flannel pajamas.

"Kick those guns away," Mustaine said. "I know none of my boys have backup pieces. How about you, Wolf? You got one?"

Wolf did not have one and he shook his head.

"Drop it now!"

"I don't have one." Wolf pulled up his pant leg, and then the other.

"What's that in your pocket?"

Wolf pulled out his multi-tool.

"Throw it down."

Wolf dropped it next to his gun.

"And phones, too," Mustaine said. "Drop them with everything else."

They pulled out their phones and put them on the pile.

"Back up. Away from the guns. Come over here, along the wall, and line up over there in front of those windows." He gestured to the bank of windows directly facing Nola and Carrie.

They walked, and as they did Wolf could see Kent more clearly. He lay on the ground, skin pale as snow, eyes closed.

Cruz sat with his hands bound behind him. His head was back, eyelids half closed, eyeballs tracking Wolf. Carrie and Nola were staring at him, too, and Wolf felt a jolt of something just short of panic. He opened his mind and let the feeling ricochet out. Then he felt a welling of anger, and he shut the door, letting the emotion boil.

"Why did you shoot him?" he asked.

"He was saying some stupid shit. Had to be shot."

"We have an ambulance on the way," Wolf said.

Mustaine said nothing for a beat, then nodded. "Yeah. He needs attention."

Wolf nodded, keeping his voice flat and calm. "You can take the gun off of Cruz."

"You're not in charge here, Wolf. You never were."

"You don't have to do this."

"I'm already doing it."

Mustaine stood up to his full height, taking the end of his barrel off Cruz's head, but kept it pointed in his general direction, the message reading loud and clear: you move, the kid dies.

"What's your plan?" Wolf asked.

"The plan is I get these people to tell me the truth."

"By shooting them?" he asked. "By beating them?"

The dogs started barking again, a muffled frenzy of claws scraping the door back near the entrance.

Mustaine's eyes were wild, pupils small. Defiance flared as he looked at his deputies. "None of this would have happened if you three cowards wouldn't have betrayed me." He looked down at Garcia. "She didn't. She understands I need closure on this. I need to know the truth. And these animals here know it."

Wolf's words were careful and slow. "What have you learned?"

"So far we've learned that these people are more willing to die than tell me what happened."

"Why did you shoot Kent?" Wolf asked.

"He was running his mouth."

Garcia turned to Wolf with a defeated voice. "He told the sheriff he was the one with Bennett. And that Bennett killed himself."

"Yeah!" Mustaine screamed the word. "Can you believe that bullshit?"

Garcia lowered her eyes, exasperation drawing her face slack.

Wolf nodded. "And so you shot him."

"If this kid is a fairy, then so be it. But he's not gonna drag my son's name into his queer back room with him."

Tears streamed down Carrie's face as she stared at her brother. Nola's face was blank, her eyes gone to a place very far from here.

"So now we're discussing the real truth," Mustaine said. "Go on, tell them what you told me, honey."

Carrie flinched and looked up at Mustaine, hatred flaring.

"Go on." Mustaine pointed his gun at her. "Tell it."

Carrie closed her eyes. "I was telling him how Valentina and I were up in his truck with him."

"Who's him? Him?"

"Bennett."

"Use my son's name when you're talking about him, you whore."

A micro smile flashed on Carrie's face, the unraveling of her psyche as she drew in a breath to speak again. "I was talking about how we left with Bennett that night. I went into his truck, and Valentina followed. We all parked up on the road. And...we were, you know, making out."

Mustaine shook his head, amazement in his voice. "Threesome. Bennett with two women." He looked at Carrie. "And then?"

"And then..." she shrugged. "We saw that Bennett had his gun underneath his seat..."

Silence descended on them, as a quiet rage seemed to build in Mustaine with each second.

"And that's where we are," Mustaine said. "She just won't

admit it. Won't tell me the truth. No matter what I say or do. You see what kind of monsters I'm dealing with, guys?" He looked at Elan, Alvarez, and Normandy, pointedly ignoring Wolf. He dug his knuckles into one eye, rubbing, a growl rumbling in his chest.

Wolf tried to think, eyeing the room. The guns were a good five paces away, lying in a group on the carpet, Kent's bleeding body and Garcia in his direct path. Mustaine was another five or so paces away, still rubbing his eyes like he was trying to smother something to death.

"The reason they're not telling you the truth is because they don't know it," Wolf said, the words flowing out without any idea how to back it up. All he had was the intention of getting this madman away from Kent and the others, saving people from injury or worse. If he could get Mustaine outside and away from the house, there was a chance for Kent and the Whitlocks, and for subduing Mustaine without collateral damage. Or, at least, any more of it.

"We figured out everything last night and this morning," Wolf said. "And the Whitlocks had nothing to do with Bennett's death."

Mustaine said nothing. In his peripheral vision Wolf saw the other deputies turn to look at him.

"And you're way wrong, I hate to say it. But the truth is elsewhere. Not up here. It's never been up here. It's down in town."

Mustaine's cocked his head. "What are you talking about?"

"I have a friend at a law firm in Rocky Points. They have an investigation division that uses a few methods that we don't. Their people aren't worried about procedure as much as—"

"Get to your point or I may decide you need to be shot."

"They have a software that gets phone records in a matter of minutes from other sources: apps or GPS data stored inside other processes, and other ways as well."

Mustaine raised the gun and pointed it at him.

"My point is we got Valentina and Carrie's phone records, and the information we got showed Carrie and Valentina told the truth. At least, Carrie did." He kept speaking, letting the words fly out without filter. "Valentina and Carrie came up here, and Carrie stayed at the house. That was it for her Friday night. But Valentina was a lot more active after that. She didn't just drive back down into town to go home, she went back to the bar. You saw the time difference between when Bennett and Valentina and Carrie said they left the bar, right? It was just under an hour. I mean, Bennett left the bar at around the same time, but he waited in his truck for almost an hour before he moved."

Mustaine said nothing, but he was thinking, doing the math. "So what?"

"So the GPS readout from Valentina's social media app shows she went straight back to the Tavern. And Bennett's GPS showed he was still there at the exact same time she showed up."

Mustaine looked like he gave up the math problem and shook his head. "And?"

"Valentina was with Bennett. That's what I'm saying. Carrie and Kent here had nothing to do with any of this. And there's more," Wolf said. "We talked to Paco Nez, me and Normandy." Wolf gestured to Normandy, who nodded on cue. "When we were talking to Paco we caught him in a lie. He said he closed down the pizza shop Friday night, and he said he left the place just before midnight. Isn't that what he told you?"

Mustaine's stare went distant. "Yeah, so what?"

"So, the guy next to him pulling pizzas out of the oven said 'No, I closed. You left at ten forty-five.' The kid didn't know he was supposed to be going with the lie, and it was clear as day to me and Normandy."

"Is that right?" Mustaine asked Normandy.

"Yes, sir."

"On a hunch I gave my person up in Rocky Points Paco Nez's phone number, too. He put the number through the wringer, and his GPS data coincided with Valentina Johnson," Wolf raised his eyebrows, "and with Bennett."

Mustaine looked at him hard, and then his eyes landed on Normandy.

"Is all this true?" Mustaine asked.

"It is," Wolf said.

"I'm not talking to you." Mustaine pointed his gun at Wolf, then at Elan. "Is this true?"

Elan nodded. "Yes, sir."

"Is this true?" he asked Alvarez.

Alvarez nodded earnestly.

Mustaine lowered his weapon, then tilted his head, looking at them in turn.

"It was Valentina and Paco with Bennett that night," Wolf said. "There's motive. Paco was in business with Bennett. There was tension, arguments, differences in opinion on how the place should be run. And you know keeping profits all to yourself is a lot better than splitting them two ways. And Valentina? We don't know the motive yet, but we have the proof. That's the important part. Mustaine, you got this wrong. It's okay. Just put down the gun and we'll change course. We'll follow the leads."

They stood in silence, and Wolf felt the urge to swallow but he fought it.

Mustaine pointed the gun at Wolf. "Show me. Show me everything you got."

Wolf nodded. "I have a printout in my vehicle outside."

"How did you get the printout?"

"Email."

"Then show me the email on your phone."

Wolf looked at his phone lying on the carpet.

"Go on, get your phone. You touch one of those guns and I'll shoot the kid."

Wolf remained where he was.

"That's what I thought." Mustaine smiled. "You almost had me going for a second. But as we all know you're from out of town and you don't know shit about what's going on around here. Paco Nez would never do that to Bennett. Do you know why? Because he knows that if he did, I would kill him with my bare hands. I already told him when they opened the place up, if he screws over my son, I'd kill him. You should have seen his face. He almost pissed himself right then and there."

"Maybe his next move was to kill you," Wolf said.

Mustaine shook his head. "I'm disappointed in this conversation."

"Not as disappointed as this family you're terrorizing."

"This family killed—"

"Shut up coward!" Wolf yelled.

Mustaine was stunned silent.

"You can't face the truth," Wolf said, "so you have to bend it to whatever freakish version you want it to be, and then you bully everyone else around you into accepting whatever you want to believe, and then what? You'll meet them out on the playground and beat them up?"

Mustaine aimed at him.

"Oh, you're gonna use your gun? What's the matter, coward? Can't come over here and face me like a man? Not strong enough to stand up for yourself so you gonna shoot me from all the way over there? Big strong man gonna punch women, tie them up, shoot kids, then what? Shoot a cop?" He snorted. "God damned coward."

"You'd better shut up real soon."

"Or what? What are you going to do about it?"

"Wolf," Elan said under his breath. "Take it easy."

"No." Wolf shook his head, contorting his face with ultimate disgust. "I'm done taking it easy on this pussy. You're soft. Always have been. You proved that yesterday when I dropped you outside on your face. Everyone saw it. Alvarez, you saw him drop face down in the dirt yesterday after I popped him, right?"

Wolf laughed.

Mustaine walked from behind the couch toward him, then stopped. His face was red, and he seemed self-conscious of it. He smiled, a fake gesture that looked grotesque. "I know what you're doing. You're trying to provoke me." He stepped around Garcia and Kent, toward the guns.

Keeping his eyes on Wolf, Normandy, and Elan, he went to the front door and opened it. Keeping his aim on them he picked up the guns and threw them outside. The faint approach of sirens floated inside, silenced by Mustaine kicking the door shut.

"Elan, Alvarez, and Normandy," Mustaine pointed toward Cruz. "Go stand where I was earlier."

They remained where they were.

"If you don't, I'll start with shooting the kid. Then I'll move to one of the women."

The three men moved, leaving Wolf standing alone.

"What are you doing?" Alvarez asked. "Are you just ready to die or something? If that's the case, go on and kill yourself. Why drag all these innocent people into it?"

Mustaine looked at Alvarez. "I'll get justice for my son before I go to hell. Now move faster or I start shooting. It's your choice."

"We're going," Elan said, ushering Alvarez ahead of him.

Mustaine put his gun in his hip holster and pointed to a spot in the room that was to Wolf's left, making a circle with his finger. "We'll keep this contained. Try to avoid landing on Garcia when you fall."

Without further warning Mustaine marched toward him, his fists balling into boulders at his sides.

Wolf shuffled left, not to follow Mustaine's orders, but it was the only direction to go.

He got ready, a stab of pain cracking in his hand as he flexed his fist. He flashed a look around the room, searching for a weapon. There was a wood-burning stove in the corner with a pair of heavy iron tongs and an iron fireplace poker next to it.

There didn't seem to be time to reach it, but it was his only chance. He lunged.

Mustaine growled and darted after him, his full mass over his toes and coming hard.

Wolf's move was too obvious, so he stopped and cut back, twisting hard as one of Mustaine's arms wrapped around Wolf's waist, a hand clutching Wolf's clothing and wrapping him in.

The room swirled as he twisted in midair, and he hit the ground with a thump that felt like it cracked his spine into a thousand pieces. His head slammed something hard, probably the ground, maybe the iron stove, he had no idea, but the back of his head felt like it was split open.

Then another blow hit him in the face, and then the side of his body.

He turned fast, leading with his fist, landing a feeble punch on Mustaine's chest that had no leverage. His lower body was pinned to the ground, so he twisted back, rebounding like a rubber band, slamming his side back onto the carpet.

Another blow, and then another. They rained down onto his head, feeling like he was being stomped by a bull. All he could do was put his arms up for cover, but when he did that

Mustaine punched him in the ribs. He tried to pull his legs up, but they were under Mustaine.

A whimper escaped Wolf's mouth as he felt ribs crack.

"You're dead!" The scream, hot on his face, seemed to split his eardrum.

Wolf's vision was blurred, going black at the edges. He could feel hot warmth leaking out across his face and over his scalp.

"Stop!" A woman's voice yelled. "Stop it!"

Mustaine climbed up Wolf, pushing the air out of him as he put his full weight down, and then he punched again.

Wolf's ear felt like it was ripped off his head.

And then Mustaine yelled, a guttural cry that sounded like it came from the lizard part of his brain.

Wolf raised his arms again, bracing himself for the blow that would persuade consciousness to leave his body for good.

"Ahh!" Mustaine's bodyweight jolted, and then let up off him.

Wolf dared a glance as he rolled back, trying to gain distance as quickly as possible.

Mustaine had regained his feet, but he was stumbling backwards, arms flailing at his sides.

Garcia had jumped onto his shoulders, one of her arms wrapped around his neck, the other hand clawing at his face. One of her fingers dug into the sheriff's eye socket to the middle knuckle.

With a scream Mustaine ripped her hand away, revealing a grotesque sight, blood spurting from his eye socket, the eyelid somehow forced open, the eyeball beneath pushing outward and turning toward the bridge of his nose, twitching uncontrollably.

"You bitch!" he said, punching behind him and landing a

blow against the side of her head. He squeezed her other arm and there was a muffled pop as Garcia cried out in pain.

Alvarez came in at lightning speed, diving hard at Mustaine's legs with a driving double-legged kick, buckling Mustaine's knee inward with an audible snap like a stick crackling in a fire.

Mustaine screamed and fell sideways, landing hard on Garcia.

She squealed again in pain as Normandy joined in with a stomp into the side of Mustaine's head, then another.

Wolf watched the tornado of flailing limbs, Alvarez rearing back with punch and delivering it into the side of the sheriff's neck, Normandy coming down with a knee on Mustaine's face. Mustaine growled, then screamed, and like a wildebeest shaking off a pride of lions he twisted, flailing his arms in a windmill that caught Alvarez in the head and threw Normandy against the wall. He grabbed for the first person he could get his hands on and caught Garcia by the hair.

"You bitch!" he said again.

With a sinking feeling Wolf watched Mustaine's other hand reach for his holster.

Wolf dove forward to stop his arm before he grabbed the gun, but Alvarez was already there, lunging across Mustaine, clutching his arm and bending it back. Wolf bounced off and landed back on the ground. He clawed back to his knees, and with a sickened stomach he realized Mustaine's gun was already out of the holster.

A deafening pop blasted next to Wolf's ear. He twisted away, heat searing the back of his neck as a spray splashed him, something he felt and couldn't see, something that could only be blood.

Elan stood over them all, aiming down, Mustaine's gun in his hand, a tendril of smoke rising from the muzzle.

There was a guttural cry of pain, and for a moment Wolf wasn't sure who it was coming from, but then Garcia crawled away, her hair freed from Mustaine's fist, and Alvarez scrambled back, Normandy too, revealing Mustaine lying on the ground gripping his chest.

Elan breathed hard, his exhales coming sharply through his clenched teeth. His eyes bulged, glaring down at Mustaine, the gun still aimed and ready to fire again.

Mustaine lay on his side, lurching, as if he wanted to roll onto his back. Blood pulsed between his hands. He looked up at Elan, horror and disbelief in his eyes, and then he focused on something else much further away, and then nothing at all.

Through the ringing in his ears, Wolf heard yelling behind him. He snapped out of it and saw Nola pointing with her chin.

"My son! My son!"

Kent was motionless on the ground, his eyes half open and vacant.

Wolf hurried to him and took his pulse. Nothing. He rolled him on his back and began CPR.

The next few minutes were a blur, with Normandy and Alvarez cutting Carrie, Nola, and Cruz free with Wolf's multitool, then Nola kneeling next to Wolf, whispering in her son's ear. It could have been thirty seconds, it could have been five minutes, but eventually blood from Wolf's wounds began dripping onto Kent, and Normandy forced him to rest while the young deputy took over.

Once the paramedics arrived, they watched in silence as two medics tried to coax Kent's soul into staying inside his body. A third medic tended to Mustaine.

"Forget him," Elan said. "He's dead. We're worried about the boy."

"I've got a pulse," one of them said.

Nola, Carrie, and Cruz knelt together, praying with their

arms around each other as they watched Kent being loaded onto the wheeled stretcher, then into the waiting ambulance.

Alvarez stood up with Garcia. "I'll get her to the ER." He looked at Wolf. "You're not looking too hot. You might want to hitch a ride, too."

Wolf sat on the edge of a couch holding his side, feeling like if he let go his ribcage would collapse into a heap of hot pain. Blood was still flowing down the back of his head, trickling down to the small of his back.

"Probably a good idea," he said.

30

Wolf opened his eyes, letting in light that burned his retinas. A noise had woken him.

"Hey, you."

He blinked, sharpening the form of Piper Cain's face hovering over him into focus.

"Hey." His voice sounded like a push broom on an old floor. The effort of talking shot pain into his right ribcage.

"Careful. You don't have to say anything." She bent down and pressed a warm kiss onto his mouth. "You're okay. Just be quiet."

He looked around, seeing fluorescent lights, ceiling tiles. He heard a machine beeping and saw a saline solution hanging, a tube running into his arm. He was propped up at an angle and wearing a hospital gown.

"What happened?" His voice was a croak now, the pain in his side still there.

"You're in the Crow Valley Hospital. You have a concussion, three broken ribs, a broken hand, and a whole lot of stitches on your head."

"Mustaine?"

"He's dead."

He lifted his right hand and saw it was splinted and bandaged. His eyes tracked to the tube in his arm.

"You were low on electrolytes."

"Geez." He still couldn't remember anything that had happened. But more than that, he didn't care. Right now he was feeling light and amazing, the pain in his body a distant whisper, like he was sitting on a warm cloud, a beautiful woman bending over him showering him with kisses.

He put his hand on his stomach, feeling a wave of pain.

"Oh yeah, you had a hernia. They sewed it up before any intestinal damage could occur. You were lucky there."

The memory of being punched in the stomach rushed back into his mind, followed by the sheriff sitting in jail, and then the rest of it.

He tried to sit up and groaned.

"What are you doing? Sit back."

"What happened to Kent?"

"Kent?"

"Kent Whitlock."

"Kent Whitlock is out of surgery and stable," a male voice said.

Normandy appeared behind her and stepped up to the bed. "The doctors had to remove one of his kidneys and his gall bladder. But he's stable."

Wolf sat back and relaxed, feeling the cocoon of warmth envelope him again. He looked up at the saline bag hanging on the rack. "What the hell are they giving me?"

"Some painkillers," Piper said. "I think it's morphine."

Oh, he thought. That's nice. He looked at Piper, mesmerized by her pretty face. "I'm sorry," he said.

She smiled. "For what?"

"For being an asshole. For not being happier that you're moving to Rocky Points. I'm so happy you're moving there." He smiled wide, and the warm tingle multiplied. "And I'm so happy you got a job in the same building as me. We can tell each other when we're going to the bathroom."

She frowned. "What?"

"I love seeing you. And if you have to pee you can tell me, or you don't need to, either."

"Um, I'm going to step outside," Normandy said. "Just holler if you need me."

Wolf's eyes felt heavy and he closed them for an instant, and then he fell into a deep, dreamless sleep.

Wolf woke up to a changed room, the walls and ceiling no longer a sterilized white, but now painted orange, the air itself seeming to be tinted a warm sepia.

He looked over to the window at a brilliant pink and orange sky, a ceiling of clouds bruised purple and red between the silhouette of two tall peaks. The sun shot rays through the window, brightening the room by the second. He stared at the rising ball of fire for a moment, realizing he was looking at a sunrise and not a sunset.

And with a jolt he realized he was home.

He was in his own bed, and the sun was rising behind the eastern mountains behind his house.

Then he heard water shut off, and only then realized there had been the noise of someone showering in his bathroom. A sliver of light leaked out beneath the door, the shadow of feet. The door opened and a beautiful creature emerged from the steam like an angel from clouds.

"You're awake," Piper said, smiling. She stood naked, drying her hair, then ducked back into the bathroom.

"Yeah." He said to himself, vaguely remembering the drive home. He'd walked with some assistance to Piper's vehicle in the parking lot, no, he'd been wheeled in a wheelchair.

"Who drove my car home?" he asked. His voice was surprisingly strong sounding in his own ears.

"What's that?" She ducked her head out.

"Who drove my car home?"

"Rachette and Yates drove me down there. We drove your car home. You and I." She disappeared again.

He stared at the ceiling while she ran the hair dryer, watching the dust motes swirl in the light.

Holding his side and pressing against the pain, he sat up and twisted his feet to the warm carpet.

She came out, now in her underwear, her long dark hair cascading down her back. "Hey, sit back. You're supposed to be resting."

"I'm sorry," he said.

"Sit back."

He sat back, collapsing on his pillow again, pain shooting through his ribs and abdominal muscles. "I'm sorry."

She smiled, patting his face. "I know. You said that. Many times on the way home."

"Well, I am."

"I know. It's okay. Relax."

He watched her move through the room, picking up clothing out of an overnight bag, slipping on jeans and a fitted t-shirt, putting on a sweater. She slipped on her socks, eyeing him with a smile.

"What?" she asked.

"You're beautiful."

"You said that, too. Many times on the way home."

He smiled. "Well, it's true."

"Thanks." She sighed and looked at him. "You've seen better days, David Wolf."

He reached up and felt gauze, some of it on his face and a patch on the top of his head. Stiff points of stitches poked through the bandage on top of his scalp.

"Sit back. Lie down." She bent over him again and kissed him. "Stay."

He remained still, allowing her to pull the covers over him.

"I have to leave," she said. "But your mother and Margaret are coming to check on you in a bit. I have the movers coming in a couple hours. I'm sorry."

He shook his head. "Don't worry about it."

"There's some fruit in the kitchen. Juice. You're supposed to keep it light with eating." She gestured to the end table next to him. "I cut up some fruit there for you. And there's some water. And next to you is your computer if you want to watch a show or something."

He saw a plate of cut fruit, the glass, and his computer. "Go ahead," he said. "I'll be fine. Wait, where are you even moving to?"

"You don't remember our conversation?"

He shook his head.

"It's okay," she said. "We have a month-to-month rental lined up just south of town. But there may be a good property coming on the market. We'll see. I don't want to jinx it."

"That's great. Awesome."

"You said that, too." She kissed him again. "Listen. I'll come check on you tomorrow."

He grabbed her hand as she walked away. What had they talked about on the way home? What did he say? What was her reaction? They had so much to talk about, but he didn't know where to begin, what to lead with.

"Have a good day," she said with a gentle smile.

He nodded and her hand slipped out of his. "You, too."

"I'll see you soon."

"Keep me posted," he said.

But his voice was hoarse and she was already outside, his statement lost behind the whoosh of the hydraulic piston closing the screen door.

31

3 Days Later ...

Wolf stopped at the door to his office and contemplated going inside. It was closed, locked since the last time he'd been there, six days ago. Nothing waited inside for him except maybe a hundred emails to sort through, so he kept walking toward the squad room.

At the mid-afternoon hour there was little activity, a few deputies milling around and sitting at their desks catching up on paperwork.

"Hi!" Charlotte stood up and walked over. "How are you doing?"

"I'm fine, how are you, Charlotte?"

"Geez," she ignored him, or hadn't heard what he said, her eyes bulging as she scanned his face and body.

He was getting used to the reaction. "That's great, glad to hear it," he said.

"Huh?" She put a hand to her own face, next to her nose. "Your eyes. My God. Can you see?"

"Yes. They're just black eyes. No damage to the eyes themselves."

She blinked and shook her head. "I'm sorry. I mean, Tom told me you were broken up, but I had no idea it was so bad." She stepped forward and gave him a hug.

He grunted. "Ribs."

"Oh yeah. Oh my gosh, I'm so sorry."

He reached out and gave her a half-hug with his left side. "Thank you for the sympathy." He eyed Patterson's office. Her blinds were closed. "Is the sheriff in?"

"She's in there again with that DA from Crow Valley. If they want you to go back down, say no this time."

He smiled and walked to the sheriff's office door. He knocked twice.

"Come in!"

He twisted the knob with his good hand and pushed the door open, revealing DA Bluthe sitting across from Patterson.

Bluthe stood up, his eyes bulging, his face going serious just like Charlotte's had. "My... oh, hi. How are you doing?"

Wolf nodded and walked in, taking a seat next to Bluthe. He took off his baseball cap, which had been perched gingerly on his head. Exposing the stitches to the open air, they began to itch immediately, but he resisted the urge to scratch, knowing that only resulted in complications.

"Holy cow. You look terrible," Patterson said. She held up two fingers. "Can you see how many—"

"Two. Two fingers. I can see just fine."

"Okay."

Wolf reached out his left hand to shake with Bluthe. The DA, still glancing at him out of the corners of his eyes, sat down.

"Thanks for coming in. I...knowing how bad you're doing, I could have come to you, you know."

"I'm fine. It's good to be out of the house."

They stared at him in silence.

"Seriously, minus the ribs, everything is mending nicely. You should have seen my face a couple days ago. I couldn't see out of my right eye because of the swelling. Otherwise, it hurts a bit to talk. And don't make me laugh."

"Now that eye is jet-black." She leaned forward, squinting. "I've never seen anything so thoroughly bruised."

Wolf sat still. "Are you done?"

Patterson sat back, clearing her throat. "Yes. Sorry."

Wolf turned to Bluthe. "How's Kent Whitlock doing?"

Bluthe smoothed his shirt, a bright red button down. A turquoise bolo tie cinched around the collar and hung down onto his chest. "He's doing okay. He's still in the ICU down in CV. I was just telling the sheriff about him. It turns out he was already in very bad shape to begin with."

"How do you mean?"

"When the doctors took off his clothing to treat him, they found his entire body was covered in bruises. His back and sides looked like your face. No offense. X-rays showed he had multiple cracked ribs on both sides of his body. He had a mild concussion, more bruises on his head."

"Sheriff Mustaine had a way with his fists," Wolf said.

"Not the sheriff," Bluthe said. "The injuries were already there. Days old when he was shot by Mustaine. He got them Friday night."

Wolf thought of seeing Kent during the investigation down south, the way he'd moved gingerly, the fall on the tractor, the way the young man's face had been a mask of pain as he sat down on the pilot seat of the big John Deere.

"How?" Wolf asked.

"Nola Whitlock started talking yesterday." Bluthe gestured to Patterson. "I sent your sheriff here the link to the interview. Maybe it's best we just watch it together. It might save you some talking." Bluthe smiled.

Patterson flipped the screen of her computer so that they could all three see it. She moused over the video player and pressed the play button. The audio crackled to life and on-screen Undersheriff Elan sat across an interrogation table from Nola Whitlock.

"—recording this interview. Do you understand?" Elan's voice reverberated in the enclosed space Wolf recognized as the conference room inside the Crow Valley Sheriff's Office.

"I do," Nola said.

There was some small talk, the undersheriff thanking her for coming in, some talk about Kent and his improving health inside the ICU. Then they got down to business.

"Do you know what happened to Bennett Mustaine on the night of Friday, October the twenty-first?" Elan asked.

She nodded. "I do."

"Can you please tell me?"

The audio hissed for a few seconds. She looked at her hands, then spoke. "Carrie came home just as she's always said, at around eleven forty-five, right before midnight. Valentina drove her home—"

"She was telling the truth," Bluthe said over the video. "We got Valentina and Carrie's phone records. They came straight to Carrie's. Carrie stayed home, Valentina went back to Crow Valley and went home after dropping her off."

Wolf nodded.

Nola continued talking on screen. "—at around two-fifteen a.m. Carrie came and shook me awake. Kent had come home and was lying on the couch in the living room. He was very upset, and he was injured. I got up, and Cruz got up, too. We all gathered around to see what had happened.

"At first I thought he had fallen on his motorcycle. I was yelling at him, telling him to stop riding that thing around. But...I realized he wasn't hurt from falling on his motorcycle. I saw there was blood droplets on him. Like, little circles, all over his face. And I realized the big puddle on his shirt didn't make sense, because he had no injuries. No cuts, at least. He was crying. Something wasn't right. He had no cuts, but he was hurt. And, you know, psychologically, he was definitely hurt. He was upset."

Elan nodded. "And then what?"

She wiped her cheeks. Elan pushed a box of tissues towards her.

"Kent told us he'd been with Bennett. And Bennett shot himself in front of him. He said they were in the middle of...you know...Kent is gay. Bennett was gay."

"I understand. But could you please tell me for the video exactly what you mean?"

"They were being sexually intimate with each other."

"Kent told you this?"

"Yes." She blew her nose and grabbed another tissue. "I knew it when he was much younger. He was never interested in girls. I loved him the same. We all did. Well... except Ken."

"Who's Ken?"

"My husband. He left five years ago." She seemed to be lost in thought for a second, then said, "Anyway, we loved Kent just the same, whether he was gay or not. But Bennett's father, that's another story."

"And I'd like to talk about that, too," Elan said. "But for now can we stick to what happened Friday night?"

She shook her head. "This is all leading up to Friday night. You want to know what happened then? You have to know their history. You want to know why I protected Kent and didn't tell the sheriff what had happened? Then you have to listen to me."

"I'm sorry." Elan held up his hand. "Please. Continue."

She paused, wiping her nose again. "Kent and Bennett used to be good friends in high school. They would hang out, dirt biking together on our ranch and out in the woods. They would stay away for hours and hours, and sometimes go overnight camping on those things. I never knew for sure, but I think they must have experimented with their sexuality with each other at that time. I didn't speak to Kent about that kind of thing back then.

"So, they were friends, and more than that as I learned later, but back then, right before college, they kind of had a falling out. Bennett left for college, to go play football out in Ohio, and I remember Kent was upset for a month or so that summer. I remember once asking him why Bennett had stopped coming over, and Kent never told me. I just chalked it up to friends going their separate ways. But I also suspected they must have had like, you know, a breakup. Again, I never asked.

"And then Bennett got injured and he came back to town. Bennett came around a couple times to hang out. They were happy together." She smiled, remembering. "You should have seen them. They were like a couple of standup comedians when they were with each other. They made all of us laugh, me and Carrie and Cruz."

Her face fell as her mind moved on to other memories.

Then the thing with Sadie Moreno happened, and the two of them stopped hanging out. I asked if Kent knew what happened between Bennett and Sadie, if he knew the truth, but Kent never talked to me about it. He said, 'No, Mom. I don't know anything about it.' But I could see that maybe he did know.

"Anyway, I didn't push it, but Kent was depressed, and he

and Bennett never hung out again. It was then that I finally got the guts to ask if he was gay. Kent said he was. And then I asked if he'd been seeing Bennett, and yes, he had been. They had been involved in a sexual relationship with each other since high school, exactly as I thought."

She wiped her nose with the tissue. "I asked him why they broke up when they seemed so happy together. He told me that Bennett was the one breaking it off, that he had broken it off a full month before the Sadie Moreno thing. I asked him why, and Kent said it was Bennett's father, Sheriff Mustaine.

"Apparently the sheriff had point blank told Bennett that he'd 'kill him if he was queer.'" She quoted her fingers. "Or something like that. Something that made Bennett break it off."

"The Sheriff knew that Bennett was gay?" Elan asked.

She shrugged. "I don't know. We didn't know. Kent didn't know. He never got an answer on that from Bennett. Bennett just pushed him away, and apparently with a lot of anger, according to Kent. Bennett was running from who he was, and of course Sheriff Mustaine was the one spurring that on." She stared at the table. "And then we heard the rumors about Sadie Moreno."

Elan cleared his throat. "So, this all leads up to that Friday night two weeks ago."

"Right," she said. "So, last Friday Kent was down at the Chicken House and Bennett came in out of nowhere, after almost two years of not speaking, and told him he wanted to talk. I guess they talked in the parking lot in Bennett's truck. They spoke about Bennett's fear, and how he was running from his feelings for Kent. I guess they missed each other. And one thing led to another and they... Bennett offered to drive him home.

"Kent took the offer, leaving his bike at the Chicken House. He said on the way home they went up High Road, to an overlook they used to like to go to. They started in the front seat, then got into the back seat, and at that point Bennett started getting rough. Kent thought it was a game at first, but then Bennett started punching him. Bennett hit him in the stomach and the chest and then on the side. Bennett was screaming at him, calling him names, and beating him, and Kent said he thought he was going to die, and Bennett just kept going."

"Can you pause this?" Bluthe said.

Wolf blinked, snapping out a trance.

Patterson paused the video.

Bluthe slid a folder in front of Wolf and opened it, then picked out some pictures. "Here're some photos the hospital took of Kent's injuries."

Wolf and Patterson bent over close ups of exposed skin, bruised deep purple, covering almost every square inch of Kent's chest and sides.

Bluthe gestured. "Okay, you can start it again."

Patterson pressed play.

"... Kent said that he pleaded for Bennett to stop, and when he finally did, Bennett was over him with a gun in his hand. He was forcing it on Kent."

"Aiming it at him?" Elan asked.

"No. I mean, he gave Kent the gun. He put it in Kent's hand, pointed the gun at himself, and told Kent to pull the trigger."

She said nothing for a beat.

"And then what?" Elan asked, breaking the silence.

She shook her head. "He didn't shoot, if that's what you mean. Kent said he dropped the gun on the floor and said he wouldn't do it. And that's when Bennett picked up the gun, put it to his head, and pulled the trigger.

"After the shot Bennett fell on top of him. And he had to crawl out from under him, out the door. Then he walked home.

And that's when he woke us up. He was hurt, shivering, covered in blood. Bennett's blood." She wiped her eyes.

"Then what did you do?" Elan asked.

She shook her head. "I just kept thinking about the sheriff, and what he was going to do. That's all I could think about. What he was going to do to my baby."

"What did you do next?" Elan asked again.

"I went up. Alone." She emphasized the word. "To look at the scene. I saw his body. He was dead. I saw the gun was lying on the floor next to his hand and he was lying face down. It definitely looked like he killed himself."

"Did you doubt Kent's story?" Elan asked.

"No. I believed every word. He would never kill a man. He's the kid who wouldn't ever kill one of the chickens growing up. His father used to shame him about that. He never liked hunting, because he felt too bad for the animals. He never liked when we sent the cattle to the slaughterhouse. He eats mostly vegetarian. He was no killer."

Elan nodded. "I understand. So, what happened next?"

"I remembered how Kent said Bennett had made him hold the gun and point it at him. I knew that there would be my son's prints on the handle. I knew there would be prints all over the place, maybe even other forensic evidence, tying my son to the scene."

She shook her head, her eyes darkening with defiance. "I left Bennett's body out there. I drove back home, and I asked Kent about Sadie Moreno. I wanted to know the truth about her. Did Sheriff Mustaine do something to cover up the truth about her and Bennett? Did Bennett attack her or not? Did Kent know the truth?

"And Kent told me he did. That Bennett had attacked her. They had spoken about it after it happened, when they had that last time. Bennett had been very upset back then, deeply depressed. He confessed to Kent what had happened, and what his father was doing to cover it up, that they could never see each other again."

"What was his father doing to cover it up?" Elan asked.

Nola hesitated. "You don't know?"

"No. I don't."

Wolf watched, wondering if she knew the secret of Sadie Moreno's aunt and uncle.

She shook her head. "I don't know. He never told Kent."

Wolf could see she was lying, and it looked like Elan could see it too.

"Let me ask a different question," Elan said. "Why did you want to know about Sadie Moreno?"

"Because I wanted to know if Bennett really had attacked her. Because the rumor was she had been attacked, and now she was saying she was injured from a fall. We all knew that Mustaine must have been behind her changing her mind. I wanted to know if that rumor was true, because if it was, it wouldn't end well for Kent. It looked like Kent shot him. There was no way Mustaine was going to follow the evidence to the conclusion that Bennett shot himself."

"What did you do?" Elan asked.

"I went back up there. Alone." Again she emphasized the word. "And I wiped the gun down. And then I saw some fingerprints where Kent had grabbed the handle in the back seat, and I wiped them. And then I wiped the front seat, and I wiped the exterior handles, and anywhere else he might have touched.

"I drove Bennett's truck up all the way up High Road. I couldn't decide what to do. I had some gasoline and matches with me. I put those into the back of Bennett's truck. And then I drove into Dry Wash. I knew that's a trail Kent had taken a lot, and knew it led out into the middle of nowhere. I figured I would drive his truck into the middle of nowhere and set it on fire.

"But when I got to the wash, when I was going to drive out into the wilderness, I stopped. I stopped and pulled out the can of gas. I was going to douse it. But then I couldn't do it. I couldn't destroy the body like that. I couldn't do more harm to Bennett. I mean, we hadn't done anything. Kent hadn't done anything wrong. He was just a young man in love. I realized I was doing the wrong thing. That I needed to tell the truth. But I didn't know..."

She didn't finish her sentence, instead descending into silence, her face blank, tears tumbling out of her vacant eyes.

"I left the truck where you guys found it. And I walked home."

Elan tilted his head, keeping his eyes on her. "You walked all the way home from up there?"

"Yes," she said, not skipping a beat.

"Carrying a can of gas?"

"Yes."

"How long did it take you?"

"Almost four hours."

"So your other son, Cruz, or Carrie, they didn't drive to pick you up?"

"No. They had nothing to do with my decision to move the body, to wipe down the truck. It was all me. Carrie and Cruz wanted to tell the truth to Mustaine, but I forced them to keep quiet."

Elan nodded. "Okay. How did you get his motorcycle from the Chicken House?"

"I drove Cruz down the next day. I made him ride it back to our house."

Elan said nothing, seeming unsure what to ask next.

Nola waited patiently. All emotion had drained from her, leaving her face stoic and determined looking.

"It was Sunday morning that some dirt bikers found the body," Elan said. "You chose to sit on the information that Bennett had shot himself, and that you had moved the body."

"Yes." She raised her chin.

"What was your plan there? Were you going to tell anybody?"

She sat motionless, then grabbed another tissue, held it in her hand on her lap. "I was going to. I really was. But I was scared. Then that detective beat up Mustaine outside our gate. I was going to come down that next morning. I thought since the sheriff was in jail that it was my time to act. But you know what happened there. He showed up to our house that morning before we'd even woken up."

She shook her head. "I was sleeping the best I ever had that night, knowing he was behind bars. I should have assumed he would get out and come for us. I should have slept with my gun. He wouldn't have snuck in on us so easily.

"And you know the rest. He broke in, put a gun to my son's head, made us all gather in the living room, tied us up, and here we are, praying for Kent to make a speedy recovery without too many complications."

The video ended. Patterson clicked the stop button.

The DA sat frozen, still staring at the now blank screen. "We still haven't made any arrests."

"What are you going to do?" Patterson asked.

"It's a sticky situation. If I'm honest with you, I'm not sure Nola Whitlock did anything anyone else in her shoes wouldn't have done. But we'll go over our case carefully, and keep you posted."

He looked at Wolf. "And I tell you what. I may have been a bit scared of Clark Mustaine, but Mr. Wolf here has inspired me to live out my final years as a DA fighting more and worrying about bruises less. I'm going to take a hard look at those involved with the Sadie Moreno coverup and bust some heads." Bluthe stood up, looking weary. "So wish me luck."

"Good luck," Patterson said. "And if you need any more help, you have our phone number."

"I do. And I won't forget your help either, sheriff."

He reached out a hand to Wolf. "Thank you, detective."

Wolf once again shook with his left hand. "You're welcome."

"Oh, and I'm supposed to say thank you from Nola Whitlock, for the bravery you showed in her living room."

"Just a second," Patterson said, sitting back, folding her arms. "So, the DA here told me Kent was shot, the rest of the family tied up, Mustaine holding them at gunpoint, and you guys broke into the house and faced him?"

Wolf nodded.

"What did you do? How did you subdue him?"

"I aimed my gun at him, but he had the upper hand and made me throw it down. Then I lied to him, tried to make him think he was on the wrong path all along. When that didn't work, I called him names. And when that didn't work, he beat me up. The other deputies jumped in and took care of him for me."

She arched her eyebrows and nodded. "Oh."

Bluthe laughed and stood up. "You're a humble man, Wolf. I have to go. I can walk myself out."

"Nonsense, I'll walk you." Patterson pointed at Wolf. "Please stay, I need to speak to you."

Wolf waved a final goodbye and settled into the chair, leaning awkwardly to alleviate the pressure on his ribs.

Patterson returned, sitting behind her desk. "Geez. You

really do look terrible, and I mean that in the nicest way possible."

"Thank you."

"I want you to take the next seven days, a full week, off, and then we'll assess how you're doing."

"I won't need a week."

"Yes, you will. And when you get back, you'll be confined to light duty."

"Confined?"

"You'll be on light duty, keeping out of any situations that might injure your ribs. Those things take a while to heal." She tented her fingers.

"When's Piper starting?" he asked.

She stared at him blankly. "I'm not following." She leaned forward. "You know she refused the job I offered her, right? She doesn't want to work at the department."

He remained motionless in his chair, but the office seemed to shift a few degrees as the news hit him. He had seen Piper twice in the last three days since being home from Crow Valley, and both times had been fast, groggy situations for Wolf, her making quick stops in to check on him.

"You didn't know she refused?"

He stared out the window past Patterson. "That's why she was talking to Michael Venus. She was looking into a job."

"She was looking into an investigator position," Patterson said. "And she refused that job offer, too, thankfully. I mean, you know Venus and what he did. I made sure she knew loud and clear he was an asshole after Rachette told me she was having coffee with him."

Wolf nodded. "Thank you for that."

"You're welcome."

"So, what's she going to..." He stopped his question and put up his hands. "I'm heading over to see her new house right now. I'll ask her myself."

"Good idea." She smiled. "But she ended up taking a much better job."

"She got a job?"

"Yeah."

He stared at her. "I'll make sure and ask about that, too."

"And I've seen the house."

"Okay." He stood up. "Good for you."

"It's a great place. I wish I had a place like that. I need to start paying myself more."

"Anything else?" he asked.

"Is that really what happened down there with Mustaine?"

He nodded. "Pretty much."

"Well, Bluthe seemed smitten by your help. Everyone seems eerily okay with Sheriff Mustaine being dead." She put out her hands. "And, hey, at least it was quick, right? It was like I said, in and out."

Wolf turned toward the door. "Bye."

"Wait."

He stopped in the doorway.

"Seriously, though, David. Thank you," she said. "And I do owe you."

"You're welcome. And don't worry about it."

32

Wolf shut off the laptop next to him and made his way old-school-style, vaguely remembering the directions Piper had given him over the phone, referencing notes in his terrible handwriting.

But he knew his way around Sunnyside well enough.

He passed Margaret Hitchens's house, and Sarah's old house, and the turnoff that used to lead to Lauren and Ella. He took a right at Fish Creek Way, getting off the main thoroughfare and onto roads that spiderwebbed through the forest.

The road crisscrossed Upper Fish Creek, whose clear and cold waters filtered from the high mountains above, down to the Chautauqua below. A decade ago, these roads would have been dirt and desolate, now much of it was paved and lined with houses.

He took a left, then another right, following his scribbled directions, and was pleased to find he was on the right track. He weaved through the woods, passing multi-million-dollar estates built with heavy slabs of wood and tons of rock. He could see his destination ahead, a house sitting among the aspens with a blue For Sale sign in front.

The house was modest sized compared to the others, a two-story design painted denim blue, accented with dark wood planking throughout and plenty of windows. The property looked to be over an acre, large considering the meteoric real estate prices these days, with skeletal aspen trees surrounding the building.

He slowed in front. "Wow," he said to himself.

Piper was sitting on the front porch. She waved and stood up as he turned into the drive and crawled toward the house.

He parked in front of the three-car garage, a luxury addition to the house in these parts, next to Margaret's Range Rover and Piper's old Nissan Pathfinder, Margaret's vehicle gleaming like polished obsidian, Piper's needing a rainstorm to wash off the mud and dust.

He parked and got out into cool air smelling of creek water and decaying leaves.

"What a place," he said.

She looked at him, concern creasing her forehead. "Geez. Your eyes. They weren't like that the other day."

"I can see out of them," he said.

"That's good." She laughed, coming close, putting her hands gently on his torso. "How do you feel?"

"A bit of pain still."

She got on her toes and kissed him on the mouth, slow and soft. He loved the way she did that.

"What do you think?" she asked.

He looked around, shaking his head. The faint sound of Fish Creek burbled somewhere in the trees. To the north there was a clear view of the Chautauqua Valley, beyond it overlapping layers of mountains dusted white. "It really is perfect."

"We thought so, too. We're lucky we got it."

"Give me a tour?"

"Yeah." She turned and led him to the front porch, up a single concrete step, and to a heavy looking front door.

Warm air billowed out as they entered a wide, vaulted entryway, a wall of windows along the back of the house letting in light.

His mother and Margaret sat outside on a built-in bench on the wooden deck. Piper's father stood, arms crossed, smiling and laughing at something one of them had said.

Piper led him through the main space toward a sliding glass door. To his left stood an open kitchen, decked out with all the modern versions of appliances he'd seen in magazines, to his right a large living room and stairway leading up to the second level. The walls had rectangular dust marks where the previous owner had hung artwork.

"David!" Margaret said as they went outside to the back deck. "Geez, your face!" She walked towards him.

"He's fine," Piper said, stepping between them. "Let's not crowd him. It's just a few stitches and black eyes. And remember the ribs, please."

Margaret backed off. She put her arms out. "Well? Did Auntie Margo do okay?"

Wolf eyed Piper's father. The man had built his dream home with his two bare hands an hour and a half from this place, over the mountains in Dredge, and they had sold it to come here. It didn't matter what Wolf thought, but he smiled and nodded, noting that Piper's father seemed pleased by his surroundings.

And, he had to admit, Auntie Margo had done okay.

The back yard had a brief expanse of grass that stopped at a wall of aspen trees, behind them a dense pine forest that climbed up the mountain. To the west was another view of the valley. You could see all the way south to Williams Pass.

"What do you think, Peter?" Wolf asked.

Piper's father looked at him and smiled. "It's beautiful."

"It's yours now," Margaret said.

Peter nodded.

"I love it," Wolf's mom said. "I can't believe how great the views are."

"The guy who sold it is from Nebraska. He never set foot in town for more than a week or so a year, so the place is ten years old, but still in pristine condition. And he's made of money. I talked him into selling for way less than it's worth."

"Thank you, Auntie Margo," Piper said. "For working this miracle."

Margaret waved her off. "You've already said thanks. I just wanted to brag to David. He needs to be reminded of my greatness every once in a while."

"Every once in a while?" Wolf asked.

Piper tugged on Wolf's shirt. "I'm going to give David the tour."

"Okay, you two lovebirds run along," his mom said.

Piper took his hand and led him inside. "I want to show you something."

He followed her upstairs to the second floor.

"There's three bedrooms," she said. "One is downstairs, and two are up here. My dad will take the one on the ground level." She led him down a hallway and into the first bedroom on the right. "This one's mine." She turned and smiled, clearly pleased with the space. It was large by any standard, complete with its own full bathroom.

"But here's the coolest part," she said, pointing out the window. "Look."

Wolf looked out the window and the view to the south came into view. From the higher vantage he could see all the way down to the valley floor.

"Oh, wow," he said, leaning into the window. "You can almost see all the way to my house from here."

He squinted, tracking the river as it cut up through the forest, and then along the treeless shrub land near his place, and into the pines where his property lay. His house was invisible with the naked eye, somewhere behind the distant trees.

He turned away and saw her staring at him.

"I'm closer now," she said. "But not too close."

He shook his head. "It's great. Listen, I don't know what I said to you on that drive back, but I love that you're close now."

"I've been lying to you, David."

"Uh, okay. About what?"

"I've been telling you that I never really had a long-term relationship before, or, at least, nothing I really felt worth discussing. But the truth is I have had a long-term relationship."

He said nothing.

"And it didn't end well at all," she said.

He nodded, a smile pulling on his lips. "I know the feeling."

"I know your history, David. You've been clear about it, and … well, you can't hang out with Margaret Hitchens for more than a few minutes without learning everything about you."

"Thank you, Margaret," he said.

She smiled briefly, then she looked at the floor. "I feel like I've been dishonest, and the more time passes, the more I feel the pressure builds for me to come clean."

"Then come clean."

She nodded, looking up at him. "His name was Jonathan."

"You've talked about Jonathan," Wolf said. "So has your dad. The guy from high school, right?"

"I never told you that we were engaged."

"Ah."

"We didn't break up in college, like I led you to believe. You know I went to Montana, and Jonathan went down to Durango. We didn't split up then. We did the long-distance thing, and our relationship lasted. So, when we were done with college, we were still…you know, going strong, I guess.

"And then I got a job up in Montana working for the sheriff's department, and we decided we would make the move up there together. He was getting into environmental work, and there was plenty of it up in Montana. So, we moved, and we lived together for the first time, and…long story short, things didn't work out."

She paused, and he asked, "Why?"

"It turned out the environmental jobs were harder to get than he expected, and so he was upset about that. Meanwhile I was having the time of my life, enjoying my work. He took a bartending job and started drinking a lot. Anyway, it didn't work out…when we broke up, he told me he resented me for wanting to leave Colorado in the first place, and for putting my career ahead of us."

Wolf nodded. Margaret howled in laughter outside, the sound muffled by the house.

Piper blinked out of her thoughts. "It was like, what? Fifteen, almost twenty years ago. And I haven't had a relationship since. It's stupid, and I was so young, but it's been tough for me to get over, if I'm being honest."

"So? Why do you say it's stupid?"

"So, I feel, like, inexperienced. You've had multiple relationships, and I've only had the one, and that crashed and burned." She looked at him, swallowing.

"I've had multiple crash and burns," he said. "If that makes me experienced, then call me Jimi Hendrix. But who wants to get into the bus with a driver who's crashed ten times?"

She smiled. "It wasn't that many times. And if you were driving, I would."

He said nothing.

"I feel like what we have going is something great," she said, "and I don't want you to resent me like Jonathan did back then."

"I won't resent you."

"And I don't want to resent you," she said, putting her hands on his chest.

He nodded.

"Just because now we're in the same town," she said, "I don't think we need to spend every night together. And, my God, can you imagine if we worked in the same building? Every time we go pee, the other knowing about it? And I know you think the same way. Those drugs they had you on the drive back may as well have been truth serum."

"Okay, you have to tell me what I said. What are we talking about here? Childhood confessions?"

She pressed her body into his. "You said exactly what I was thinking. That's what you said."

He nodded. "Okay."

"Minus the taking a pee part, which you were talking about a lot for some reason. I actually pulled over once, thinking you had to go."

They laughed.

He shook his head. "But I don't want you passing up the job at the sheriff's department so that I won't resent you. That sounds like a recipe for you resenting me, doesn't it?"

"I didn't want the job. The only thing available is bottom of the totem pole. I would have been working overnights for six months, minimum. I'm done being on the bottom. I did that back in Montana and worked my way up already. I told Patterson thanks, but no thanks."

He read her face. She was passionate, telling the truth. "So, tell me about Michael Venus."

"Yeah, that was a mistake. He's starting a law firm in town and hiring an investigator. I had coffee with him to hear about the position. I had a bad feeling about him. And then Heather called me and told me his story. Wow."

"She told me you took another job, though."

Piper smiled, eyes narrowing with a glint. "I took a different investigator position. For Leary, Crouch, and Shift."

Wolf nodded, thinking back at Patterson's own stint as an investigator at the biggest law firm in town. She had hated the job, quitting and coming back to the department after a year.

"I know, I know, Heather hated the job," Piper said, apparently reading his expression. "She was very upfront, it wasn't for her, but I think I'll enjoy it." Her eyes lit up. "They have twenty-seven locations around the west. I would be stationed here in Rocky Points, but there would be occasional travel. Which I'm great with.

"The job description is right up my alley. I like that I'll be working with a lot of other people, but I'm totally independent as well. I totally got along with Patterson's old boss...my new boss. He's a hard-ass, but a likeable hard-ass, you know? And the benefits are great and will cover my dad's health expenses, and the pay is phenomenal. What else? Oh yeah, I'll get a vehicle."

She shook her head, then smiled. "I'm excited."

"That's great." He grinned. "Seriously. That's cool."

She reached up and kissed him again, and they pressed against each other.

"David!" Margaret's voice echoed up from downstairs. "Piper! You two had better be decent! We want to go to dinner! David, you're invited!"

They ignored her.

"Hello?"

"We'll be right down!" Piper said, pulling away. "Well? What do you say? You want to go get a fancy dinner on Auntie Margo? Oh, wait. Is your stomach okay to eat now?"

He nodded. His gut had been fine for the last few days, and he was ravenous.

"What do you think?" she asked. "It will probably be quick. In and out."

He smiled.

"What?" she asked.

"Nothing. It's just I've heard that one before."

"Do you have somewhere else you need to be?"

"No." He pulled her close, ignoring the pain in his ribs, and kissed her softly. "No I don't."

Thank you for reading High Road. I hope you enjoyed the story, and if you did, thank you for taking a few moments to leave a review. As an independent author exposure is everything, and if you'd consider leaving a review, which helps me so much with that exposure, I'd be very grateful.

CLICK HERE TO LEAVE A REVIEW

I love interacting with readers so please feel free to email me at jeff@jeffcarson.co so I can thank you personally. Otherwise, thanks for your support via other means, such as sharing the books with your friends/family/book clubs/the weird guy who wears briefs around the house sitting next to you right now, or anyone else you think might be interested in reading the David Wolf series. Thanks again for spending time in Wolf's world.

―――

Would you like to know about future David Wolf books and other projects, such as the new Ali Falco series the moment they are published? You can visit my blog and sign up for the New Release Newsletter at this link – http://www.jeffcarson.co/p/newsletter.html.

As a gift for signing up you'll receive a complimentary copy of Gut Decision—A David Wolf Short Story, which is a harrowing tale that takes place years ago during David Wolf's first days in the Sluice County Sheriff's Department.

READ ON *for a sneak preview of THE COMO FALCON, book one in a new series starring Ali Falco, an Italian detective, and for another sneak preview of DEAD CANYON, book 16 in the David Wolf Series ...*

ALSO BY JEFF CARSON

Gut Decision (A David Wolf Short Story)– Sign up for the new release newsletter at http://www.jeffcarson.co/p/newsletter.html and receive a complimentary copy.

THE DAVID WOLF SERIES

Foreign Deceit (David Wolf Book 1)

The Silversmith (David Wolf Book 2)

Alive and Killing (David Wolf Book 3)

Deadly Conditions (David Wolf Book 4)

Cold Lake (David Wolf Book 5)

Smoked Out (David Wolf Book 6)

To the Bone (David Wolf Book 7)

Dire (David Wolf Book 8)

Signature (David Wolf Book 9)

Dark Mountain (David Wolf Book 10)

Rain (David Wolf Book 11)

Drifted (David Wolf Book 12)

Divided Sky (David Wolf Book 13)

In the Ground (David Wolf Book 14)

High Road (David Wolf Book 15)

NEW Dead Canyon (David Wolf Book 16)

THE ALI FALCO SERIES

NEW The Como Falcon (Ali Falco Book 1)

This is a work of fiction. Names, characters, businesses, places, events, and incidents are either the products of the author's imagination or used in a fictitious manner. Any resemblance to actual persons, living or dead, or actual events is purely coincidental.

Printed in Great Britain
by Amazon